W9-ARW-344

DARK ROAD HOME

DARK ROAD HOME

A GIN SULLIVAN MYSTERY

Anna Carlisle

CROOKED
LANE

NEW YORK

Copyright © 2016 by The Quick Brown Fox & Company LLC

Published in the United States by Crooked Lane Books, an imprint of The Quick Brown Fox & Company LLC.

Crooked Lane Books and its logo are trademarks of The Quick Brown Fox & Company LLC.

Library of Congress Catalog-in-Publication data available upon request.

ISBN (hardcover): 978-1-62953-604-0
ISBN (paperback): 978-1-62953-636-1
ISBN (ePub): 978-1-62953-605-7
ISBN (Kindle): 978-1-62953-665-1
ISBN (ePDF): 978-1-62953-676-7

Cover and book design by Jennifer Canzone

Printed in the United States.

www.crookedlanebooks.com

Crooked Lane Books
2 Park Avenue, 10th Floor
New York, NY 10016

First Edition: July 2016

10 9 8 7 6 5 4 3 2 1

1

The trick was to get to the Forest Preserve late in the afternoon, after the mommy brigade had packed their strollers into their SUVs and headed home, and before everyone else got off work. When Gin Sullivan hit it just right, she could put in six miles without seeing more than a few other people. Later in the summer it would be impossible—the sweltering Chicago heat and humidity would drive even the most dedicated runners off the trails in the heat of the day—but so far, this June had been cool and pleasant.

Gin pulled into a spot vacated by a frazzled-looking woman in a Suburban and was on the trail by 4:30. The occasional early departure from the office was one of the perks of working as a medical examiner. After clearing the day's case load, Gin had left with a clear conscience, knowing that new arrivals to the morgue would not mind waiting until tomorrow.

Patience, in Gin's opinion, was a virtue of the dead.

Besides, she had been in the office before anyone else arrived, and she'd spend several hours working on a journal article tonight after a shower and a quick dinner. This time on the trail was the single indulgence she would allow herself today.

If "indulgence" was the right word for it. Gin kept up an easy, steady pace for the first mile, until the path came to a T, the right branch continuing along the picturesque Cal-Sag Channel.

Gin took the left branch. The terrain quickly became much more challenging, rising up into a rocky, mountainous mound. Thanks to the engineers who'd dug the channel almost one hundred years ago and dumped out the dirt next to it, the preserve provided some of the only decent trail running for hundreds of miles.

Gin headed up the trail, modulating her breathing and increasing her pace, aiming for the narrow space between exhilaration and exhaustion. In those moments, her thoughts splintered and faded and her mind emptied, and there was nothing but the slapping of her feet on dirt, the pain in her lungs, and the faint roar of the interstate in the distance.

She picked her way across a rocky quarter mile before the trail flattened out into a meadow with views of the skyline far in the distance. She paused at her customary turn-around spot, doubling over with her hands on her knees, breathing hard under a stand of aspen while a squirrel chattered angrily from an overhanging branch.

Gin drank in the cool, fresh air, free of the faintly unpleasant odors that filled her days at work: the chemical disinfectant, the ammonia-like formalin, the metallic-sweet-musty smell of decomposition. For these few precious moments, it was just her, the hill, and the weak yellow sunlight streaming through the trees, the past a blur that might have belonged to someone else entirely, the future open and unknowable.

She was stretching out her hamstrings in preparation for the steep descent when her phone rang. She dug the phone from the pocket of her running shorts, wishing she'd left the damn thing in the car.

An 814 number. *Shit.* Gin's thumb hovered over the keypad. The 814 area code included Trumbull, and there wasn't anyone in Trumbull she wanted to talk to. The number was unfamiliar, however. If it had been either of her parents, the choice would have been easy—let it go to voice mail, tackle it later when she'd had time to prepare herself—but Gin couldn't think of anyone else in Trumbull who would want to talk to her.

As a forensic pathologist, Gin had developed an exquisite sense of the fragility of life. And while Richard and Madeleine Sullivan had been perfectly healthy during their last conversation several weeks ago, and though they were still fairly young and stubbornly fit, Gin couldn't think of them without feeling the twin burdens of guilt and responsibility.

She sighed and leaned against the smooth bark of a tall white oak, wiping the perspiration from her forehead with the back of her arm before answering.

"Virginia Sullivan."

"Gin?" a man's voice asked.

And in just that one syllable, everything that Gin had worked so hard to bury deep in the past came crashing back.

* * *

When Gin was in medical school, she had briefly worked as a graduate assistant for a professor who was doing research in speech perception. She learned that speech perception was based on an astonishingly detailed palette of information— not just pitch, gender, and dialect, but also speaking rate, emotional state, and a dozen other indexical properties.

So even though it had been almost two decades since Gin had heard Jake Crosby's voice—he'd be thirty-six now, a few months older than her—it only took that one word for her to know that the voice belonged to the first and only boy she'd ever fallen hard for. But the emotion accompanying that realization was not love or affection or even nostalgia, but a roiling mix of dread and resentment.

"Yes, this is Virginia," she said, to buy herself time. "How can I help you?"

"Gin, it's Jake. Jake Crosby."

"Oh." She squeezed her eyes shut and grimaced. *Play this easy,* she ordered herself. *He doesn't mean anything to you.* "Wow, Jake, I haven't talked to you in ages. How are you?"

"I'm, well, I'm okay, I'm fine." He hesitated, and Gin could picture the way he used to run his hand through his dark, unruly hair when he was flustered. "I'm afraid I've got some, uh, potentially upsetting news."

Mom? Dad? Gin shook her head, clearing the ridiculous fears; there was no reason in the world Jake would have news of her parents. He had ceased to be a part of their lives many years ago.

"Oh?"

"They found a body out in the woods west of town, by the old water tower. They think . . . look, Gin, I'm going out on a limb here, telling you, because no information's been released to the public yet, but it looks like it could be Lily."

Lily. Oh God . . .

The breath caught in Gin's throat; the spring-green world around her lost focus. *Oh, Lily.*

She had to say something, but to speak now would betray her, would destroy the barriers she had built with such care.

"Gin, I'm so sorry," Jake began, and she could hear in his tone that he had his own armor, his own walls. But he had had the time to prepare for this call, and she hadn't. He had probably practiced it in his head a dozen times, the way he'd once practiced his AP English presentations, kicked back in that old beanbag chair in his father's rec room with his hands behind his head while Gin sat at the clunky keyboard working on her college application essays.

Of all people to tell her, of all the gossamer threads that should have been cut long ago—why did it have to be him?

"Okay. I see." Her voice tasted metallic and she knew she probably sounded cold. She'd heard it often enough in her performance reviews at work—her matter-of-fact delivery, a defense against the emotional intensity of her work, made her seem uncaring. "Thank you for letting me know."

"Gin, don't—"

"I'll make some calls."

"Dad will be expecting to hear from you."

Was he warning her, or giving her permission? She wouldn't be surprised if Jake was breaking his father's confidence; he probably shouldn't be telling her anything at all. After all, he was a contractor, not a cop.

But Lawrence Crosby had blurred the lines long before Jake was old enough to do it himself. He always put people first, even if that meant bending the rules. As a small-town chief of police, Lawrence had always tried to do his best by everyone.

Not the best quality in a police officer—something Gin had had to move almost five hundred miles away, and spend years working with big-city cops, to understand.

Memories of Lawrence—his big, sunburned hands with square fingernails cut short; his voice, so gentle, when he had come to their door with his hat in his hands that rainy summer night, water dripping down his face.

"Jake, I . . . appreciate it. Who found it?" Not *her*. Gin wouldn't let it be a her. A body, as she knew better than anyone, was only an awkward and often unlovely assemblage of muscle and fat, bones and teeth.

"Hikers." Jake cleared his throat, perhaps attempting to disguise the faint quaver in his voice. A quaver that could be grief . . . or something else entirely. The old doubts crowded back into Gin's mind along with all the other emotions Jake provoked. "Couple of kids from Duquesne University, hiking

5

along Bear Creek. They had a dog with them. The dog, I guess it got to digging."

"How deep?" Gin asked, surprised. A body buried close enough to the surface for a dog to scent it would have been discovered long before seventeen years had passed.

"I don't know exactly." She could hear him take a breath, all those miles away. "Not far, though, maybe a foot or two. Dad—Lawrence—said the dog was likely going after a bird carcass. But it got down a ways and hit the lid of a cooler. The boys pulled the dog off it but then they got curious themselves. Cleared the dirt off the lid and opened it up."

"A cooler," Gin said, a sick feeling creeping into her gut. "By the Bear Creek trail?"

"Yeah," Jake said. "I know what you're thinking. There's a good chance it was ours."

2

Gin inhaled deeply as she twisted the corkscrew, trying to focus on the wonderful, savory aromas issuing from the kitchen. Behind her, standing at the six-burner Wolf gas range in a Lincoln Park townhouse that cost three times as much as the largest house in Trumbull, Clay Toeffler was searing two tuna steaks. Clay had spent thirty dollars on the fish alone, the sort of extravagance that Gin was still getting used to almost eight months into their relationship.

"Perfect," Clay announced, shutting off the gas. While he slid the steaks onto mounds of sautéed chard, Gin poured the wine, the two of them moving around the small kitchen in practiced harmony.

They were good together—as well-matched as the hand-painted tile backsplash was to the Brazilian granite countertop. Gin was one of the most respected pathologists on staff at the Cook County Medical Examiner's office, and Clay was one of the youngest partners at a leading Chicago law firm. Each had the respect of their colleagues, the admiration of their peers, and more disposable income than time to spend it. Clay was striking in a hard-planed Nordic way, with piercing blue eyes and blond hair, in contrast to Gin's dark brown hair and green eyes, and he had a good five inches on her lean, toned, five-foot-eight frame. They both enjoyed the extensive collection at the Art Institute, and in the eight months they'd been dating, they'd attended the symphony, the opera, three Cubs games, and a handful of charity events that required Clay to put on a tux and Gin to spend her lunch hours shopping for gowns.

Despite being the daughter of a former debutante, and the great-granddaughter of a steel baron, Gin had grown up believing she was ordinary to a fault. Boring, even. She'd never imagined that she would end up with someone like Clay.

"Everything looks delicious," she said as they sat down to dinner.

"You deserve to relax, after the day you had." Clay raised his glass in a toast.

In addition to being articulate and ambitious, Clay was unfailingly considerate. He invited her to dinner at least once a week, knowing she kept almost nothing in the refrigerator in her apartment, which was in a considerably less swanky neighborhood in Hyde Park, ten miles to the south. She spent many more nights at Clay's place than he did at hers. It wasn't just nicer—it was also fully furnished, something that Gin had never managed to get around to since trading her studio apartment for a larger unit the year she finished her fellowship and the Cook County Medical Examiner's office offered her a job.

Tonight, however, despite the beautiful meal and the good wine and Clay's attempts to draw her out, she was having trouble keeping up her end of the conversation. She had fully intended to tell him about the phone call from Jake, but now she was having trouble finding the words. There was simply too much that she had never shared with him.

Clay set down his glass and gave her a quizzical look. "I was going to say, here's to the weekend," he said. "But you look like your mind's still back at work."

"I'm sorry," Gin said, raising her own glass and taking a sip. She managed a smile. "Everything looks fantastic."

"You know I enjoy cooking with you."

She speared a bit of the fish and put it in her mouth, chewing mechanically. It *was* good—and yet it was all she could do to swallow and put down her fork.

"Tough case?" Clay said. "Want to talk about it?"

"Yes . . . actually, I might have to go in over the weekend." Even as she silently scolded herself for her cowardice, Gin scrambled for an excuse, calling up one of her tougher cases from a few years back. "A newborn infant came in with burns over eighty percent of her body. They've arrested the mother."

"Oh, wow, I'm sorry."

Gin froze, her fork halfway to her lips, as it sunk in: had she just lied to Clay? It was the first time—and to her, a serious breech. Gin had been unfailingly honest since adolescence, and other than occasionally stretching the truth to ease social interactions, her few transgressions had been lies of omission.

"Yes," she stammered, "I mean, I—"

Her phone buzzed again in her handbag. The ringtone was the one she'd assigned to her mother—the trilling first measures of a Mozart flute concerto. "I'd better get that," Gin apologized, folding her napkin and setting it on the table next to her plate. She didn't meet Clay's gaze as she reached for her bag; she didn't want to see the kindness and concern in his eyes.

"Hi, Mom," she said as she walked down the hallway, her stocking feet silent on the polished wooden floors. "Give me just a second, okay?"

Clay's office was located in the back of the townhouse's ground floor. She let herself in and shut the door behind her, curling up in his leather desk chair. "All right, I'm here."

"Virginia, I hate to have to tell you this, especially over the phone. Your sister's body has been found."

9

Lily. Seconds ticked by as images of her little sister, who would never be older than sixteen, crowded Gin's mind. All that unruly, sun-streaked hair, the ragged hand-woven bracelets she wore on her wrists and ankles, the doodled "tattoos" she inked on the insides of her wrists at school when she was bored. Glitter shoelaces in her Converse sneakers; a pale scar on the inside of her calf from when she'd tried to shave her legs at the age of eight with their father's razor.

Her smile. Oh, Lily's dazzling smile, even when she was mad at Gin, even when they'd been arguing, even when she swore she'd never speak to her sister again. And her hugs— all arms and elbows, she somehow always managed to bump Gin's chin or nose or poke her in the eye, but she put everything she had into those embraces. With Lily you always knew you were loved, a hundred and ten percent.

"Virginia? Are you there?"

"Mom . . . sorry, I—"

"I know it's a shock."

Gin realized that her mother didn't know Jake had called already. But how would she? Jake was dead to them. Gin pinched the bridge of her nose, composing herself.

"Are *you* all right, Mom?"

"Yes, I'm fine, honey. In a way—I mean, we've only just found out, of course, and I suppose your father and I are still processing, but we've known for a long time that this day was coming."

"Dad's doing all right, too?"

A dry, humorless laugh. "Oh, you know your father. He's in his garden. He's handling it in his own way, but you don't need to worry about him."

"All right." Gin realized she should be asking questions, perpetuating the fiction that she was only just hearing the news. "Where . . ."

"Some hikers discovered the body out by the water tower. I don't know any details yet. Lawrence came by. He couldn't tell us much, but he promised that he'd inform us of any developments as soon as he could. And he's going to work with us to deal with the media, of course." Her mother's voice went quieter. "Thank God for Lawrence."

"Mom—how did they ID her?"

"Oh, honey." Madeleine sighed, and Gin detected a note of exhaustion in her tone. "They still had the dental records from the original investigation. And the clothes she was wearing. Lawrence described them to me and your father."

"Right. Okay." Gin cut her off abruptly, because she knew exactly what Lily had been wearing that day, and she couldn't bear to hear her mother describe the Third Eye Blind T-shirt and the hand-me-down jeans from Gin that Lily had embroidered with daisies on the pockets.

Given the condition of the body, there was no reason they would have to do the autopsy right away; a few more days would make little difference, and considering the high-profile nature of the case, Gin knew the ME's office might well take the precaution of trying to find a pathologist with expertise in advanced decomposition. Grateful for procedural details to focus on, Gin shifted seamlessly into her professional mode, thinking through the process that lay ahead.

Several years earlier, Gin had taken a leave of absence to join a Red Cross team that traveled to the mass graves in Srebrenica where victims of Bosnian ethnic violence were buried. There, she had helped exhume hundreds of bodies and learned more about decomposition than she ever would have in an entire career at Cook County.

She had volunteered for the task at a time when her life had seemed especially devoid of meaning, when a mild, chronic depression had sapped her of vitality. Certainly, the work had given Gin a sense of purpose, but she had never imagined that the skills she'd acquired overseas would come into play in such a personal way. But part of her mind was already reviewing the special considerations for bodies that had been buried for extended periods of time.

"I'll leave tomorrow morning," she said. "I can be there by dinnertime."

"Oh honey, there's no rush. Dad and I are going to have our hands full planning the service. Unless you . . . would you want to help?" There was the faintest note of hope buried in Madeleine's cool competence, but they both knew that Gin and Madeleine collaborating on anything was a bad idea, even with Richard there to referee. Gin's own emotional state would not be soothed by helping pick out a casket, ordering flowers, or talking to caterers, whereas Madeleine excelled at that sort of thing and might find it a comfort. Long before she ran for city council, she had developed formidable organizational skills as a PTA member, Girl Scout leader, and a volunteer for a variety of charities.

"No, Mom, you go ahead without me. I'd just be in the way. I'll call when I'm close, okay?"

"All right, sweetheart. Drive safe. And . . . Virginia?"

"Yes?"

"I love you."

"Me, too," Gin said, wincing as she hung up the phone.

For a moment she sat very still, staring at the darkened screen of the large monitor on Clay's desk.

Lily's disappearance all those years ago had turned Gin's world upside-down. Before, she had been planning to be an environmentalist and work to clean up the threatened upstate watersheds where she'd attended summer camp as a child. Jake was going to be a mechanical engineer, studying robotics so he could help make American manufacturing competitive again.

How idealistic they'd both been.

And how terribly naïve.

* * *

There were eleven pathologists on staff at the Cook County Medical Examiner's office, not counting the chief and the deputy chief, and in any given year, they conducted nearly 2,500 autopsies. So in theory, a month-long leave of absence would, if the workload was evenly distributed among her colleagues, mean an average of two extra cases per person.

Gin did this calculation in her head as she drove east past the Portage exit on I-80 the next morning, the sun glinting prettily through the passenger window of her navy-blue Touareg. Gin had been awake early, tossing and turning until she gave up and got out of bed at dawn.

She'd never managed to tell Clay about the discovery of her sister's body. After helping with the dishes, she'd claimed a migraine and begged off the rest of the evening. That was lie number two. Lie number three was when Clay had asked if everything was all right at home, and Gin had said that her mother was calling to let her know she was planning a birthday party for her father.

Gin was dismayed at how easily these lies tumbled out of her. She knew that Clay would do everything he could to support her, that he would do his best to give comfort, maybe even offer to make the trip home with her. But after the unsettling call with Jake, her head was full of too many disturbing memories and emotions. It was simply better to keep it all to herself. And it had been easy—she was sure Clay didn't suspect a thing. Maybe she should have given in to the lure of dishonesty years ago.

She needed to work on her prevarication skills, though. It would have been smarter to invent a medical emergency—claiming Richard had a minor stroke, for instance—so she would have an obvious reason to leave town. Eventually she was going to have to come clean with Clay, perhaps as early as this afternoon, when he would call to politely inquire if she was feeling well enough to go to the film they'd been planning to see.

The call to her boss had been easier. Reginald "Ducky" Osnos, Cook County's chief medical examiner, was nothing like his lighthearted nickname: a lugubrious, somber man with a hidden but deep vein of kindness, Ducky was starchily correct even with his closest colleagues. "It's—it's a family thing," Gin had told him, after apologizing for calling him at nearly ten o'clock on a Friday evening to say she needed some time off.

"Of course, of course," Ducky had said, accepting her excuse without demanding any further explanation. "Is there anything I can do?"

She'd assured him that there wasn't, promised to update him in a day or so, and said she hoped it wouldn't be more than a week or two until she returned.

Gin stopped for gas and coffee at the Sandusky exit several hours later. As an afterthought, she bought a Hostess cherry pie and ate it in the parking lot with her windows rolled down and the radio picking up WLEC. An old Suzanne Vega song came on, something she'd listened to in high school. She hadn't heard it in years, but she knew every line; she could envision her friend Christine dancing in the clearing by the water tower, barefoot, her Indian-print skirt swirling around her ankles, her twin brother Tom playing air guitar in a cloud of weed smoke. *Night is the cathedral / Where we recognized the sign.*

When she had finished the pastry, she licked the gooey red filling from her fingers and got out of the car to throw away the trash. A thickset old man in a stained T-shirt and suspenders tipped his greasy cap at her as he got into the cab of an ancient pickup.

The music, the junk food—there were more chemicals in that pie than Gin had probably ingested in the entire past month—the flat Ohio accent. So many memories. As Gin threw her wrapper and Styrofoam cup in the trash can next to the gas pumps, she thought guiltily of Clay, with whom she'd shared so little of her history. She pulled out her phone, fully intending to call and catch him up on everything that had happened, but with her thumb hovering over his name in her favorites, she couldn't quite bring herself to dial.

What did that mean about their relationship? If Gin couldn't tell him about the worst thing that had ever happened to her, how close were they, really?

Typing quickly before she changed her mind, she texted an excuse that would buy her a little more time.

I think this migraine's turning out to be something else. Summer cold? So sorry but I think I'd better stay home tonight.

She dropped the phone back into her purse and got back in her car. As she eased back onto the interstate, she resisted the urge to glance in the rearview, back toward Chicago. It felt as though the life she'd built with such care and determination was shattering, and the past was circling around her, like a fog that seeped through invisible cracks.

3

Gin made the Pennsylvania state line by late afternoon. She could count on one hand the number of times she'd returned to Trumbull since leaving for college. It had been easier to invite her parents to visit her, planning rushed, busy tourist weekends so the three of them never had to sit too long together, forced into conversations none of them knew how to have.

But this time was different. This time, there was Lily.

Half an hour outside of Trumbull, Gin noticed something new. A massive Wal-Mart suddenly loomed large where there had once been a roadhouse whose bartenders didn't card, especially if you slid a folded five across the bar. Tom had talked them all into going to the roadhouse a few times. He'd worn them down one by one, first Christine and then Jake and then, finally, Gin. No one ever needed to talk Lily into anything—Lily was always game. The riskier the adventure, the better.

Gin dialed her mother's number. Madeleine picked up before the second ring.

"Hi, sweetheart, are you close?"

"I'll be there in half an hour."

"Wonderful!" The joy in her mother's voice sounded real—but then again, sincerity was a skill her mother had worked on as hard as Richard Sullivan had worked to introduce regenerative medicine to the Trumbull Surgery Center. "I've got cold cuts."

"Sounds good."

"And your room's ready."

"Oh, you didn't have to—I hope you didn't go to any trouble." Gin steeled herself, gripping the steering wheel tightly. "I was thinking I'd check into a motel tomorrow. So I don't get underfoot, with all the planning and everything."

"Virginia." Her mother sounded genuinely aggrieved. "Don't be ridiculous. We're not having people back to the house, anyway. I mean, we're not going to have a wake, especially since the investigation's still going on. It'll be a memorial. Dad was thinking maybe we could use the Grange."

"Oh." In the anxious hours since Jake's call, Gin had simply assumed that her parents would wait until her sister's remains were released to hold a traditional service. But Madeleine was on the city council now, with connections all over town. Even their large home wouldn't hold all the people she'd want to invite. "All right. See you in a bit."

Gin hung up and forced herself to take a deep breath and exhale slowly, consciously relaxing her body. To Madeleine, the line between public and personal matters wasn't just blurred; it had become practically nonexistent. It was one of the profound differences between a mother and daughter who had always had to work hard to find common ground, ever since Gin had been a little girl.

Gin was grateful for the darkness as she drove through the outskirts of town and turned down Hyacinth Lane. Back at the turn of the twentieth century, when the founders of Trumbull planned for a brighter future for the town than it would go on to enjoy, Hyacinth Lane was to be the grandest address of all, with views of the Monongahela River half a mile away. A handful of stately homes had been built for the men who ran the steel and coke processing plants, the largest of which belonged to Theodore Gault, the founder of Gault Steel. Gin pulled into the circular drive, noticing some subtle changes in the blocky Indiana limestone mansion.

The bars on the basement windows had obviously been selected to be as unobtrusive as possible. The steady decline of the town had swept in a tide of low-income residents who brought with them the drug trade that had caused the local crime rate to skyrocket, something Gin's parents had been loath to acknowledge until Madeleine got into politics.

Madeleine and Richard were standing at the front door, her father's hand resting protectively on her mother's back. Her father's neatly trimmed beard had more silver in it than Gin remembered, though maybe it was just the light from the porch fixture. Her mother was wearing a wraparound dress and heels, and her hair was styled into a smooth, chic blonde bob. In their late fifties, the Sullivans were the picture of health and vitality.

Gin fixed a smile on her face and got out of the car, taking a deep breath. Then she walked into their embrace.

Everyone had loved her parents when she and Lily were kids. Richard worked long hours as a surgeon, but on his days off, he was always ready to drive a carful of kids out to Brandywine Lake or down to Tastee-Kone for ice cream. Madeleine had been a devoted mother. She cut grilled-cheese sandwiches into four perfect triangles; she made the girls' beds every morning after they left for school; she patiently braided their hair and bought them umbrellas that matched their lunchboxes.

Her parents folded her into their embrace. Gin inhaled White Linen and her father's pipe tobacco, felt her mother's spray-stiffened hair brushing her cheek and the tight weave of her father's plaid sport shirt. Classical music drifted from the living room, something light, maybe Vivaldi. A faint buzz signaled doom for the moth that had flown into the bug zapper bolted to the porch roof.

"Thank God you're home," her mother whispered, and that very un-Madeleine-like comment was Gin's first clue that things were not as she had expected.

*　*　*

"Trumbull Police Department. How may I direct your call?"

Gin didn't recognize the voice when she called the police department the next morning, but then again, Lois Szabo, who'd answered the phones back when Lily disappeared, would be around eighty now.

"May I speak to Chief Crosby? This is Virginia Sullivan."

A few seconds later, Lawrence himself came on the line. "Ginny-girl!"

That was Lawrence—she'd always been Ginny-girl to him, just like Lily had been Lily-girl. The memory lodged like wet tissue in her throat. "Lawrence, it's good to hear your voice."

"Oh darlin', don't I wish it was under different circumstances. It's a hell of a thing."

"I was wondering if I could come by, if you had a few minutes—"

"Tell you what," Lawrence said, turning brisk. "I promised your mom I'd come by this afternoon. Can we talk then? I should have a little more information for you."

He was giving her the brush-off, and Gin understood. But she was operating on a tight timeline. As soon as the cause of her sister's death was determined to be suspicious—and since she'd been found buried in a cooler, that would be a foregone conclusion—the Allegheny County Police would take over. The mobile crime unit would have been dispatched from Pittsburgh within hours. The Trumbull officers would be relegated to the sidelines. Lawrence might remain involved in the ongoing investigation, but he wouldn't be in charge, unlike when Lily was assumed to have run away all those years ago.

When Gin had been growing up, the Trumbull police department had consisted of Lawrence and a half dozen other officers. Now, after Trumbull's precipitous fall from grace, the department had doubled in size, making Lawrence's tenure there somewhat surprising. An old cowboy cop who'd spent most of his career rounding up check forgers and town drunks didn't seem like the ideal candidate to battle the bloody gang rivalries being played out on the streets of Trumbull.

"Listen," she said, trying to keep her tone as light as possible. "I thought I'd give Harvey Chozick a call."

"You know him?" Lawrence sounded surprised that Gin would know the chief Allegheny County medical examiner.

"Not in person," Gin hedged. "Professionally, I've heard of him, and I'm familiar with some of his published work. But I thought—they're bound to want to talk to me anyway."

Getting anywhere near the investigation would be difficult, except for one thing: there was unlikely to be anyone on staff whose expertise with decomp cases rivaled her own. And in a case that was likely to draw a huge amount of media attention, the ME would be doing everything he could to ensure the integrity of the investigation.

"Yeah, probably. You kids . . . that was a heck of a summer. All of you thick as thieves."

"Yes." For a moment, Gin let the silence stretch. The investigation had the potential to unearth all kinds of forgotten things. She made a snap decision. "Look, Lawrence, I just thought maybe—I mean, later, with Mom there, I don't know . . . It's just, the cooler."

"Ah."

"I mean—was it ours? Could you tell?"

She could hear his breathing—heavy, just this side of labored—in the silence. "Look, honey, let's just wait until this afternoon, okay? I've got another call, I've got to take it."

Another man might have hung up then, but Lawrence was old school. Polite, even in the face of everything.

"Of course," Gin said. "I'll see you then."

But really—who else's could it have been?

Gin pressed the phone thoughtfully to her hip. She had walked out to the backyard to make the call, and she stood now surrounded by the dew-heavy hostas lining the brick patio and the bud-laden camellias that would soon burst into glorious bloom.

By the time she'd woken that morning, her parents were both already gone for the day. She knew her father would have insisted on keeping to his surgical schedule; her mother was probably in her office downtown. They both found solace in their work, a trait Gin shared.

She had the house to herself, but she'd already begun to feel suffocated by it. The two smaller bedrooms upstairs shared a Jack-and-Jill bathroom, and while the doors from the bath and hall to the other bedroom were both closed, Gin knew what lay behind them: her sister's room, exactly as it had been left the day she disappeared.

Not so Gin's room, which Madeleine had redecorated while Gin was in her residency. The heavy drapes and the quilted coverlet and mounds of pillows were tasteful but anonymous, and still Gin couldn't stand to be in the room.

Next door, Lily's room still held the echo of joyful chaos. The white-painted bed with its Dotted Swiss canopy was still unmade, the quilt kicked to the bottom of the mattress the way Lily always used to do when she had one of her frequent stomach aches. The matching bookcase held her Beanie Baby collection; her bulletin board was covered with photos and notes she'd passed with her friends.

Lily had disappeared before the advent of texting, before she ever owned a cell phone. The evidence of her life was forever frozen on the cusp of a world that had completely changed. What would she think, if instead of spending the last two decades in the lonely grave not two miles away, Lily were to return today? What would she make of her mother's success, her father's constancy?

What would she think of the woman her sister had become?

Gin paused on the wide landing at the top of the stairs, staring down the hallway at the closed door to her parent's bedroom. It took up the left wing of the house, a lovely room with a glassed-in porch and arched windows. The door had been kept resolutely closed all through Gin's childhood, entrance by invitation only. Richard never emerged from that room unless he was showered and neatly dressed; Madeleine stowed her exquisite treasures—gloves and perfume atomizers and hair ornaments and dance cards from her debutante season—in the furniture she had brought with her from Philadelphia. Led by Lily, the girls had investigated on a few occasions, looking for clues to their mother's unknowable depths.

Gin entered the bathroom she'd shared with Lily and stripped, dropping her clothes on the floor. She turned on the shower as hot as it would go and stood under the stinging spray, thinking about the afternoon when she'd come into the bathroom to find her sister, huddled naked in the corner of the shower, crying so hard she couldn't speak.

4

The next morning, dressed in jeans and a black T-shirt she'd hastily packed the day before, Gin decided to walk into town for breakfast. From the house to the intersection of State and Elm, where Veterans' Park was bounded on three sides by the carcass of the old downtown, was a lovely, tree-lined walk of less than half a mile. The worst of Trumbull's disgrace was to the east of town, a grid of run-down buildings and shuttered shops in the shadow of the old cola-processing plant.

A modest renaissance, championed by her mother, had taken tenuous hold downtown. Last time Gin had been here, a little organic café had appeared where the copy shop used to be, and Gin headed for it, hoping to get some decent coffee.

She was waiting for one of the town's three stoplights to change when the truck pulled up in front of her. Big and hulking and exactly the same shade of green it had been twenty years ago, the old Ford was like a stone tossed from the shore of her past, landing with a resounding splash—and there was Jake at the wheel.

He did a double take that might have been comical under other circumstances, old friends meeting by chance. But they weren't old friends, exactly. They had been so much more—until they were nothing.

Jake. Fury welled up inside her, hurt so powerful it had a taste, like rust in her mouth. As for Jake, his expression darkened even as he flashed a thin smile, then passed by her to park.

She walked toward the truck as Jake climbed out, fixing what she hoped was a neutral expression on her face while the old engine popped and banged. They looked at each other uneasily. "Hello, Jake."

He reached for her hand, pressing her fingers between his large, callused palms. She jerked her hand back after a second.

"You got in last night?" he asked.

"Yes. Mom and Dad stayed up."

"They must be . . . I'm glad you're back here, for them."

His voice was steady, with no trace of the bitter barbs that had once landed between them. He had retained the wholesome good looks from his high school years, but maturity had brought a kind of hardness to his features, a few lines to his sun-burnished skin. Same stick-straight thick brown hair, a few strands of silver at the temples.

She hadn't been prepared for the emotional impact of seeing him again. Madeleine had slipped in allusions to Jake's welfare over the years, always from a safe remove. Usually, she mentioned him in an e-mail, which was the default form of communication between the three surviving Sullivans.

Saw Jake at the records office pulling permits.

Judge Banner told Dad that Jake's added another crew. They got the demolition job. Imagine, no more roller rink!

Ida mentioned Lawrence got that flu. Seems like folks are getting it this year whether they got the

vaccine or not. Lucky he's got Jake to look in
on him.

"You look good," Gin said, recovering her composure. She
could do this—she could act like seeing him meant nothing.

"You—well, no one would believe that almost twenty years
have gone by." Jake shifted his weight restlessly. "Listen, are
you doing anything right now? Want to get a cup of coffee?"

Gin cast her gaze across the park, where a handful of
young mothers were gathered with their toddlers and babies,
and a small group of teenagers were clustered by the basketball
court. She could turn him down. She *should* turn him down.
Except that everything she thought she knew about Jake Crosby
had been flung violently into question again, the moment the
cooler was unearthed. The old doubts were exposed, the painful knotted threads of loyalty and loss, blame and longing. If
there was a chance to find out what had really happened to
Lily, it once again looked like Jake might hold the key.

"Yes, actually," she said. "Mom's still making the decaf she
gets in a can at the grocery store."

"There's an organic coffee company in Trumbull now."

"Still no Starbucks?"

"Not on your mom's watch."

That made her laugh despite herself, and Jake joined in,
and for a moment her defenses wavered. "God, it's good to see
you," he said, and then before she could respond, he added,
"The Triangle's still probably our best bet," and walked into
the street to stop traffic for her, as though it was 1960 and
Trumbull was still thriving and they were just a couple of nice
kids with time on their hands.

* * *

The Triangle Diner was only vaguely triangular. It was more of
a blunt-tipped polygon carved from what had been the lobby

25

of the old theater. When the multiplex cinema had opened in the new mall in nearby Greensburg in the seventies, the theater closed, and a handful of businesses had tried to make a go in the beautiful old building.

Only the Triangle survived, though the faces were all new to Gin. They were greeted by a young Asian man with full-sleeve tattoos. The girl who seated them was pretty enough to walk a runway in New York City, but when she opened her mouth, her flat accent gave her away as a local.

"Hi, Mr. Crosby," she said. "You want the buckwheat and over hard?"

"That'll be great, Ell," he said. "How's your mom?"

"Good, I guess." The girl looked shyly down at her order pad. "Ma'am, what can I get you?"

Gin glanced at the menu chalked on a board behind the register. It had been updated some since the nineties, one side still devoted to eggs and flapjacks, the other venturing bravely into organic fare. "How about the spelt French toast?"

The girl nodded and left them alone.

Jake was watching her carefully. "Gin . . . I don't even know where to begin. I would say I know this must be a shock to you. I mean . . . it is for me. I never thought—I guess I never thought they'd find her."

Gin's emotional state had been chaotic in the months after Lily's disappearance. Anger, blame, grief, and loneliness—a toxic brew of emotions too complex for any adolescent to untangle, much less one like Gin who'd never been good at showing her feelings. When she went away to college that fall, it was a relief to shut her former life out, to lie to her new friends and say that she was an only child. As for Jake . . . when the girls in her dorm asked if she had a boyfriend at home, it was easy to shrug and say no.

Jake was staring at her, waiting for her to respond. "It'll be good for Mom and Dad to have closure," Gin said woodenly, a

variation of the things she and her colleagues said when they
had to interact with the families of their cases. No one liked
dealing with the families—forensic pathology tended to draw
introverts, people more comfortable behind the mask in the
noble silence of the morgue than outside it.

Jake quirked one eyebrow up. He wasn't fooled. "Look, I'm
glad I saw you today. I didn't know if it would be . . . welcome,
for me to come around to see you. How your folks would feel."

Everyone knew how Richard Sullivan felt about Jake. What
surprised Gin was that Jake would want to see her at all. "Your
dad's coming over this afternoon," she said, avoiding the topic
of her father. "Look, Jake, have you had a chance to find out?
Is it our cooler?"

He nodded, running his hand through his hair in frustration. "Dad already called Lloyd in, and he gave a statement
to the county cops. Dad offered to step off, but so far they
haven't taken him up on it."

"And Lloyd . . . ?"

"Took one look and pointed out where he'd carved his ini-
tials with the wood burner. But he also told the detectives he
didn't have any idea what happened to the cooler when he got
rid of it. His memory's not what it used to be."

Gin's own memories of Lloyd were of a kindly old man,
but he couldn't have been more than sixty then. A lifetime
of sun damage spotted and creased his Irish skin, but he still
took off every chance he got to fish and hunt. He'd been Lawrence's partner before Lawrence got promoted to chief, and to
hear them tell it, they'd spent as much time hunting deer and
drinking beer as working in the old days. After his wife left,
Lawrence was too busy raising Jake to hunt, but Gin remembered more than one Sunday dinner at the Crosby's when
Lloyd arrived wearing a clean shirt buttoned up to his chin,
his hat in his hand, with a couple of plucked and cleaned ducks
ready to throw on the grill.

Jake had found the cooler on Lloyd's trash heap after Lloyd decided to treat himself to a new one, in anticipation of a fishing trip down to the Florida Keys. The older man encouraged Jake to take whatever he liked before he drove the rest to the dump. It had been so long ago, no wonder the details were murky in Lloyd's mind.

"Well, that pretty much put the matter to rest. The county boys questioned Lloyd for an hour or so, Dad said, but in the end he couldn't really give them much."

"They can't think *he* had anything to do with it—"

"Of course not. Look at it from their perspective, Gin."

She thought about it for a moment. Jake had fired the first volley—acknowledging the ugly question between them. "I guess from their perspective, you're still their best bet," she said coolly. "Since you were with her that night."

He nodded. "I imagine they'll want to talk to me today. Dad told me to keep my phone handy."

What are you going to tell them? Gin wanted to ask, but another question crowded her thoughts:

Will it be anywhere close to the truth?

5

July 3, 1998

Gin was helping her mother make red, white, and blue crepe-paper starbursts to decorate the porch when Tom and Christine arrived. Her fingertips were blue with the dye from the paper when they walked in the door.

The twins were slathered with sunscreen, smelling like piña coladas. Christine had a summer job at the medical center, filing and answering phones for her dad, and could only work on her tan on the weekends, so Tom was well ahead of her. His blue eyes sparkled with life and his hair had gone a peculiar green-tinged shade of pale blond from chlorine, a side effect of his lifeguarding job. The last two Septembers, he'd ceremoniously shaved his head for the pep rally that kicked off the school year, and this year—his senior year—he would be a cocaptain of the football team.

But the pep rally was still two months away, an eternity when measured by the slow, sultry clock of summer in Trumbull. Gin had been helping her mother set up the backyard all day; tomorrow at ten o'clock, a few dozen friends and neighbors would gather for brunch, and then they would all walk to town to watch the parade. Tomorrow night there would be fireworks in Veterans' Park.

Tom and Christine didn't bother to knock. They'd been regular visitors to this house for years, ever since their father, Spencer, had arrived in town, a grieving widower with infant twins in tow. Spencer and Richard had worked together in Chicago, and Richard convinced him to take the director of clinical operations job at the surgery center he was starting.

Madeleine had cared for the twins along with baby Virginia, since they were all born within months of each other. When Lily came along, Madeleine said she barely noticed, so busy was she with diapers and bottles and laundry.

"Hi, Mrs. Sullivan," the twins called, their voices an echo of each other, separated by an octave. Christine pulled her tank dress self-consciously lower, trying to cover up her bikini; Madeleine frowned on skimpy swimsuits. Madeleine came out of her little office off the laundry room, wiping her hands on her apron, already reaching for the list tacked to the fridge with a magnet, and kissed them each absently.

"Hi, kids. Listen, Virginia, will you ask Jake to bring the ice on the way back? I'll give you some money. I think three of the big bags will be enough, and your father can get more in the morning if we need it."

Gin accepted the folded twenty that her mother dug from her big white purse, and then they all clattered up the stairs and into Lily's room.

It had always been the four of them. They had taken baths together, napped together, gone on camping and Disney trips together. At first, Mr. Parker had come along on these adventures, the Sullivans folding him into their own family as though their hale goodwill would be enough to cure him of his melancholia. And it had seemed to work. Gin remembered countless summer evenings chasing fireflies with her sister and their friends while the three adults talked and drank wine.

Occasionally Mr. Parker brought a friend of his own, some woman who taught school or worked in a bank or sold real estate, as exotic as a spy in her summer dress and lipstick and cloud of perfume, and then the children would skulk solemn and tentative at the edges of the yard, watching. But these girl-friends never lasted long. Mr. Parker seemed destined to be a bachelor forever, and Gin's parents seemed content to be the shore on which he perpetually washed up.

That phase ended, of course. Gin couldn't remember the change, so gradual had it been, but each of the adults seemed to find their own distractions. All four kids started school, and the years ticked by. Tom was good at every sport he picked up, Lily was in trouble as often as not, Christine was in student government, and Gin was content to be left to her pursuit of good grades. The dynamics of their four-way friendship ebbed and flowed, leaving room for fits of pique and moody détentes, screaming battles and passionate apologies, pranks and dares, betrayals and crushes. When Gin started dating Jake halfway through her junior year of high school, their little quartet had made room for him, his presence barely causing a ripple in the placid surface of their friendship.

Gin had thought of the twins as family right up until the day she found Tom and Lily kissing in the garage over Christmas break, when Lily had just turned sixteen and Tom was weeks shy of his eighteenth birthday. But that, too, seemed inevitable in retrospect. Reckless, passionate, bubbly Lily; popular, headstrong Tom—the two of them seemed to understand each other. Even their parents were delighted, with the exception of Madeleine, who was dead set against the pair's romance; but the rest of them laughed her off, much as they'd laughed off her idea of a cotillion at the country club or her pleas for Lily to cut her hair or for Gin to take Latin.

Now it was summer, and it was dawning on them all that life as they knew it was coming to a close. Jake and Gin had been accepted to Ohio State, Christine was going to Temple, and Tom seemed remarkably unfazed to be headed to Duquesne after none of the athletic scholarships he had hoped for materialized. Only Lily would be left behind, and—in typical Lily fashion—she was expressing her displeasure with frequent fits of temper interspersed with moody afternoons sequestered in her room, complaining of mysterious pains that inevitably turned out to be nothing.

At the moment, as the rest of them burst through her door, Lily was leaning out the window, her toes barely touching the floor. Gin's heart flew to her throat as only an older sister's can: she'd been in charge of wild Lily's safety since Lily was an eighteen-month-old determined to climb out of her crib.

"Lil!" Gin shrieked, while Christine sorted through the tray of barrettes on Lily's dresser—the three girls were constantly trading hair accessories that summer. Tom seized Lily around the waist, picked her up, and twirled her. Lily shrieked and held on, laughing, and Gin bit back the scolding that had been on the tip of her tongue.

She took Lily's place at the window. There, idling in the circular drive in front of the house, was Jake Crosby in the old truck he'd bought with his lawn-mowing money. His arm hung out the window, and he was craning his neck to look up. When he saw Gin, he tapped his lips—shorthand for a kiss, and a promise for later.

Gin smiled down at him and felt her heart swell up like a sponge soaking up pure sunshine. Jake was hers—finally she had something that no one else had.

"Look what I got from Lloyd!" he called. In the bed of the truck was the biggest, filthiest cooler Gin had ever seen, a dented plastic box plastered all over with bumper stickers. "We can take it to the creek. Keep the sodas cold."

He winked when he said it, and Gin knew it wasn't soda in that cooler. Tom and Jake liked Heineken when they could get someone to buy it for them, but mostly they settled for PBR, $2.99 for a six-pack at a gas station on the far side of town.

An hour later, they were sitting on the long, flat sand bar in the middle of Bear Creek near the water tower, their feet in the water, sweating in the humid afternoon. A storm threatened in the distance; the sky to the east was thickening with clouds. No matter; it would be gone by tomorrow. Secretly, Gin wished for a storm, for the excitement of the purpling sky, the plummeting temperature, the whipping of dust into the air and green acorns shaken from the trees to roll down the creek bank into the water.

Even more than a storm, Gin wished for the ability to capture this moment in time, preserve it forever, and take it with her when she and Jake left for college. Lately, Lily had been petulant with her; only Christine seemed to be able to talk her out of her moods. But today was perfect. If it weren't for the future Gin had planned with Jake, she might have wished that the five of them—six, if you counted Ben Blankenship, Christine's latest boyfriend—could just stay here by the creek for the rest of their lives.

Lily was sprawled in Tom's lap, her bare feet dirty, as far from the water as she could get; she said the reeds along the shore gave her a rash. She was lazily weaving one of her bracelets; this one was red and orange, a gift for Christine to go with her new sundress. Christine was climbing the narrow metal ladder attached to the old water tower. Ben, several rungs ahead, had talked her into it. Watching them, small as beetles in the distance, halfway up the ladder, Gin knew Ben was in for a disappointment. No girl allowed herself to be lured up that ladder unless she was planning on being kissed, but Christine was never distracted by a boy for long.

Jake tickled Gin's cheek with a fringed stem of Queen Anne's Lace. She was lying on a smooth rock, enjoying the heat of it on her spine; she'd changed from the Speedo that her mother made her wear into the bikini she'd bought with her allowance. Gold-toned rings joined the fabric at her hips and between her breasts. Seeing her skin through the rings made Gin feel sophisticated in a way she couldn't explain.

Jake was leaning on his elbow beside her, watching her. She tilted her head to avoid the direct glare of the sun, happy to be watched. The smell of wet leaves was sweet on the air.

Lily leaped up from the rock and plunged into the creek, breaking the perfect moment. She came up for air laughing and drenched. "Save me!" she yelled, splashing water at Gin.

Tom got up and went in the water after her, and if only Gin had known it would be one of her last afternoons with Lily, she might have done the same.

6

The French toast arrived, drizzled in aromatic honey and garnished with an artfully sliced and fanned strawberry.

"Wow," Gin said. "Things have come a long way around here, at least in the food department."

"Here, anyway." Jake upended the hot sauce bottle on his scrambled eggs. "Out there . . . well, some things haven't changed much at all."

"Why do you stay?" Gin asked abruptly. Her curiosity was genuine. "Why put yourself through this?"

He held her gaze, his expression shadowed. "By *this*, do you mean the shitty economy, watching this town give up and die, get taken over by meth heads? Or do you mean living in a town of six thousand people, nearly all of whom probably think I'm a murderer?"

"You stay for Lawrence," Gin said, sidestepping the question.

Jake shrugged. "Lawrence doesn't need me now. I stay because my work is here, my whole life. My guys do good work; there's always someone ready to hire us. And as for the people who won't . . . well, if they need a building boarded up, they can hire a few guys at Home Depot and buy a bucket of screws and a stack of plywood, get the job done by noon. If they want the place burned down so they can collect on insurance, there's people they can hire for that, too."

"I never said—"

"Listen, it was tough at first, I admit that. Dad wanted me to go back to school before he was fully recovered. I wanted to make sure he wasn't trying to do too much, too soon. But we figured it out. We got by. I started picking up renovation work when the economy turned around. Thirty miles to a job site is nothing when someone wants to put in a seventy-five-thousand-dollar kitchen, you know?"

"None of that's going to help you if the county cops come after you," Gin said. "Have you got a good lawyer?"

The corner of his mouth twitched. He reached across the table and put his hand over hers, pressing down. The gesture wasn't meant to be tender. "So you still believe I could have done it? Killed Lily?" he asked, very quietly.

She winced, wishing she hadn't agreed to this conversation. She wasn't really sure what she'd been hoping to get out of it. If the investigation led to conclusive proof of Jake's guilt, then she was sure to regret every second she spent in his company.

The door opened and three men in shirts and ties and city haircuts came in, laughing at something one of them said.

A change came over Jake. He laid his silverware across his plate and crumpled up his napkin. Then he reached for his wallet, tugging out a couple of bills and pushing them under his plate, more than enough for the whole bill.

"I've got to run," he said. "Truth is this probably wasn't such a hot idea."

He was up and out of the booth before Gin could react. His hand rested on her shoulder so briefly that she felt the aftershock of his touch more than the touch itself.

"No matter what happens," he said, "the things I said then are still true now. But I'll do my best to stay out of your way."

He ducked out the side door, and Gin stared at her plate, wondering which things he meant. His protestations of innocence? Or something else?

Gin took a sip of her coffee. The three men headed for a big, square four-top by the back. When they passed Gin's table, one of them stopped. His face was florid and pink from the rapidly warming day.

"Gin?" he said. "Oh my God, it's you."

But she didn't recognize him. Until he pulled her out of her chair, into his arms, making a choking, sobbing sound into the crook of her neck. "I'm so sorry," he said hoarsely as he pulled away, and Gin suddenly realized that underneath thirty extra pounds he could have done without, it was Tom.

7

"I can't believe it's you," Gin said.

Tom laughed self-consciously. "Neither can my personal trainer. I think he's going to quit if I don't lose a few pounds by fall. He's got me signed up for a ten-K. Kind of a tough love thing."

"No no, you look wonderful," Gin said, though it was only selectively true. Tom had held onto his hair and the wholesome good looks he'd gotten from his mother's side, the mother who'd died giving birth to him and his sister.

But he'd also started to take on the florid complexion with broken capillaries that signaled a drinking problem. Gin had plenty of experience seeing the ravages of addiction on her cases, and she wasn't too surprised that Tom's habits hadn't changed. By the summer after their senior year, he was putting away a six pack and a half every night they were together. The version of the stories that reached her over the next few years, filtered first through Spencer and then through her mother, had a decidedly "boys will be boys" tone to them. Tom had gone Greek at Duquesne, and there had been fraternity pranks as well as an extra semester to make up for some academic probation.

But she hadn't anticipated his physical decline. In the Christmas card Spencer had sent a few years ago, before Christine's divorce, Tom still looked like the golden boy he'd always been.

"Listen." Tom put his hands on her shoulders, digging in with his fingers. "I can't even begin. I mean . . . Lily. God."

"Thank you, Tom, but—"

"I don't even know how to put it into words. I mean, I'm just so sorry, Gin. She's . . . it's like, it brings it all back again, you know?"

That was Tom: unparalleled master of the obvious. He'd never been capable of much depth. Seventeen years ago, he had been a bit like an adolescent Labrador, tearing around after Lily and looking for excitement. He didn't think about the future; he had rarely seemed to think past the next ten minutes.

But when Lily disappeared, Tom had shut down completely. It was the only time in his life that he'd refused even to talk to his twin sister. Christine had implored Gin to help, but Gin was so consumed by her worry about Lily that she'd shut her out.

A wave of guilt passed through Gin. This was what she had chosen to leave behind—people who were struggling, people who weren't strong enough to devise strategies for dealing with loss.

"But listen to me," Tom said, seemingly genuinely stricken. "I mean, you and your family, God, I know I can't imagine what you're going through. I just, if there's anything I can do, seriously, Gin."

"Tom. Thank you." Her words had the soft, spongy quality of checked tears; Tom's eyes were shiny and pink, too. "How is Christine?" she asked, to change the subject.

"Well, you heard she and Brandon split up."

"Yes, actually, Mom mentioned it." Although Gin would have been hard pressed to come up with his name—that was one of the weddings she'd skipped. "I'm sorry to hear it."

"Nah, it's probably for the best. Got a little ugly there; Brandon had some extracurricular activities, if you catch my drift."

"How are the kids doing?"

"Aw, they're awesome. Especially Olive. I mean, Austen is cool, too, but he's still kind of too young to be good at anything. I get Olive out there shooting sometimes—she's got real potential." He mimed a free throw. "Lucky she got her dad's height."

"That's great, Tom." Gin meant it, even as she thought sadly that of the five of them, only Christine had become a parent.

"What about you? How are things in the Windy City?"

"Oh, you know. Fine." Just once, Gin had invited Tom and Christine to come up and visit. It was during her first year in Chicago, when she was a first-year resident at the University of Chicago. But the visit never happened, and Gin had wondered since then if it had already been too late. If their friendship had already disappeared, along with Lily.

"It better be fine, after all that school." Tom gave a mock shudder. He hated studying and had barely graduated from Duquesne. He wasn't stupid, but he had the work habits of his teen self.

"Work is good. I like it."

"And you were dating a lawyer, right?"

"Clay's an attorney, yes," Gin said. "He works for one of the big downtown firms."

"Aw, I'm glad you found someone, Gin."

She didn't miss the wistfulness in his tone. "What about you? Seeing anyone?"

"Me? No, no. I mean yeah, a couple people. Nothing serious. Work, long days, you know how it gets." His discomfort was evident in his lowered gaze, his rapid speech.

"You just haven't found the right woman yet." Gin smiled kindly. Tom had been a heartbreaker before ending up with Lily, and her mother implied he'd made the rounds of the sororities while at school. Since then, though, he'd been stuck in the ever-shrinking pond of Trumbull. Gin almost felt sorry for him.

"You going to see Dad while you're here?" He blinked, and seemed to catch up a half-second later. "Wait, I guess that would be . . . I mean, hell, it's time they all get over that, right? Especially now."

"I'd love to see the whole family," Gin said diplomatically. "You're coming to the memorial on Saturday, aren't you?"

"Of course. Dad called this morning—he said you're having it at the Grange."

Gin nodded. "It can accommodate a lot of people. And Mom was able to bring in the caterers she wanted."

"Not local . . ."

"I'm not sure, actually. We didn't have much time to talk last night. I imagine I'll find out more this afternoon." She sighed. "I don't suppose I can talk you into coming for dinner, can I? Dealing with the two of them on my own can be . . . challenging."

Now it was Tom's turn to look uncomfortable. "I love your folks, but I always feel like I'm on the verge of disappointing them. Of course, that's how I feel around my dad, too. Anyway, I'm afraid I can't make it over tonight, but thanks for the invitation. A rain check?"

"Absolutely."

"You going to be around for a while this time, Ginny?" His voice had softened and there was sadness in his eyes.

"I'm not sure. Probably through the end of the week, anyway. It depends on . . . on whether there's anything I can do here."

"For your folks?"

"Well, that, and . . ." Gin decided it would be best not to voice her intention to lend a hand with the investigation. "And just reconnecting with people," she finished awkwardly.

"Like Jake? I saw him when I came in. I'm sorry I didn't come over right away—things are still . . . awkward, between us. Which is kind of tough, as you might imagine, given the size of this shithole town."

"Jake still holds you responsible for the accusations against him back then?"

Tom looked increasingly uncomfortable. "Not just me . . . well, maybe mostly me. He never believed me, that I didn't really think he did it. Not deep down, because of the stupid things I said. I tried to apologize, you know . . . It's just, these things take on a life of their own."

"Well, I'm glad you're coming on Saturday. I'm hoping Lawrence will be there, too," she said carefully. "And Jake may make an appearance. I hope that won't be uncomfortable for you . . ."

"Aw, hell no, of course not," Tom said, forcing a jocular tone. "We're all adults. It was so long ago—and now the important thing is to give Lily the peace she deserves, let your parents and you grieve."

"All of us," Gin said with feeling. "You, too."

"She was special," Tom said quietly. "I've never met anyone like her. I doubt I ever will."

Gin felt her eyes mist over, and rubbed at them impatiently. She wasn't going to fall apart—not here, not in front of the whole town.

"You know, there's bound to be questions about that cooler," she said, changing the subject. "The only people who knew it was there—"

"Was half the senior class," Tom finished her sentence. "Not to mention anyone who ever fished or dirt biked or went walking out there. Wasn't like we ever tried to hide it."

"It was too big to hide," Gin remembered. At first they'd planned to haul it back and forth in Jake's truck, but then they decided that the sheer size and unwieldiness of it would be

42

deterrent enough to anyone taking it. They'd dragged it close to the pilings under a rustic footbridge over the creek, carrying in their ice and beer and sandwiches.

"Did we even notice it was gone?" Tom asked. "I can't remember now."

Gin thought back: after her sister's disappearance, she'd never returned to the clearing. And two months later, she left for college.

"I don't think I ever went back there," she said softly. "Not that summer. Not ever."

They were quiet for a moment. Then Tom cleared his throat. "Well, I'd better get going. I'll see you Saturday, if not before. And Gin? It's really good to see you again."

"You, too." That, at least, she really meant.

8

When she got back to the house, a Trumbull police vehicle was parked in the drive behind her mother's Volvo. It was disconcerting to see that it was a hulking Explorer; gone were the Impalas that Gin remembered from her high school years.

Letting herself in the front door, she could hear Lawrence's voice in the kitchen. She found him sitting with her mother over untouched slices of coffee cake.

"And there she is," Lawrence said with forced cheer, pushing back from the table and getting up, the process slowed by his arthritic joints. Lawrence, who would now be in his late sixties, was older than the other parents, something that had made him seem especially avuncular when Gin was young.

Gin was dismayed to see how old he looked: his back was hunched, and deep lines had taken over his face. He had finally given up the comb-over, the strands he'd kept plastered across the smooth dome of his bald, freckled head all those years, and he somehow looked more vulnerable with the close crop of gray hair. He had been in his thirties when Jake was born, and Jake had confided to Gin once that his much-younger mother had blamed Lawrence for robbing her of her youth, before she left them both for good.

"He told me he figured it was a little too late to give me back," Jake had reported wryly. It was local legend how Lawrence had let the boy ride along in the cruiser on school holidays and vacations. Some of town gossips had clucked that it was a disgrace, only to have to eat their words when Jake graduated at the top of the class, second only to Gin.

Jake had had a bright future, once.

Gin held back when hugging Lawrence, all too aware of the sharp edges of his shoulder blades, the thinness of his biceps. But Lawrence gripped her hard and murmured fiercely, "You are a sight for sore eyes, Ginny-girl. We're all so glad you're here now."

"Thank you," she murmured, swallowing her feelings of guilt over the suspicions she couldn't quash, the resentment she still felt toward Jake.

"This—this awful thing, it's devastated all of us," Lawrence continued. "I was just saying to your mom, not a day has gone that I haven't thought of your sister."

Madeleine got up and went to the stove, busying herself with cutting a slice of pastry from the white bakery box. "I'll make more coffee," she said.

"Not for me, Mom. Is Dad around?"

"No, sweetheart, he took a run up to the Burgh to finalize things with the caterers."

The Burgh—what they'd called Pittsburgh in high school, lacing their voices with contempt for a city fifty times the size of their town but nowhere near big enough for their dreams. She had never heard her mother use the term before.

"Didn't he want to be here?" Gin asked. "To hear what Lawrence has to say?"

"I'll fill him in later," her mother said, sidestepping the question.

"We've just got started," Lawrence said tactfully. "You haven't missed much."

"Have the county police already taken over the case?"

"Yep, fella name of Stillman's in charge. Good guy, been a detective nine, ten years now. I knew him when he was still a beat cop. Then they got this young guy, Witt. Sharp as a tack. Liam's his first name, he came up from downstate."

It was like Lawrence never to say a bad word about a colleague. It was impossible to know how he really felt about the detectives.

"And their team processed the scene?"

"Yes, the crew was down here within a couple hours of the locals calling it in, I got to hand it to them. Course we didn't do much other than take pictures and secure it. But Stillman and me, we're working close on this one. We've set aside the big conference room for the team." He grimaced. "Me and him'll be doing the press conference together tonight."

"The press," Madeleine said tightly. "It's bad enough just dealing with the Pittsburgh crews. Now it looks like they're coming from as far away as Chicago. *People*'s sending someone up here to take a look. They called the office."

"Now don't worry, we're going to keep them in check," Lawrence said, patting Madeleine's hand.

"It really makes no sense to report it now." Madeleine's cheeks were pink with anger.

"Lawrence." Gin would have preferred to do this away from Madeleine; she didn't have a sense of how much her mother could handle. "What can you tell me about Lily? Did the initial examination reveal anything?"

"Now, Gin," Lawrence reproved her gently.

But Gin knew that if she backed off now, she'd be setting the tone for every future interaction with Lawrence, who probably had trouble accepting that she was a grownup, a professional. And the dark, gnawing anxiety she'd felt since Jake's call had not diminished. She had to be involved. Had to see for herself what had been done to her sister.

Gin was not about to waste her chance to help identify Lily's killer. Perhaps the county police were competent, perhaps they were even excellent, but Gin wasn't going to leave anything to chance. She was determined to make sure that nothing was missed at autopsy by a pathologist unfamiliar with the effects that being buried for seventeen years would have on a body. She was hopeful that Harvey Chozick would see things the same way.

At the same time, she couldn't risk alienating Lawrence in any way. Given their family's friendship, and her one-time involvement with Jake, he might bend some rules for her. The county officers would have no such incentive.

She took a breath. "Lawrence, I'm not going to say anything to anyone, you know that. My only—*only*—goal here is to help. I need to know what happened to my sister. And I knew her better than anyone, so I might have a unique perspective."

The older man nodded slightly. "Ginny. Honey. This is me speaking to you as a friend, you understand. I don't need to tell you I could lose my job for giving you confidential information."

"No, you don't."

We're in this together, Gin was tempted to add—her family, the Crosbys, and the Parkers. Three families, or what was left of them anyway, their histories knitted together in ways they might try to forget but could never undo.

Lawrence sighed and shifted uncomfortably. "She had a head injury. The condition of the body made it hard to say much more than that, but the skull was fractured."

"Mom, don't feel like you have to stay for this," Gin said.

"It's all right."

"They won't know more until they do the autopsy, but one of the crime-scene guys showed me, he called it a depression fracture. More like a, I guess you'd say like a dent, not a crack."

"When is the autopsy scheduled?"

Lawrence's forehead creased. "Ginny, sweetheart, you *know* you can't be there."

"I know . . . I know, Lawrence. I just wondered."

"It was supposed to be this afternoon, but they ended up delaying it," Lawrence admitted. "Case like this, they're being extraordinarily cautious. They're not going to make a move until they're sure they've lined up the right experts, considering the condition of the—of the remains. They can put it off practically indefinitely, since it's not like a delay's going to change the outcome. Fellow who caught the case is supposed to give me a call tonight."

"Not Chozick?" Gin asked.

"Lawrence," Madeleine interrupted, setting down the glass of seltzer she'd been sipping. "Virginia is just trying to help. She won't get in the way."

Gin tried to contain her annoyance at her mother speaking for her. "I'm sure he knows that, Mom."

"But," Madeleine continued, ignoring her, "you have to know she's good at what she does. The *best*. Let her help. She can help figure out who did this. I just know she can."

Her mother's voice wobbled on the last few syllables, to Gin's surprise. That endorsement—and the emotion that accompanied it—were completely unexpected. Were they evidence of her mother's desperation, the splintering of her careful composure?

"I hear you, Madeleine, I do," Lawrence said. He had always been powerless to stand up to her. "I can't promise anything at all—hell, I don't know if *I'll* be on the case tomorrow."

"We appreciate everything you're doing," Madeleine said. "You have to know that."

"I do." Lawrence pushed back his chair. "Now Gin, if you'll walk me out, I'll look up the name of the pathologist who's doing the autopsy. It's slipped my mind at the moment, but I've got it in the car."

"Sure. Mom, I'll clean up when I get back."

"No need," Madeleine said, already stacking the dishes, scraping off the uneaten pastry.

Outside, Gin waited until they were halfway down the walk to touch Lawrence's arm. "You didn't forget his name. You've never forgotten a name in your life."

Lawrence dipped his head in acknowledgment. "You always were a smart one. And you know I can't give you that name, either, even if I wanted to. I just didn't want to say this in front of your mother. Here, walk with me, make it look convincing, because Madeleine's no dummy."

He opened the passenger door and took out a sheaf of papers. "Now listen, Gin. You probably don't need me to tell you this, but Jake's right back in the crosshairs. Stillman's already asked me if it's going to be a problem. I'm dancing as fast as I can here, but there's a real danger they'll remove me."

"I . . . understand," Gin said, guilt coloring her words. She couldn't bear to voice her suspicions of Jake to Lawrence, but pretending to agree with him was little better than a lie. "I mean, there's reason to hope that the autopsy might . . . take them in another direction."

"That's what I'm hoping, but for now, what they're looking at, it was his cooler," Lawrence said. "I mean, sure, he got it from Lloyd, but there's a handful of people in town who are still going to remember how you kids used to hang around down by the water tower. And the people who thought it was him all those years ago—well, now they'll think they have proof. When word gets out about the cooler, half the town is going to be convinced all over again that he did it."

"But so much time has passed. I mean, he's got one of the most successful businesses around—"

"By hiring from out of town, and doing most of his work elsewhere in the county. People don't forget that, even if they're the reason he was forced to go outside in the first place.

Truth is, there are quite a few people here who'd like to see him fail. Who still won't give him the time of day, much less their business."

"I never knew it was that bad," Gin admitted.

"We've got friends," Lawrence shrugged. "I don't mean to paint too negative a picture. Lots of folks believe in him. But there are those who don't, and others who never really made up their minds. You'd be surprised."

"But anyone who ever knew him," Gin started, then realized she couldn't complete the thought. She'd been in love with Jake—she'd planned to share her life with him. They'd talked about getting married someday, about the future they'd build together.

But then Lily had disappeared, and the lies had started to pile up. Late that afternoon on the last day her whereabouts were known, she had been seen walking with Jake—a fact he disputed for days, until the county police brought him face to face with the woman who'd claimed to have seen him. The woman who, it turned out, had given a perfect description of him, right down to what he was wearing.

Then he'd finally told the truth. But not before he'd lied to Gin.

After that, everyone knew that Jake Crosby was the last person to see Lily alive. But only Gin knew that two nights after her disappearance, he had held Gin while the tears coursed down her cheeks, swearing that it was all going to be okay, which counted as the second lie he'd told her.

After that, Gin had begun to wonder if her father had been right about Jake all along, when he called him shifty and irresponsible, and worse. Things she'd dismissed as meaningless began to seem suspicious and even sinister: The increasing amount of time he'd been spending with Lily, his unwillingness to tell her what they talked about. Lily's moodiness, the nights she disappeared after curfew. The times Jake didn't call when he said he would.

Gin had never allowed herself to fully believe that Jake had harmed Lily. But she became convinced he knew *something*, that he was involved in some way, even if it was just trying to keep Gin from knowing the truth.

"Look, I don't blame people for what they think," Lawrence said. "I don't have the faintest idea how Lily died or who was responsible. I don't know why the killer used that cooler. Why anyone would hurt your sister. But I do know that what people want now is answers. That's just human nature, when something like this happens. Our hearts aren't big enough for the grief, is the way I've come to see it after all these years on the job. And so we do the next best thing: we start looking for answers, trying to find someone to blame, so we can understand."

Gin nodded, not trusting herself to speak.

"There's something you should know, Virginia, honey," Lawrence said gently. "Your dad isn't at the caterer's. He left the house because of me. He left because he blames my son. He still thinks Jake killed your sister."

"Lawrence, Dad's just . . ." Gin floundered to find the words. Standing outside her house with this gentle man, in the driveway where Jake had kissed her good-night so many times, her own doubts about his innocence blurred in a haze of confusion. "He just never understood Jake."

Lawrence made a sound that was half grunt, half sigh. "I was far from a perfect father," he said gruffly. "I take the blame for that. His . . . ways. He didn't have a mother looking after him."

Gin toed the ground with her shoe, silenced by the insurmountable weight of the past. She knew what Lawrence meant: In high school, Jake had run as wild as possible while still making the honor roll and staying out of juvenile hall. His hair had been too long, he made a point of riding his skateboard over every municipal building, he cut class when he was bored—which was often—and he committed the grave sin of refusing to call her father "Dr. Sullivan" or even "Sir." The first time he took Gin out, he brought her home an hour after curfew, and when her father came out into the driveway to berate him, Jake looked him in the eye and told him he figured Gin could make up her own mind. After that, it was only Madeleine's intercession on her behalf that prevented Richard from outright forbidding Gin from seeing him.

Time had seemed to soften her father's distrust of Jake, as their romance blossomed and Jake was named salutatorian of their graduating class. Gin had held out hope that someday the two might be close—a hope that ended when Lily disappeared.

"None of this is your fault," Gin said fiercely. That, at least, she believed with all her heart. "You were a great father. And my dad, he can be rigid. And after everything with Lily, well, I think it was just easier for him to lash out than to accept that we might never . . . might never know . . ."

Lawrence pressed the back of his hand to his forehead, suddenly looking exhausted. "Ginny-girl, your father is a good man, a fair man. But there are things you don't know. Things that were said, back then . . . you didn't need to hear all that, especially because it didn't make it into the official investigation."

Gin was quiet for a moment. She stared down the road, wondering where her father had gone, if not to the caterer's. But that was an easy one—Richard had found an unexpected passion when the town had created community gardens a number of years earlier.

"Lawrence . . . I'll talk to him."

"I don't know if that's wise, sweetheart," Lawrence said. "He's as stubborn as I am, and that's saying something. Give him his space, a little time to think things through." He dug in his wallet and handed her a card embossed with the logo of a local roofing contractor. "Now, your mom's watching out the window, so just play along here. Tell her all we talked about was the ME's office. No need to mention the rest. The last thing I want is to add to their pain. I offered to talk to your mom at the station rather than coming here, but she said . . . well, she knows him best, I guess. She thinks your dad will come around."

"He *will*," Gin said with as much conviction as she could muster.

"I hope you're right. Lord, I really do."

Lawrence went around to the driver's side and got into the SUV, hanging his arm out the window and smacking the door. "All righty," he said, a version of good-bye that he'd been using as long as Gin had known him.

She watched him drive away, the SUV's tires spinning gravel into her mother's impatiens, before heading back into the house.

Now she had another reason to get involved. She wanted to ease the burden of a kind man who had dedicated his life to helping others, only to have his community turn on him.

But the tiny, hard kernel of doubt refused to go away. Deep in the night, when the grief and horror of loss churned endlessly in Gin's mind, it couldn't help snagging on the damning facts that were just too much for coincidence. Jake, the last person to speak to Lily before she disappeared. Jake, who couldn't account for where he'd been that night. And Jake's cooler, interred in the earth where he'd brought them all a hundred times.

Once before, Gin had allowed that tiny seed of a doubt to poison her feelings for Jake.

Last time, it had destroyed the love they had shared.

What was left for it to destroy now?

9

G in planned to drive the back way to the community gardens to find her father, but there was something she needed to do first.

Clay had texted her back yesterday afternoon, saying he was sorry she wasn't feeling well and that it was a shame she'd miss the movie, and maybe if she was better they could try for the Sunday matinee. But now it was Sunday and she still hadn't come clean with him.

As she rummaged in her purse for her phone, the thing started ringing, and somehow she just knew it was Clay. She'd been too slow—she'd lost the chance to call him first and make things right, to explain herself, and now he had the upper hand; he was the aggrieved one.

After four rings the call went to voice mail, and Gin's feelings of guilt turned to relief. She needed to talk to him, just not now. After she talked to her father, maybe, when she had a chance to compose herself. And she would apologize, of course. For lying to him that night at his condo—and for leaving town without bothering to call and explain.

She waited until the ding alerted her that Clay had hung up, then hit play on the voice mail.

"Gin. It's Clay. I'm . . . I don't know what to say. I saw it on the news. They showed a family photo. That's your sister, isn't it? Lily? I can't believe you never—I mean, didn't you feel like you could tell me?" Gin winced—it hadn't occurred to her that the discovery of the body would be reported in Chicago already. Clay sounded both wounded and angry that she had lied to him, though he was clearly making an effort to suppress his emotions. "Look, I'm sure things must be a madhouse there, but call me, please, when you can."

When you can. Well, Gin thought, turning the key in the ignition, evidently she couldn't yet. It was wrong to keep Clay hanging like that, but she felt like she was unraveling at the edges, and if she started down the rabbit hole of history with him, she wouldn't be able to stop. It would all come out at once in a flood of emotion, and Gin just couldn't afford to go there just now. Just a little longer, and she'd make it right, she'd tell him everything.

She drove down the hill through town to the patch of land across from the plant's smokestacks and parked along the rutted shoulder, her tires sinking into the soft earth. The company offices had stood on this spot when the plant was running at full capacity. The buildings had been demolished and the earth turned and composted, but traces of the steel company's shadow remained. Two edges of the foundation remained, repurposed as markers for the bright-green rows of snap peas, tomatoes, lettuces, and other plantings. A scarecrow wearing someone's hand-me-down Carhartts oversaw the garden, but there was only one other lone figure bent over a row of feathery young carrot seedlings.

Gin got out of the car, glancing at the clouds forming to the east, and detected a faint rumble of distant thunder as she picked her way through the rows.

Her father had always believed that anything was achievable, given focus and hard work. She'd heard that lecture dozens of times as a child, though usually it was directed at her sister. All that natural talent, Richard scolded Lily—such a waste not to develop it! Next to dazzling Lily, Gin had often felt dull, plodding, unartful. Still, she worked hard, taking her father's lesson to heart—but every accomplishment lost its shine next to Lily's spirited, attention-seeking behavior.

Gin had always felt a kinship with her father, but oddly, it seemed to her that he never felt it in return. She thought that wound had finally healed, as her career flourished, but as she watched him dig carefully for weeds, tossing them in a plastic bucket, she wondered how much of her success she owed to him after all. Richard was admired in Trumbull in a way that few outsiders were. Trumbull credited him for bringing the clinic to the town, creating jobs while his wife led the charge to revitalize the downtown, but it was more than that. His brand of unvarnished hard work was appreciated here, both by the old-timers who still remembered the days when steel kept the local economy thriving and by the younger generation who'd been born too late to profit from it.

Lily, meanwhile, was a magnet for people's affections. A pretty, convivial baby, she had grown into an irresistibly sunny adolescent. It had been easy for Gin to understand why her mother preferred Lily. After all, they shared a natural charisma; each understood—innocently, innately—how to use their charm. Both had been beautiful and each seemed bewildered by those who were not—how did one manage, they seemed to wonder, when one was given only ordinary graces? Madeleine had received three marriage proposals before accepting Richard's, and seemed to believe that Lily was destined for a similar fate. Maybe that was why she'd been so negative about Tom: at sixteen, Lily would have years to spend spurning suitors before settling down.

Richard set his spade in the bucket and started walking toward her, wiping his hands on his pants. Gin stayed outside the garden, mindful of her shoes, letting the winds blow her hair around her face.

"The garden looks great, Dad."

Richard smiled, embarrassed even by this small accomplishment. "I guess it'll do. Mom send you out to fetch me?"

"No, I just felt like talking. Just me and you, for once."

Richard's expression showed he didn't believe her, but he didn't argue. "Want to pick some radishes? I've got some interesting heirloom varieties."

"Dad, you know I don't have your green thumb."

"Oh, but you could. Get that investment banker boyfriend of yours to put some raised beds in his backyard. Clay, wasn't it? How is he?"

She swallowed her guilt. "Yes, Dad, his name is Clay, and he's fine, and he's not a banker, he's an attorney."

"Close enough."

Surprised, Gin examined her father's face more closely. Was it possible—was he *teasing* her? It seemed unlikely, especially now, with tragedy clinging to the family once again. She'd never found it easy to talk to her father; now it seemed nearly impossible.

"Now look here, Virginia," Richard went on, taking a rag from his tool caddy and wiping off his hands. Nearby was a basket of lettuce that he'd picked. "I made my peace with losing Lily a long time ago. I never expected her to come back, not like some folks did. I guess I knew . . . well, there was a moment, that day. I've never told this to anyone. I was at the clinic, between surgeries. I was down at the vending machine getting a cup of coffee. Two, actually; I was getting one for Spencer, because we'd got in a habit of taking a break together in the afternoon, checking over the construction. They were putting the new wing on that summer, remember?"

"The regenerative medicine department. I'd forgotten."

"That's right. I mean, here it is seventeen years later and everyone still calls it the new wing, but back then it was exciting to go down where the courtyard used to be and see all those fellows with hard hats hard at work. Spencer generally just fretted about the budget and the schedule, but me, well, I guess I never did outgrow my fascination with dump trucks and the like." He laughed, looking at his hands. "An occupational hazard for guys like me, I guess, feeling like we missed out on something.

"Anyway, they'd started framing it out that week, and I was looking forward to going to check out their progress with Spencer. My next case wasn't for an hour. It was Mrs. Madigan with a knee replacement, which I remember because, what with everything that happened, she ended up going up to Pittsburgh to have it done, and it gave out on her five years later and we were the ones who went in and fixed it.

"I was standing there waiting for the coffee to fill—there was a trick to that machine, you had to wait a little extra time after you thought you were done, or you'd end up getting your hand burned with that one last spurt. And suddenly I felt like—I don't know how to describe it, but like I was kicked hard from the inside. Like—like my guts, all my organs, like someone just hit me with a roundhouse as hard as they could."

Gin kept her expression carefully neutral. He was right—she'd never heard this story, and she doubted her mother had either.

"I grabbed the counter—knocked over a stack of those Styrofoam cups. It wasn't pain exactly, what I was feeling, but more of an urgency, a sense that something terrible was about to happen. This pressure inside me, I knew it was a signal that I had to do something, something important, maybe even heroic, but I had no idea what. You know? I had never felt this way in my life, that something important depended on me. Not during my surgeries, not when you girls were learning to drive, or when your mother had that ski accident—in all of those times, I felt like I was in control, like I knew what to do next. Like autopilot took over and I trusted all my training, my judgment. But this wasn't like those other times. This was . . . terrifying."

His face had gone ashen, and he was gripping the handle of the bucket tightly. Some of the weeds dangled over the side, about to fall out, but Richard didn't seem to notice.

"I called your mother, but she didn't answer. I'd bought her a cell phone, but she didn't want to use it back then. It was something of a tug of war between us. Maybe her way of asserting her independence a little, what with you girls getting older. Anyway, I decided that after my surgery, which was the last one of the day, I'd come straight home. I even thought I'd call my brother—Uncle Randy, you probably don't remember him, he died the next winter—and see if everything was okay with that branch of the family. But you know what?"

He was staring down over the vast stretch of plant operations, seemingly unmindful of the first spatters of rain that had begun to come down, stinging their faces.

"I never once thought to worry about the two of you girls. Isn't that crazy? But I knew you were with the twins, and—well, I guess I thought the four of you were so tight that you insulated each other against anything that could go wrong. I mean, I knew you were growing up, I had the usual parental concerns, and you know how I felt about Jake. That I didn't trust him. I figured it was just a matter of time before I'd take him out for another talk. Hell, maybe I already should have. It's just, I thought I had time. I thought . . ."

He stopped speaking and compressed his lips into a thin line. A blast of cool wind delivered a smattering of raindrops as lighting broke, still miles away. Richard touched his face, his fingertip coming away wet.

"Anyway. Like I said, I never told anyone that."

"Oh, Dad." Gin's heart was heavy with regret. Men like her father didn't reach out for help, even when they most needed it. And women like her mother didn't encourage them to seek counseling, to find an outlet for their feelings. What must it have been like for him to carry this secret? How could he possibly have held himself responsible?

"But now." Richard tossed the contents of his bucket onto the compost heap, shaking the dirt free. "Now I'm not going to ignore my instincts like I did back then."

"What does that mean, Dad?"

"It means that Jake Crosby has been walking around this town free as a bird for seventeen years. Seventeen years when my daughter was left like trash under the damn ground. When all of us were suffering, wondering what happened to her."

"Dad. You can't—"

"It's what I've thought all along," Richard said grimly. "Only this time, maybe he won't be able to weasel free. Don't you see, Virginia? I might not have been able to stop him, but somehow—and I'm a man of science, so don't ask me to explain it. But I was given a sign that day, and I didn't do anything about it. Didn't do one goddamn thing for my baby girl."

"They interviewed Jake," Gin said. "There wasn't enough evidence against him"

"Hell yes there was," Richard spat. Gin was shocked to hear him swear, to see his eyes flash with fury in his tanned, lined face. "He lied in an official inquiry. He never did bother to come up with an alibi that could be checked out. Why would he do that, if he didn't have something to hide? He was the last person to see her. The *last person*, Virginia." He seemed close to tears, clutching his bucket as though it were a buoy keeping him from drowning. "And now it turns out he knew exactly where she was all along, because he stuffed her in that dirty old cooler. Didn't even bother to bury it deep—it's a wonder it stayed hidden as long as it did."

"But you don't know *he* did it. Anyone could have gotten to that cooler—"

"*Virginia.*" Richard fixed her with an anguished glare. "Please. You know what they taught us in medical school: when you hear hoofbeats, think horses, not zebras."

"I don't recall ever learning that in med school—"

"Don't be obstinate. Please. Just think about it: he was with her at the park entrance that day; he had been using that cooler all summer. Yes, it's *possible* that someone else—with no discernable motive and no reason to know about the cooler—might have come along after Jake and your sister had their private little walk. But that's zebra thinking." Richard sighed, and suddenly all the anger drained out of his voice. "And no one's going to convince me this isn't a horse."

He's angry at himself, Gin realized. *He blames himself for allowing it to happen.* "There's nothing you could have done," she protested. "None of us could."

Richard turned to her, and in the sunken hollows under his eyes, she caught a glimpse of his pain. "Other fathers do," he said. "Other men protect their families. I was too busy building some kind of—of memorial to myself. The medical center. Ha."

"Let's not rush to judgment, okay?" Gin tried, lamely. "They still haven't finished processing the scene. It'll be a couple weeks at the earliest before they get the results of the tests back. Dad, you know the media's going to be all too keen to play this out in the press before they have all the facts. Let's not make it worse, okay?"

"How can it be a proper investigation when the murderer's father is the one investigating?" he demanded. "It was bad enough Lawrence handled it the first time around. If they'd let the county boys run things then, maybe we wouldn't have had to wait so long to bring her home."

The pain in her father's voice was real, but Gin couldn't believe that Lawrence Crosby would ever do anything to interfere with an investigation, no matter how close to home it hit. But Gin had never been a parent. The bond between a father and son was strong; could it be strong enough to make a man ignore his principles? His responsibilities?

"Dad, the county police are handling it this time. Lawrence is assisting, but he isn't in charge. Even if he wanted to interfere with the investigation—and I don't see how you can suspect one of your oldest friends of something like this—he wouldn't be able to."

"Virginia. You've been away a very long time. With all due respect, you don't know how these things work here. Lawrence is friendly with a lot of them."

"Dad, I've worked with law enforcement agencies for the last decade. I've testified in dozens of murder and wrongful-death cases, some of them from very small towns, very insular corners of the county. Not to mention that I grew up in a small town." Which was more than he could say; Richard had been born and raised in Boston, and had often complained about the pace and cultural deprivation of small-town life. "I think I know how things work."

"But you haven't lived in *this* town in a very long time." If Gin didn't know her father so well, she might have missed the anger buried under his tightly controlled expression. "We're a forty-five minute drive from Pittsburgh, but it might as well be the other side of the moon, when it comes to law and order. They leave Trumbull alone because for the last century, Trumbull has been determined to police itself. You know how it is in this county: they have a hundred little municipalities who don't talk to each other. And now? Sure, they come in and haul off the latest idiots who shoot each other over drug deals gone wrong, and the townspeople don't complain because deep down, none of us really consider the gangbangers to be part of our community. They're a plague, no better than a swarm of cicadas.

"But when it comes to one of our own, the county boys are on the outside looking in. And most of the time, it works out. Lawrence has kept the peace for almost forty years. Only, this time, we can't count on justice being served. Because Lawrence is going to protect his son."

He looked at her intently. Flecks of icy blue brought fire and energy to eyes that were otherwise dulled with exhaustion and pain. "It's what I'd do. You do know that, don't you, Virginia?"

A strange chill came over Gin, starting in her fingertips and radiating through her body. What was her father suggesting?

"You—you and Mom will always be there for me," she stammered. "I know that, Dad, and I'm grateful, and I'm sorry I don't always—"

"That's not what I meant," Richard said, narrowing his eyes. He reached for her hand and gripped it tightly. "Of course we love you. Of course we'll always do everything we can to help you. But what I am saying is that if any child of mine were ever accused of a serious crime—if there was even a hint of suspicion—I'd do everything I could to squash those accusations. I'd defend my child to the death . . . no matter what. Do you understand?"

Shocked, Gin tugged her hand back. Her father released it, but he didn't drop his gaze.

He had just told her that he'd protect her even if she'd been accused of doing something terrible. That he'd stand by her . . . whether she was guilty or not.

Richard had always blamed Jake for the loss of his precious younger daughter. But Gin had never imagined that the day would come when he could blame her as well. Did he think she had been complicit somehow? That she knew, that she'd helped cover it up? That she'd been capable of carrying a secret like this for all these years?

"I . . . I heard you." She picked up his tool caddy and slung it over her shoulder. "I'll walk you back to the truck, Dad. Mom's making dinner and we should probably get back."

"Yes, those casseroles are her version of slaughtering the fatted calf," Richard said, taking one last look at his garden as he retrieved the basket of lettuce. "You mustn't hold it against her that her repertoire hasn't expanded in the last decade. Tell you what, you make do with home cooking tonight, I'll take you both out for prime rib tomorrow."

That was Richard's way of navigating his domestic life, using humor and grace to accommodate his wife's career once she made it clear that she intended to have one. And it was also his way of ending the conversation.

They reached their vehicles, and Gin got into her car and eased back onto the road, glancing in the rearview mirror to see Richard's truck keeping pace, their tires kicking up a cloud of dust in the late-afternoon sun as they left the small garden plot behind.

Her radio was still set to the NPR affiliate out of Erie, and the evening news summary played through a layer of static. She snapped it off in the midst of a traffic report, knowing it was just a matter of time until they turned to the investigation here in Trumbull. Gin didn't need to hear it just now.

Her father had just admitted how far he was willing to go to protect her.

But had he also just accused her of having something to do with her sister's death?

10

Saturday dawned clear and bright after two days of cloudbursts and occasional heavy rain. The temperature was balmy and the air was crisp and lilac-scented, a perfect summer day.

By unspoken agreement, Gin dressed early and headed for the hall with her mother to check on the arrangements. Richard promised to return before the memorial was due to start, after picking up his mother from the nursing home in Donora where she was living through the middle stages of dementia.

Gin threw herself into helping out behind the scenes while her mother, elegant and even imperious, directed the caterers, the servers, and the boys they'd hired to park overflow cars. Gin was setting out napkins near the flower arrangements anchoring either end of the buffet tables when Madeleine approached, her tasteful midheeled pumps clicking on the hardwood floors.

"I think we'd better get ready up front," she said. "People are beginning to arrive."

Gin looked through the tall windows overlooking the park. Cars were lined up in a slow, somber procession into the drive that circled around to the parking lot in back. Out on the street, traffic backed up halfway down the block, waiting to make the turn; Gin's gaze landed on the drug store where she'd once shoplifted a Jolly Rancher on a dare from a fellow Brownie girl scout and where, much later, she bought tampons at lunch during high school. She blinked away the memories, fixing a smile on her face for her mother.

"I'm ready," she said.

"All right, good. I think we should stand here, to the right of the doors, don't you agree?"

Gin could imagine how her mother envisioned it: the family lined up with her father at the front, then Madeleine, then Gin, then Grammy seated in a folding chair. Three generations of contained, modest grief, with a nice buffet luncheon to follow.

Gin knew that her mother's pain was real. But she also knew her mother would never reveal her private feelings here, in front of their neighbors and friends, in front of the town that she hoped would vote her into the mayor's office.

Gin made one last effort to escape: "Mom, do you want me to stay back here and keep an eye on things?"

"That's what the caterers are for, Virginia," Madeleine said crisply. Then she adjusted the neckline on Gin's simple navy dress with her manicured fingers. It was a conciliatory gesture, her version of the hug another mother might give. "I think they've got it all well in hand. It'll be fine."

Gin followed her mother to the wide French doors at the front of the large room, open to the sultry breeze. The scent of the floral arrangements was layered faintly with the river's smell, the fecund combination of tar and fishy rot and sun-baked mud, but her mother's perfume masked it when she turned.

"Here's good," she said, guiding Gin to a spot next to her. "And when your father gets here, he'll go—oh look, there are the Madigans."

Old Mr. Madigan, who could always be counted on to buy a glass of lemonade from the stand Lily and Gin set up in front of the house, shuffled toward them on his cane. Mr. Madigan always told Lily she was as pretty as a princess as she poured the lemonade into a paper cup, while Gin felt invisible next to her, manning their cigar-box cash register.

She breathed deeply and reminded herself that she could get through this.

*   *   *

Forty minutes later, the room was filled almost to overflowing. Gin recognized some people immediately, and others after she'd dug through her memories and accounted for the passage of nearly two decades. A girl she'd been in band with came with three little girls in matching dresses. One of the nurses who'd worked with her father had lost at least fifty pounds.

But more than half of the mourners were unfamiliar to Gin. Everyone seemed to know who she was; they pressed her hand between their cool ones and bent close to murmur their sympathies, their sorrow. Despite their kindness, each encounter felt like an invasion.

After she'd been stiffly greeting people for half an hour, Gin caught a glimpse of charcoal linen, a wide silver cuff, the glint of sun off strawberry-blonde highlights. The woman heading her way trailed two appealing children, their pale hair and clear green eyes making them a matched set. Only when the woman was upon her did Gin realize who it was.

"Christine!" she gasped, as her oldest friend in the world scooped up her hands in hers and squeezed. Then they fell into a hug, Gin breathing in the powdery scent of Christine's subtle perfume.

"Oh, Gin, I don't even know what to say," Christine said when she finally pulled away. Her eyes shone brightly with tears, but she brushed them away impatiently with a handkerchief.

"Are these your children?" Gin asked. The pair waited patiently, wearing appropriately solemn expressions. The girl appeared to be about thirteen or fourteen, and was on the gangly awkward cusp of growing into her features; in a few years, she would be stunning. The boy had managed to smudge his otherwise immaculate blue button-down shirt and one of the tails hung out over his trousers, but his hair had been slicked smooth and his tie was expertly knotted.

"Oh, yes. This is Olive, she's going into high school this fall, and Austen, who is going to be in Miss Krane's fourth-grade class next year, if you can believe it."

"It's a pleasure to meet you both," Gin said. "Your mother and I . . ."

Her voice trailed away as she realized how unprepared she was to finish that sentence. What would Christine have told her children about her? How would she explain away the silence, the fact that Gin never called when she was in town, that she hadn't sent holiday cards despite the fact that Christine never missed a year—even two years ago when Brandon's absence from the family photo was the only indication that they'd divorced.

"Miss Sullivan and I were inseparable," Christine said, rescuing her.

"Oh, please call me Gin."

"What does 'inseparable' mean?" Austen said. He'd shaken Gin's hand dutifully, and now he shoved his hands into his pockets like a young version of his uncle.

Olive tossed her long, shiny hair impatiently. "Austen. Think about it. As in, separate? Can't be separated?"

"Olive," Christine said, a mild rebuke.

Gin couldn't help smiling at this first reprieve of the day. Christine's children—bossy older sister, pesky younger brother—reminded her of the dynamic between her and Lily. She'd so often felt plain and prissy next to her willful, beautiful sister, but in truth, she'd also missed few opportunities to belittle and nag Lily.

"Did you really get the Gault Scholarship?" Olive asked.

It took Gin a moment to place what the girl was talking about. When the steel baron's daughter had grown up, she had bequeathed a scholarship to be awarded each year to a female graduate of Trumbull High School for the furthering of her studies at a time when college had been a questionable goal even for wealthy and privileged young women. When seventeen-year-old Gin won, unaware that in a few months her life would change forever, she'd mocked the prize and its small cash award, and been roundly rebuked by her mother, who had been its recipient twenty-eight years earlier.

"Yes, it's true," she said, smiling.

"Lydia Gault is kind of my hero," Olive said, her face turning pink with embarrassment. "Did you know she was the first woman to have a front-page byline in the *Examiner*? I'm going to be a journalist, too."

"That's our Olive," Christine said forcefully, putting her manicured hand on the girl's shoulder and propelling her forward. "And Austen is going to be a professional soccer player."

"*Mom!*" he wailed in protest as he was ushered along. "I'm not either!"

"Please excuse us," Christine said. "I don't want to hold up the line now, but I'd really love to catch up."

"Me, too," Gin said, surprising herself by how deeply she meant it. "As soon as I can get away, I'll come find you, okay?"

Moments later, when the line had finally died down and all the mourners were gathered around the photo boards and the tables laden with quiches and bagels, Madeleine turned to Virginia. The change in her expression was instant, her shoulders slumped and worry lines around her tight grimace. "I just can't understand what happened to them."

Gin had already tried her father's phone twice, with no answer, and she wondered if her father was dawdling for the same reason she'd been dreading the memorial—having to face all the people. "I'm sure that—"

That was as far as she got; before she could come up with some soothing reassurance for her mother, she heard the crunch of footfalls outside, and her father's raised voice.

"—no goddamn good reason why you have to come here and—"

Another voice cut in, low and murmuring, attempting to placate. Then her father's angry response, his words incomprehensible as he tried too late to keep his voice down.

Gin took two steps toward the doors, putting herself between her mother and the commotion outside. Three people stood on the sidewalk: her father in his navy blazer and the gold cuff links her mother had given him on their wedding day; Grammy, supported by her son with an arm slung around her shoulder; and on the other side, with Grammy clinging to his arm, Jake.

"I'll go," Gin said to no one in particular; her mother was already stalking over to the long table where the servers were loading coffee urns and restocking sandwich platters. Madeleine, an accomplished delegator, was undoubtedly about to dispatch some helpless waiter to "help" with Grammy, in order to get Richard away from Jake.

"Dad," Gin called as she strode outside. Jake turned in her direction, raising his hand halfway before letting it drop at his side.

She couldn't look at him, not here, not now. For a moment she felt some of her mother's indignation, the complex swirl of emotions from seeing him again yesterday giving way to irritation that he'd upset her family. "Grammy," she said deliberately, bending to be at eye level with the old woman. "Oh my, it's so good to see you."

But the old woman showed no recognition as she patted the hem of her acrylic cardigan nervously. Grammy had been a prickly, hostile woman, a very occasional presence in their lives when she'd been healthy; now she was a fragile, feather-light, mute doll. She was trying ineffectually to break out of her son's grip, but her feet merely shuffled in place as he held on.

Grammy eyed Gin and pointed vaguely in the direction of Jake. "He, he," she said, spittle flying delicately from her wrinkled lips. Someone had made sure her hair was done for the occasion, and it curled crisply to her head, a dignified note that belied the slightly haphazard nature of her outfit: a skirt that didn't match her blouse; pale, thin knee socks; brown slip-on loafers. Who, Gin wondered, had helped the old woman dress this morning? And following that thought, the inevitable guilt chaser that trailed every memory of Gin's past: what kind of granddaughter lets three years go by without a visit?

"Dad, Mom's been worried," she said, slipping between them and taking her grandmother's arm. The old woman batted weakly at her hands, and Jake caught her around the waist to help keep her balance.

"Keep your hands off her," Richard snapped. Grammy pulled away from Jake and stumbled over her own feet in their ugly footwear, pitching dangerously forward before Gin caught her. She was shockingly light, little more than a leathery wraith with a chemical hospital smell rising from her processed hair.

"Dad, he's only trying to help," Gin said.

"Yeah, well, we don't need his help, Virginia. We talked about this."

"*You* talked about it."

"Look, I'll be on my way," Jake said. He sounded genuinely remorseful. "I never would have come if I thought—"

"You didn't think, though, did you," Richard said bitterly. "That's just it with you. You don't *think*."

Jake held the older man's gaze, the muscles in his jaw working. "I mean no disrespect," he said quietly. Gin could tell how much effort he was putting into staying calm. "I loved Lily, too."

"That's enough!" Richard practically shouted, lunging for him.

"*Dad!*" Gin was shocked, but she couldn't let go of her grandmother or the old woman would fall. She reached for her father's arm and managed to hold onto his sleeve. "Please. Mom needs you. I'll take care of Grammy."

Richard glared at Jake for a moment more, then turned on his heel and stomped up the steps.

"I'm sorry," Jake said. The change in him was immediate; the defiance left his face, his body slumped. "I was hoping—I mean, I see now that it was a stupid idea. I just thought . . ." He stared at the ground and shook his head angrily. "I thought you might need the support."

"I'm fine," Gin muttered, but she was taken aback by his words. He'd come . . . for her? "Look . . . I need to go."

"How long are you going to be here?"

For a moment, she thought he was asking about the service—how long she could endure the murmured plati- tudes, the egg-breath questions from the old busybodies, the awkward greetings of people she'd left behind. How long it would take before she bolted—the one thing she could always be counted on to do.

Then she realized that Jake was asking her how long she would be in town. "To be honest, I'm not exactly sure," she said. "I thought I would try to find out where they are with the investigation. See if . . . if there's a place for me to pitch in."

He looked at her in surprise. "But I thought they'd already done the autopsy."

"Not yet," she said. "They're still lining up experts. It's not like the physical evidence is at risk of further damage after all this time."

She didn't add that it would be highly unorthodox for her to be chosen as one of those experts, considering that she was related to the victim—especially since she herself would have been considered a suspect if she hadn't had an airtight alibi, having been at freshman orientation a couple hundred miles away.

"I'll be here for at least a week," she amended. "I'm going to take some time off from my job."

"I'll call you tonight," Jake said. Not a question—a promise. He was already backing away, toward the parking lot jammed with cars. "And Gin—I'm so sorry. Really. I wish I could make today easier."

She watched him go, standing at the doors hidden behind tall brass planters full of wisteria. He crossed the street to his truck parked on the opposite side, got in, and rolled down the windows. For a moment, he sat motionless, staring out at nothing, his hands loose on the wheel, until he finally shook his head and turned the key. Seconds later, he was gone.

11

Gin sat with her grandmother, keeping a careful eye on her parents, who seemed to have resolved the matter of Richard's tardiness without rancor. Gin held a paper cup of punch to her grandmother's lips, wrapping her hands around her grandmother's trembling, waxy fingers. In truth, she was grateful for the distraction, the excuse not to mingle.

"Hi, Mrs. Sullivan. Hi, Gin."

Olive stood in front of them, smiling shyly.

"Olive, it's so nice to see you. But I'm not sure my grandmother can understand you. I'm sorry, honey."

"Oh, I know that. I just like to say hello anyway."

"You've met each other before?" Gin was surprised; until Grammy's move to assisted living several years ago, she'd been famously private, eschewing the garden and bridge clubs and senior-center bus trips that the other seniors in town enjoyed.

Olive nodded. "I interviewed her for a class project on Trumbull history when I was in fourth grade. She was really nice."

"I . . . I'm glad," Gin said. Yet another thing that was not as she remembered.

Picking up on her surprise, Olive shrugged. "I've heard people say that she used be, you know, kind of mean. But my dad says some people have trouble showing their nice side, but it's still there."

"Your dad sounds like a smart man," she said gently, wondering if it had been Christine herself that he had been talking about. It made her sad to think that Olive might find her own mother aloof, but Christine had always been the most reserved among them, a counterpoint to Lily's unbridled and uncensored moods. "Would you like to join us?"

"Sure." Olive sat primly, tucking her skirt under her. "These shoes hurt my feet. They're new."

Gin admired the shiny, black platform sandals, and imagined the argument mother and daughter must have had over the heels. She repressed a smile, remembering how Lily had clomped up and down the stairs in the high-heeled clogs she bought with her babysitting money.

"Would you care for a cookie?" Gin offered Olive the plate she had filled for her grandmother.

Olive helped herself and took a dainty bite. "Were you and my mom really best friends?"

Gin was caught off guard, unsure how to answer. Certainly it had once been true, but would Christine still see it that way? There had always been a distance between the two of them, one that waxed and waned depending on how Gin and Lily were getting along and, later, Lily and Tom. "We were very close," she settled on saying.

"I've seen your picture," Olive said. Her eyes darted nervously up and back to her lap. "You were so pretty. I mean, you're still pretty."

"Oh, honey, that's very kind of you," Gin said, embarrassed by the girl's clumsy compliment. "It was a long time ago."

"Uncle Tom says you were the smartest kid in the whole school. He says I take after you."

"Really?" Gin smiled. "You know, he and your mom were pretty smart themselves."

"Yeah, but Uncle Tom says you could have done anything you wanted. He says I shouldn't go into writing, because print's dead. But if I do, he says I will find a way to succeed, just like you did." She peeped up under long, luxurious lashes. "What I'm going to do is write, for like, online media."

"That's—that's a great goal," Gin said, wondering when kids had stopped reading newspapers. "I bet your mom's proud."

"I guess. I mean, Austen's a lot of trouble."

Again Gin found herself suppressing a smile. Many of her colleagues in Chicago had kids, adorable little toddlers who careened around the few barbecues and birthday parties that Gin was invited to. But she didn't know any teenagers, and she was surprised at how much she liked this one. "Your brother's a pain, huh?"

"Oh my *God*. He's like totally ADD and he has no respect for boundaries." Olive sighed dramatically. "Four more years."

"Until you go to college?"

"Until I can get away from him." Olive flashed a small, conspiratorial smile. "And this stupid, boring town."

"You don't like it here?"

"Did *you*?"

Gin laughed out loud. "Okay, you got me there." She had been dreaming about leaving since her first memory of visiting Pittsburgh, of the skyline looming in the distance as they drove up through the Mon Valley. "So you're not a small-town girl, huh?"

Olive shook her head adamantly. "Mom's taking me to New York City next year for spring break. Dad's going to take Austen to spring training, so it's only fair. They're crazy about the Padres." Another weary sigh. "I don't care for sports."

Gin was getting a sense of this girl: bookish and serious, like she herself had been, but without the crushing self-doubt that plagued her. Good for Christine, for raising her daughter to be confident.

"Well, I'd better get going," Olive said, so much like her mother that Gin felt a pang in her heart. "Are you coming to my birthday?"

"Your birthday?"

"My party? I'm pretty sure you're invited. I mean, I can invite you, can't I?"

"Why—sure," Gin stammered. "Although I'm not sure how long I'll be in town."

"It's next weekend," Olive said. "We're having make-your-own sundaes. You'll still be here then, won't you?"

"I'll do my best," Gin promised, as one more invisible thread wrapped around her, pulling her back into the shadow land of her past.

12

"Help me with these, will you?" Madeleine asked, when they arrived home to find a collection of neatly labeled Pyrex pans in shopping bags on the porch, defrosting in pools of water. Small-town condolences were expressed with covered dishes meant to sustain the family through their difficult times. Madeleine herself had made countless lasagnas for new mothers and shut-ins, labeling them neatly with masking tape and tucking them into Kauffman's-department-store bags.

"I don't know if there's room in the freezer for all that," Gin said doubtfully.

"No, just dump them. Your father can't eat any of this. And you and I shouldn't." Madeleine patted her stomach as though some pudge had managed to sneak onto her size-four frame when she wasn't looking. "Make sure the labels stay on anything I need to return, if you don't mind. I'll wash all those dishes later."

Gin dutifully picked up the bags, following her mother into the quiet house. Her father had headed back to the nursing home with Grammy, looking as exhausted as Gin felt. She'd almost offered to go along with him, but the truth was she wasn't sure she could bear the silence.

Instead, she pretended that Madeleine needed her.

She was standing at the sink with the disposal running, scraping soggy noodles down the drain, when her mother came back into the room wearing navy yoga pants and a matching pullover. She went straight to the refrigerator and pulled out an unopened bottle of white wine. "Want some?"

"Sure." Gin had drunk one diet soda after another at the service, just to give her hands something to do. She dried her hands on the dishtowel her mother kept neatly folded by the sink and followed Madeleine out to the screened porch.

Evening was falling slowly, ushering in the fireflies and the scent of charcoal, the shouts of children carrying over the neighbors' fences.

"I like to sit out here and watch the river," Madeleine said, settling into a chair and putting her feet up on the matching caned ottoman.

Gin settled on the love seat next to it. "I don't remember you ever taking the time to sit out here before."

"Wait until you've got a bunch of kids running around underfoot and a husband who's never home," Madeleine said. "With the twins here so much . . . I was lucky to get five minutes to myself to shower."

"Did you resent that, Mom?" Gin had never really considered those early days from her mother's point of view. "I mean, having to watch over kids who weren't even yours while Dad and Spencer worked all that overtime?"

The name still felt funny on her lips. After calling him "Mr. Parker" her entire life, Spencer had insisted she call him by his first name when she came home to visit the summer before she started medical school. "You kids are all grown up," he'd said, raising a toast at the barbecue he hosted for the two families. Then, cutting his gaze to Tom, he'd added, "Well, some of you, anyway," which had prompted laughter from everyone but Tom.

"Not really," Madeleine shrugged. "I mean once you've got two, a couple more . . . well, it's more work, but not *that* much more. And I mean, poor Spence, widowed with two newborns. Nowadays it's a different story, but back then there weren't many options for single dads. I guess your father and I just felt it was the right thing to do."

"I'm surprised he never got remarried. If nothing else, it would have been easier, with the kids."

"When was he going to date anyone long enough for it to get serious? Those two—back when they were trying to get the surgery center going, they barely came home to shower and sleep."

"Mom, you should demand reparations," Gin said, only half kidding. "Even if he only gave you minimum wage for all that childcare, you could probably retire."

Gin regretted her words the minute they were out. But trying to apologize—to convince her mother that she took her political career seriously—would be even worse.

Her parents would have more than enough money to last the rest of their lives, even if neither worked another day. Richard earned well as a surgeon, and as far as Gin knew, her parents had never even touched her mother's inheritance. Each worked for their own reasons, even if those reasons were murky. Richard still racked up as many as twenty joint replacements a week, in addition to tirelessly campaigning for the still-nascent regenerative-medicine department. As for Madeleine—whether her mother worked to give her life meaning or to give her an excuse not to face the gaping hole left by Lily's absence, Gin had never known.

Guilt, guilt, guilt—every interaction with her parents seemed rife with it. Gin drank her wine, letting the tart, cold liquid slide down her throat, welcoming the pleasant blur it promised.

"Listen, Virginia." Her mother set her wine down on the little glass patio table and leaned toward her. "I think it would be best if you avoid Jake while you're here. Lawrence, too, as much as possible. Your father . . . well . . ."

She didn't bother finishing the sentiment: *Your father gets so upset, it's best if we try to stay out of Daddy's way.* Old excuses made during the sisters' teens, when Lily's clattering joyful presence sent Richard's blood pressure through the roof. His angry door-slamming when she failed a test or ignored a curfew.

"Mom . . . I know Dad's angry, but we don't know that Jake did this. He was investigated, and they let him go."

"He's not the only one who thinks Jake got off easy," Madeleine said, and Gin couldn't bring herself to ask if she herself was among his doubters.

"I thought I'd go up to the county offices on Monday."

"Have you talked to anyone up there yet?"

"Only about my statement, so far." The detective who'd come had talked to them each individually, drinking tea on this very porch. Gin hadn't had the nerve to ask her parents what it felt like to have their statements read back to them all these years later, but for her the experience had been both discomfiting and strangely blurring. "You say here that you know your sister was still at the school at four o'clock because she was working on a theater set," the detective had said, prompting a sudden sharp memory of the streaks of blue paint on her sister's wrist, from painting clouds on a canvas backdrop. Details she'd forgotten had the effect of erasing the time that had passed, so that she felt seventeen again as she talked to them.

"So you think you'll be able to talk them into letting you help?"

"I hope so, but it's complicated. What will work in my favor is that they are going to need a very particular skill set as the investigation moves forward."

81

"What skills exactly?"

The back screen door opened, saving Gin from having to explain that exhumations of long-buried bodies posed particularly difficult challenges at autopsy, as decomposed tissues often disintegrated when they were handled, something she hoped to shield her parents from having to know.

Richard came out onto the porch, carrying the jacket he'd worn for the service. His shirt was wrinkled and his face bore glints of silver where his five-o'clock shadow was coming in.

"Hi, Dad."

"Did Lawrence call?" he demanded, not bothering to return the greeting. "On the day of her *service*, for the love of God."

"Richard . . ."

"No, no one called," Gin said. "Why don't you get a glass and join us? It's been a long day."

"I just . . ." Richard shook his head, and turned to go back into the house. Then he changed his mind and turned around again, stumbling against the outdoor dining table. Gin wondered if he had been drinking, just as the smell of strong liquor reached her nostrils.

Her mother had smelled it, too. She was up out of her chair instantly, watching him warily. "You're back sooner than we expected."

Richard shrugged, then slumped into one of the dining chairs. The jacket landed on the table in a pile. "Gordon offered to take Mom back."

Gin exchanged a worried look with her mother. Gordon was her father's cousin, a timid man who owned several fast-food franchises in Pittsburgh. She hadn't heard either of her parents mention his name in years. It seemed unlike her father to entrust his elderly mother's care to someone who was virtually a stranger.

"But I saw you leaving with her," Madeleine said.

"Gordon met us in the parking lot."

"But—where did you go? We've been home almost an hour."

"Had a drink with Spencer and Tom." Richard's petulant tone was out of character. With a sickening feeling, Gin wondered if this was evidence of something worse, something deeper between her parents. Naturally tempers were stretched thin now, but had things been deteriorating between them even before the discovery of Lily's body?

"Not just one, it looks like," Madeleine shot back.

"Well all right, sue me, I'm guilty as charged," Richard said angrily. "Only in this town, I guess that doesn't mean much. You can kill people and walk around like you own the whole goddamn joint."

"Dad, don't. Please."

He was breathing hard, his shirt sticking to his neck. It was damp under the arms, and Gin wondered where he and the Parkers had gone—somewhere without air conditioning. Maybe they'd had a drink on Spencer's back deck, although neither was big drinker. Tom was a different story.

"I'm sorry, Virginia, but someone's got to say it. Or there won't be any justice for anyone, the way this is going."

"Dad, they've barely reopened the investigation. They've delayed the autopsy, and they won't get results back from the lab for another week at least. These things take time."

Her father regarded her with unfocused eyes, his jaw working. "Now look here, I don't know how they do things up in Chicago, but you need to remember this is a small town. Lawrence has been running things for thirty years, and he's tight with those county detectives. And he's got a hell of an incentive to keep this covered up."

"*Dad.* Please. I know you have your doubts about Jake. But let the investigation take its course. Lawrence isn't going anywhere, and I'm sure they'll be questioning Jake closely."

"But you don't think he did it." Richard pointed at her with his index finger, shaking his head. "Or else you don't care. From the first day that he walked into this house, he did nothing but throw my rules in my face and lie to all of us. Virginia, when are you going to open your *eyes*? What did he tell you, that it was an accident?"

"Dad!" Gin gasped. She looked to her mother for support, but Madeleine had gone ashen, gripping the arms of her chair.

"You could never see the truth about him," Richard said. "None of us could ever say one word about that boy before you'd rush to defend him."

"Dad, he was my boyfriend. But that doesn't make me blind to—"

"You both need to just *stop* this," Madeleine said, finally finding her voice. "Richard, you're drunk and you're making a fool of yourself. I'm not going to sit here and listen."

Gin looked from one parent to the other. She'd never seen her father like this—not even in the dark days after Lily's disappearance. He'd always hidden his pain, tried to bury it with his work. Watching her parents battle, Gin felt the pain of loss mix with her guilt over having been absent.

Madeleine got up and pushed past them, jostling the table and knocking her wine glass over. It fell to the slate floor, smashing into shards, as she raced into the house.

"Dad," Gin begged, bending to pick up the biggest pieces of glass. "You've got to calm down and let the authorities handle things. Don't get Mom so upset."

Richard awkwardly crouched next to her, clumsily reaching to help. "She just needs to listen," he said. "You both have got to *listen* to me."

"Let me get this," Gin said. "You'll cut yourself."

"Nobody listens," Richard mumbled, holding up fingertips red with blood.

13

G in pulled into the cracked driveway in front of a modest, white-sided ranch house with black shutters. On either side of the flagstone walkway leading up to the front porch, tractor tires had been put into service as planters, overflowing with red and white geraniums. An American flag flew from a polished brass pole. A carved wooden sign on the wall next to the door said, "A Bad Day Fishing Beats a Good Day Workin'."

Gin knocked tentatively, wondering if it had been a poor idea to come here, but Lawrence came to the door immediately, peering out over half-moon reading glasses.

"Ginny-girl," he said politely, as though he wasn't surprised to see her the evening after her sister's memorial, a memorial he hadn't attended. "Come on in. You've caught me in the middle of the crossword, actually, and it's been kicking my butt."

"I'm sorry to barge in on you. I should have called."

"This is a tough day for you, I expect," he said, leading her to the living room, where he offered her a seat on a velvet couch that was faded from the sun.

Gin took a deep breath as she sat down. The best way to get through this was to be direct and focused. She had often advised medical students on how to deal with the family members of the dead, emphasizing that a matter-of-fact delivery is far preferable to letting one's own emotions bleed into the exchange.

"My father is still convinced that Jake had something to do with Lily's death," she said, forcing out the words despite knowing they had the power to hurt the old man. "And I have to admit that he makes a . . . reasonable case."

Lawrence paused in the act of lowering himself to his recliner. For a moment, he kept his head bowed, a frown tugging at his wrinkles. Finally, he merely nodded as he sat down. "I see."

"But you don't believe it. Please. Help me understand why you're so sure."

"He's my son. So anything I tell you—why would you believe what I say?"

Virginia had no answer for that. "I'm not sure. But I still want to hear your thoughts. Anything you can tell me about the investigation. I mean, not the official part but . . . I guess I'm just asking you what you believe in your gut."

Lawrence gave her the ghost of a smile. "An unusual request coming from a doctor. If I remember my lessons, the scientific method doesn't leave a lot of room for intuition."

Gin returned the smile, glad for the note of humor to lighten the discussion. "I guess I'm not here as a doctor today. Maybe as a . . ." A sister? A daughter?

A woman who had reached the age of thirty-six, the years passing like pebbles under the wheels of the job that consumed her, without any idea who she was supposed to be? "A friend," she finally settled on.

He nodded. "All right. Well, you have to remember that our unofficial assumption was that she had run away, especially after you and your mom figured out that some of her things were missing."

"Her old backpack," Gin recalled. "And a couple of changes of clothes. But we didn't even notice that for a few days. And Mom insisted that she could have left them at a friend's house, or lost them somewhere—she was constantly losing things."

"Yes, but from our perspective—let's just say that the missing items confirmed our initial assumption, that Lily had taken off intentionally. Even out here in the sticks, we'd seen plenty of runaways over the years. Even kids from nice families."

"I know," Gin said. "I can see how you would have reached that conclusion. Especially because it's what everyone wanted to believe."

"But now we need to take a fresh look at everything. Let's start with who could have done it. Have you come up with your own list?"

"I've . . . had some ideas," Gin said carefully, not wanting to admit that the question had kept her up in the middle of the night ever since she'd learned Lily had been found.

"It's just me and you here, Virginia, we're just talking. Tell you what. Would it help for us to go over the whole sequence of events again, walk it through together? This old, creaky brain and your sharp insights?"

Gin felt her tight muscles relax fractionally in the face of his encouragement. "I'd like that," she said. "It's kind of hard to hear myself think sometimes, over at Mom and Dad's."

"Well, sweetheart, we've got all the time in the world. At least until this old codger falls asleep in his chair." He chuckled. "Happens more often than I'd like to admit."

Don't let your guard down, Gin cautioned herself, despite feeling at ease for the first time since coming back into town; Lawrence hadn't risen to chief in this town by being as harmless as he let people believe. He had a powerful reason to convince her of Jake's innocence—and she had an equally compelling reason to dig out the truth, no matter whose guilt it revealed. So she would do well to remember their interests weren't necessarily aligned.

"All right," she said carefully. "Well, in the days leading up to Lily's disappearance, I remember that she was acting . . . different. She was moody, emotional, more unpredictable than usual." She thought of telling Lawrence about finding her sister sobbing in the shower, and decided against it; it didn't change any of the other facts. "And she was definitely spending more time with Jake. Before that, we were all together a lot, of course. But for the first time, I'd see them off together, just the two of them, sitting up on the trail above the creek talking. Or she'd go along with him in the truck to get sandwiches while the rest of us stayed back."

Lawrence frowned, tugging at the collar of his ancient western shirt, but said nothing.

"Did he say anything to you?" she asked. "About Lily? About . . ." She felt her heart twist at the thought, but this was the time for truth, the time to lay it all out. "Him and me? Was he, you know, unhappy? Getting ready to break up with me?"

Already Lawrence was shaking his head. "I didn't know anything about any of that. I promise you, Ginny-girl, Jake never said anything about being unhappy with you, or fighting with you. I mean, I'm just an old thick-skulled dolt when it comes to women, but to hear my son talk, the two of you were in it for the long haul." He sighed and ran an age-spotted hand through what was left of his hair. "He was crazy about you, my boy was."

Gin felt the tug of his words, the longing to believe that fantasy of young love—and pushed back against it. "But he was also eighteen. Come on, Lawrence, we were just *kids*. I didn't know my own mind back then either, didn't have the faintest idea what love was." *Another lie,* her conscience chided her; she ignored it and spoke more forcefully than she intended. "What about that morning? Did he say anything, do anything, out of the ordinary?"

"You know, I've thought about that a thousand times, trying to see if there was something I missed that day. But no, Jake was up early like always, got in some time with the weights and a run around the neighborhood before he had to head to work. I'm not sure I even saw him before I left the house. A lot of days, I didn't."

Gin watched him carefully, and could see no signs that he wasn't telling the truth. "All right. Well, I guess the same was true at our house. I don't remember anything unusual, other than I was getting ready to go up to freshman orientation. My ride was picking me up at noon, and I'd spent much of the night before ironing and packing, so I was tired. Lily slept in, as usual, until Mom made her get up. Mom made us breakfast, Lily refused to eat it, she wouldn't help me clean up, she wanted me to walk with her to the drug store because we were out of conditioner . . . I probably snapped at her. I just couldn't wait to leave, to get on the road."

"So nothing happened before you left?"

"Well . . . Jake came by. To say good-bye." Gin felt the twinge of painful ambivalence and took a breath. This was the memory she'd revisited so often when she thought about that day. "I was only going to be gone through Sunday afternoon, but we were . . . anyway, he made up some excuse to run to the hardware store and came by in the truck."

The memory was so exquisitely clear—except memory lied. Science had proven that, over and over again; humans convince themselves of versions of events produced in their own rich imaginations. So the memory of Jake picking her up and swinging her around, the memory of the warm, tan skin of his neck against her cool cheek, the smell of laundry on a line mixed with his shampoo and sweat—were these real? The faded green of the truck, the blue of his eyes, the flash of white teeth in his smile before he kissed her—they were exquisitely real in her mind. She could practically feel his lips brush against hers, his strong hands at her back.

With a start, she realized she'd let her eyes drift shut, and she snapped them open. "He only stayed a minute. Mr. Nelson kept a close eye on him at work. Anyway, Lily had already left for school by the time he came by—she'd had to repeat her English class during summer school, so she was gone three mornings a week. That was the last I saw of either of them. I had the house to myself until my ride came."

"All right." All the humor had drained from Lawrence's voice. As they talked through the day, it was impossible to forget that they knew how it ended. "I didn't see Jake at all, not until the next morning. Nelson's crew was working on that apartment complex out on Second Street and they were framing that week, so he kept the whole crew busy through quitting time." Other days that summer, when the work was slow, Mr. Nelson occasionally sent Jake home early. "Nelson backed him up on that: Jake wasn't out of his sight until a little after five."

"And then two people saw Lily and Jake in the truck together between five thirty and five forty-five."

"Yes. Guinevere Morgan and Archie Chin. Their statements were nearly identical: they said Jake was driving well under the speed limit, and that Lily looked upset. Mrs. Morgan was sure she was crying."

"But that's—Lily was so dramatic. I mean, she used to cry over commercials on TV!" Gin heard the defensiveness in her voice and closed her mouth. She was here for the truth . . . whatever it turned out to be.

Lawrence nodded. "After that we've only got Phyllis Bannon's statement."

"That she saw them when she was walking her dog . . ."

"Correct. And unlike Mrs. Morgan, Mrs. Bannon refused to speculate on what frame of mind either of them might have been in. They were at the creek. They were talking. He had his arm around her. That's it."

"I remember," Gin said. "So many people jumped to the conclusion that Jake and Lily were, you know, *involved*. Romantically."

"Which is a reasonable guess, based on the fact that they were touching."

"But it could have been anything. I mean, Lily . . . she was sunshine and storms, you know? There wasn't a single person who knew her who hadn't seen her get upset about some meaningless incident, and then five minutes later she was laughing again. If Phyllis Bannon had walked past them five minutes later . . ."

She was doing it again. Trying to find a version of the story that didn't implicate Jake.

That had to stop.

"Right, right," was all Lawrence said. "We were aware of that, of course. By then it was a county case, and some said I shouldn't have even been allowed to sit in on the interviews. But you know, I'm glad I did. I needed to hear it all to be sure. I—I never believed that Jake had it in him to do something like that. But knowing what I knew, about witnesses, about how we perceive what we see, I could easily understand how people came to suspect him."

"Well, to be fair . . ." Gin said carefully. "People knew that he lied. In an official investigation."

Lawrence glanced down at the table. "He wasn't under oath . . . but yes."

"So in the first interviews, he said he was working on the shed." That summer, Jake had been stripping the wood siding on the old shed behind their house, intending to repaint it. Gin realized that she had no idea if he'd ever gotten around to painting it, since after Lily's disappearance, she'd never gone back to the Crosby house. Not until today.

"They brought him back in after they talked to Chin and Mrs. Morgan. I didn't attend that interview—at the county's request, or perhaps 'insistence' is a better word—but I saw the transcript. The minute they confronted him with the witness statements, Jake reversed himself. He admitted that Lily had called him right after school and asked to talk, he'd picked her up after work, and he'd taken her to the old mall parking lot. But he said they only talked for a while, that she was, in his words, 'rambling.' They pressed him on whether she'd been drinking, if they'd been smoking marijuana, but he swore that none of that happened. Jake said she was obviously upset. At one point, she started crying and he did his best to comfort her, but she wouldn't say what was wrong . . . only that it would all work out one way or another." He paused, and looked at Gin intently. "You've never figured out what it might have been about? Trouble with your parents, boys, anything?"

Gin shook her head. "No. I mean, like I told you guys back then, she'd been kind of moody, but that wasn't anything new. The thing is, Lawrence, I'd seen her crying, too."

She didn't look at him while she told him about that day, about how she'd seen Lily huddled on the tile floor of the shower, sobbing while the water streamed down her face and hair. How she'd returned to her own room without Lily knowing she'd been observed. Gin couldn't tell their parents—Richard wouldn't have had the faintest idea how to deal with a hysterical daughter, and Madeleine would have overreacted and probably dragged poor Lily off to her therapist.

"I just . . . pretended it never happened," Gin said in a small voice. "If only I'd talked to her . . . tried to find out what it was, you know? Maybe then . . . maybe she . . ."

Her voice thickened with emotion, and Lawrence offered her the box of tissues on the coffee table. "You can't think that way," he said. "No one could have prevented what happened."

Gin took a tissue and twisted it around her fingers. "It's just, when people started saying Jake and her . . . well, it would have explained it, right? If she'd gotten involved with him, it would have given her a reason to be upset, because she would have known it would . . ."

She couldn't finish. Couldn't say the words *break my heart*.

"Ginny-girl. Look at me." Lawrence's voice was beseeching. When she peered up at him through her unshed tears, he looked stricken. "Jake loved you. I might be wrong about everything else—all of it. But there wasn't any other girl for him. Not then, and sometimes I think never again. Just . . . no matter what happens, don't ever doubt that."

Gin dabbed at her eyes with the tissue and nodded. But she hadn't come here for reassurance, didn't want to think about what went wrong with Jake. She was here for answers. Truth. No matter how painful.

"So the other witness statements? The hitchhiker?"

"All discredited. Well, or at least, no evidence ever came to light to support them."

"But the sex offender . . ."

"Yes, there was a man who matched the one description we got. But he had an alibi for that night. Of course, now they've got another shot to get DNA and other evidence."

"Okay. Then . . . well, there's Tom."

Lawrence was nodding. "The obvious choice, but we couldn't put a hole in his alibi back then. He'll be questioned again, of course. Who else?"

"Um . . . I guess me and Christine? Since we knew the area well and used the cooler?"

"Good. Let's leave you out for the moment. Why would Christine want to harm Lily?"

"I . . . I mean, maybe she didn't want Lily dating her brother?" Gin thought back to that summer, the excitement the four of them were feeling about college. Lily had been thrilled

93

when Tom had chosen Duquesne, since he would be only a little more than an hour away, close enough to visit frequently. But Christine had not been nearly as enthusiastic. "I mean, she kept insisting it would be better if they broke up before Tom left for school. She said it was inevitable anyway . . ."

"What did Tom think?"

"He just mostly ignored her. Tom was used to getting his way. To getting everything he wanted."

"Well, then maybe, if he thought Lily was thinking of breaking up with him . . . ?"

"Possible, I guess," Gin said doubtfully. "But Lily loved him. Thought she did, anyway. I never heard her voice any doubts about their relationship."

"But then again, there were obviously things she didn't tell you."

Gin tried to ignore the sting that his comment brought. "Okay. Well, so I guess that points right back at him. As for Christine, she definitely thought they didn't have a future, and she wasn't afraid to say it. But that was just the way she was. Opinionated, you know? And not always the most tactful."

"Anyone else? Like I said, we're just brainstorming," Lawrence said. "The wider you allow yourself to think, the better. Teachers who took a special interest in her, neighbors who maybe acted strangely in regards to her, girls at school who might have been jealous. Boys she rejected."

"It was so long ago," Gin said.

"Didn't she see a psychiatrist for a while?"

"A psychologist, and it was only a few sessions and only because Mom made her go. I guess she thought therapy might get Lily to calm down and focus on school, but you remember how well *that* worked."

Lawrence smiled sadly. "She sure was a spitfire. It's a shame, though—since we ended up filing it as a runaway, we didn't talk to all the people we might have if we'd had a body. But spend a little time thinking about this, all right?"

"I will," Gin promised. "But you have to know that none of this will help Jake if we can't prove who the killer is."

"I know," Lawrence said. "But I'm willing to take the gamble."

"Lawrence," Gin said, wondering if she should ask the question that had been haunting her. "How can you be so sure? I mean . . . deep inside, how can you be certain if someone is telling you the truth?"

Lawrence pushed his glasses up on his forehead and leaned back in his chair. "About a hundred years ago, when I was in the academy up in Pittsburgh, they brought in this specialist. Can't remember now where they found him, some university, but his specialty was body language. How to tell if a suspect was lying. All this nonsense about if they looked up or down or sideways, that was supposed to mean something. Tell you what, that never did me one lick of good in all my years as a cop."

Gin had encountered similar theories in a psychology class in college—and like Lawrence, she found them suspect. "Every person's different. Their reactions, their gestures, their tics."

"I figure folks have been lying to me pretty much since the first time I pinned on the badge," Lawrence continued. "And not to brag or anything, but I've had a pretty damn good record for knowing when they do it."

"Lawrence, with all due respect, you can't expect me to go on the strength of your track record—no matter who the suspect is."

"I appreciate that, young lady. But that's not quite the point I was trying to make. I feel like I learned more from my mistakes than anything else, and I've been fooled plenty times. But now I've learned what makes for a really successful liar. The thing is, they don't give themselves away when they're lying to you—it's when they're telling the truth."

"I don't understand."

"They drop their guard, is what I'm trying to say. They reveal who they really are. You pull a guy over for speeding and he says he's racing to his elderly mother's house because she took a fall, well, okay, that's a pretty good excuse. But in the next breath, he snaps at his wife, sitting in the passenger seat? Talks to her like she's lower than the dirt on the bottom of his shoe? Well, that doesn't add up. A devoted son isn't generally going to treat his wife like that. You follow?"

It was an awfully precarious argument, but Gin nodded. "I think so."

"Well, after Lily went missing—and I mean, the very next night, when your folks were calling around to find out if anyone had seen her—Jake overheard me talking to your father. He put it together, what had happened, from hearing my end of that conversation, and by the time I hung up he had his jacket on, ready to go looking. He was out half the night, scouring the town from one end to another."

And two days later, when they organized groups to search the trails, the woods above town, the creek, and Gin had returned from the orientation weekend, he had been there, too—dark circles under his eyes, tight-lipped and grim. He'd barely spoken to Gin, which was the start of the hurt and doubt that ended their relationship. His obsession with Lily's disappearance was, paradoxically, the root of her suspicion of him.

"I can understand why that might not mean much to you, Gin," Lawrence said heavily. "But I know my boy like no one on this earth. Growing up without a mother like he did . . . well, I was both mom and dad to him. I was all he had, when he needed to talk."

The pain inside Gin twisted sharply. *He had me*, she wanted to shout, but she had never been enough for Jake. He'd never opened himself up all the way to her. There was always some part of himself that he kept closed off.

96

At eighteen, reeling from her sister's disappearance, it had been easiest to hide the pain of rejection by turning him away. At the time, she justified it to herself as payback for him shutting her out. But when people speculated about his relationship with Lily, her guilt morphed into something colder. Meaner. Uglier.

And when people accused him—at kitchen tables over coffee, in the line at the grocery store, after church—she stopped defending him. Stopped telling people she was sure he couldn't have had anything to do with it.

And now? After all these years, could she still suspect him of something so evil? Could he have fooled his own father along with everyone else?

"Lawrence," Gin said carefully. "I don't know what I believe. I wish I could tell you that I share your certainty . . . but you have to admit there is a lot of damning evidence."

"Like Lloyd's old cooler? Listen, Virginia, I'm taking a chance here, talking to you about it, but it's pretty clear why I haven't said anything about it to the detectives. Question is—why haven't you?"

"The detectives already know who the cooler belonged to," Gin said. "Lloyd ID'd it."

"But he didn't tell them he passed it on to Jake. Truth is, I think Lloyd forgot. At any rate, they haven't brought Jake in yet for official questioning. They've kind of shut me out, so this is just speculation, but I figure they're waiting for lab results before they go down that road. When they do . . . well, you know my boy as well as anyone, I guess."

Knew, Gin thought. Past tense. She hadn't known Jake for a long time. Maybe ever. "You think he'll tell them."

"I'd stake my life on it. Which . . . well, this is where things get a little gray for me. I mean, I can't stop my boy from speaking the truth, and I wouldn't if I could. That leads me to you."

"Me?"

"Virginia, you may not remember, but when you and Jake were in fifth grade, you made it to the county spelling bee."

"I remember."

"You represented Trumbull Elementary, and Jake was your alternate." He chuckled. "Man, he was unhappy about that. Couldn't stand to be whupped by a girl back then . . . Anyway, I watched you two up on that stage up in Pittsburgh. Both of you nervous as ticks, and Jake tugging on his necktie like it was strangling him. He got eliminated in one of the early rounds. You hung in there until the very end. But when it came down to the last word, suddenly you looked as cool as a cucumber. The principal gave you your word, I don't remember what it was now, and you looked up at the ceiling and thought for a few seconds and then you gave it your best shot, perfectly calm, like there weren't three hundred people in that auditorium."

"But I got it wrong," Gin said. "I still remember, the word was 'inoculate.' I spelled it with two c's."

"Well, if you say so," Lawrence said. "But it wasn't the winning or losing that made such an impression on me. It was your focus. I imagine that served you well, all those years of medical school. You were just about the most ferociously determined kid I ever met. And now I'm hoping you'll direct some of that focus at finding out who killed Lily.

"You can't tell me you haven't been thinking about this night and day," Lawrence continued. "And now I'm counting on you. The county chief wants this closed, badly, before the media starts talking about departmental incompetence. In a situation like this, there's always the danger they'll make a hasty arrest. Jake's already got enough stacked against him without him being tried in the press. I need your help, Virginia. I know I said the other day that you should steer clear of the investigation, but I need to find the real killer and I can't do it alone."

"But even if I discovered anything, all I could do is report it to the detectives."

"Of course. I'm not trying to go around those fellows, but they've pretty much pushed me out of the official investigation. Truth is, I don't have any skills that they don't. I'm about as useful to them as an udder on a snake. You, on the other hand—well, I know how to use the Internet, Ginny-girl, and I've made a few friends over the years. I did my research after our conversation, and I know you're good. I know you've been consulted on cases far outside Cook County. I know you've developed a reputation for your work on exhumation cases."

For a moment, neither of them said anything. Out in the backyard, a cat meowed loudly, and several houses away a mother called for her kids to come in for dinner. Gin had been in this house a hundred times, long ago. Watched TV on the comfortable plaid couch. Eaten dinner at the oak kitchen table.

Shared stolen kisses with Jake when Lawrence wasn't home.

Lawrence cleared his throat. "If you'll excuse me for a moment, I need to go take my blood-pressure pills. I'll be just a few minutes." He stood and pulled his phone from his pocket, setting it carefully on the coffee table between them. "This damn thing, I try to shut it off at night. Don't feel like taking calls when I'm off the clock, you know?"

At the foot of the stairs, he paused. "Speaking of pathologists," he said, not meeting her eyes. "One of them called me this afternoon, not half an hour before you came over. Course I couldn't help him much, seeing as the county crew had already turned in their paperwork, and I didn't have anything to add. Guess he had a few questions before starting the autopsy, some things he couldn't sort out. Oh, and he had a memorable name—Stephen Harper, just like the former Canadian prime minister. No relation, I'd suppose."

Then he was climbing the stairs, his boots heavy on the wooden treads.

Gin stared at the phone, her mind swirling with thoughts. Had Lawrence really just given her the name of the pathologist who was going to autopsy Lily's body?

Was he asking what she thought he was asking?

If she was right, he'd intentionally left her alone with his phone. Gin picked it up and tapped it on. There was no passcode, and she checked his recent calls.

Right at the top was a number with a 412 area code. Gin dug a pen from her purse and jotted the number on one of her business cards. She'd just stashed it and set the phone back, face down, when Lawrence came back down the stairs.

"Sorry," he said, "I'm taking so many pills these days I probably qualify as a scientific experiment myself. I do appreciate you coming by, Virginia. I wish it was under better circumstances."

"Me, too," Gin said, standing. She would have liked to say more . . . there was so much unsaid between them.

So many questions. So few answers.

"I'd better go," she said. "Mom's going to need help with all the food people dropped off."

"I'd ask you to give them my regards," Lawrence said sadly. "I don't expect they're welcome, though."

Gin held out her hand; it felt like an inadequate gesture, but Lawrence took her hand in his large, callused one. "These are hard days," he said quietly, every one of his sixty-something years suddenly reflected in his face.

Gin was halfway back home before her heart returned to a normal rhythm. She was really going to go through with it. She was about to interfere in an official investigation. Even if she could talk her way into examining the body, any evidence she found could be deemed inadmissible because of her personal connection to the victim. She risked blowing the whole case.

But for the first time since coming back to Trumbull, she felt a spark of hope. Hope that she might be able to learn what happened to Lily. Hope that, for the first time in seventeen years, she might find some sort of peace.

As she drove, thoughts roiled in her mind, memories and contradictions and questions, too much to keep straight. Only after she had arrived at home and was getting out of her car did it come to her—the word that had gotten Jake disqualified from the spelling bee.

Vengeance.

14

Gin turned off her headlights before pulling into the driveway. Her father's truck was parked behind her mother's Lexus, so she knew they were both home. She hoped they hadn't noticed her arrival; she wanted privacy to call the number she'd taken from Lawrence's phone.

Stephen Harper didn't pick up, but Gin could tell from his voice mail message that she'd reached his private number. She expressed her request as succinctly as possible and asked that he call her back as soon as he could.

Then she bit her lip and dialed Ducky Osnos. At this point, she had nothing to lose by letting her boss know that she was getting involved—and asking for his help.

He picked up on the first ring. "I saw the news," he said, not bothering with a greeting. "Why didn't you tell me?"

It had taken her almost a year to tell him about Lily, and that was only because her fellowship had ended and she was being hired fulltime as a pathologist. She had been afraid that the story would be unearthed in the reference check, and she confided in Ducky in hopes of convincing him not to tell anyone. He'd promised to keep it just between them and had never mentioned it again.

"I need your help," she said, ignoring his question.

"Anything."

When she'd explained what she hoped to do, Ducky whistled. "You're sure about this? I mean, I can get you the time off, no problem. You'll owe a lot of favors when you get back, but you've built up a lot of goodwill."

Gin had covered for just about everyone over the years. She was one of the few staff who had no children or spouse to get home to.

"I'm sure."

"You know all I can do is vouch for your skills," Ducky said. "I can't change protocols."

"I would never ask you to. Ducky, I can't tell you how much this means to me. I just—I mean, I guess it's like the families always say. That they just want to know the truth."

"Virginia . . . I'm so sorry. For your loss, for the way it happened, for you having to find out like this. I'll be praying for you. For your whole family."

"Thank you, Ducky."

"Good luck."

After they'd hung up, Gin rested the phone on her thigh and stared at the old house that had been the only true home she'd ever known. Through the kitchen window, she could see her mother moving around, setting the table, taking dishes from the oven. She'd soon call Richard in from the den, where he would be watching the evening news.

It was a good excuse to simply go in, to put off this call for yet another day. Instead, Gin took a deep breath and dialed.

Clay picked up on the third ring. "Where have you been?" he asked, sounding both irate and concerned.

"I'm so sorry, Clay. It's been hectic."

"Too hectic to let me know you're all right? Sorry," he amended almost immediately. "I don't mean to snap at you.

And I can understand why you didn't want to talk about it that night. But I've been worried."

"It was really thoughtless of me," Gin concurred. "And I'm so sorry that I lied. I just—I guess I was in shock, at first."

"It's all right," Clay said, his tone softening. "I just wanted to know that you were okay."

Briefly, she described the memorial service, the many people who'd expressed their condolences. She left out any mention of Jake, telling herself it was too complicated to explain—and knowing that wasn't the only reason.

"Do you really think there's any chance they'll find out who did it after all this time?"

"Well, it all depends on what they're able to find. If the killer left any DNA on the body or the cooler, they'll cross check it with CODIS."

"But that only helps if he's been arrested before, right?"

"Yes, more or less. Depends on the state where they were arrested and a few other variables. But they'll also be able to use it to rule people out."

"Yeah, I guess . . . but there are a lot more people who didn't do it than did."

Welcome to my world, Gin resisted saying, remembering how his eyes would sometimes glaze over when she talked about her cases. "I'm going to stay for a while," she blurted.

"A while," he repeated. "Is that like a few days? Or a month, or . . . ?"

"I'm not sure yet. I'm sorry, Clay, I wish I could be more specific. I just—" She squeezed her eyes shut before telling a lie. "It's just that I think I need to be here for my parents."

There was a pause before Clay said, "I understand." His tone implied otherwise.

"I'll try to do better about checking in."

"I'll see if I can get someone to take the opera tickets," he said, a little stiffly.

She'd forgotten—they were supposed to see *Der Rosenka-valier* next Friday at the Lyric. The tickets had been a coveted perk, a gift from the senior partner at Clay's firm. Clay had made reservations at Brindille for before.

"I know that evening is a big deal," she said. "And I was really looking forward to it, too. I'm sorry, Clay. I just . . . everything is a little overwhelming right now."

"Do you want me to come? I can rearrange my schedule—"

"No." She hadn't meant to sound quite so abrupt. But the idea of Clay coming here, seeing her hometown, her family, the complicated and painful echoes of a past she had never fully shared with him . . . it was just too much. "I mean, thank you, really. Maybe I'll come back next weekend for a day or two."

But she wouldn't, she suddenly realized. She wasn't going back to Chicago until she could make some kind of sense of Lily's death, no matter how long it took.

"That would be great. We can . . . whatever you need to do, Gin. Talk, or—or whatever."

But the awkwardness in his voice underscored the distance that she had kept between them; they never really talked. Not about the most important things. She had held back so much: not just what had happened to Lily, but how it had changed her, changed the course her life had taken. Her fears that she would never really be whole again.

Other than Lily, there was only one person in the world that she had allowed to know her that deeply. Only one person had understood who she really was, and loved her for it.

"Well, I'd better go," she said, pushing away the unwelcome thoughts of Jake. "Mom's got dinner ready."

"Right. Take care of yourself, Gin. Good night."

"Good night," she said, hanging up.

Neither of them had said "I love you."

Gin headed for the house, into the comforting aroma of her mother's latest casserole.

*   *   *

Her phone rang as she was loading the dishwasher.

"Hi, this is Stephen Harper returning your call," he said when she picked up. In the background, she could hear a child's shriek. "I got your message."

"I'm so sorry to disturb your evening," Gin said, wiping her damp hand on her jeans and hurrying to the laundry room where she wouldn't be overheard.

"No, don't worry about it. I also spoke to Lawrence Crosby earlier in the day."

"Again, I regret taking up your time with—"

"You're a godsend, to tell you the truth. I've never had a case like this. I gotta ask, though—I mean, it's your sister. Are you sure . . . ?"

"I'm sure." She wasn't, of course. She had no idea what she would feel when confronted with the physical reality of her sister's death. But it didn't matter—she was committed to doing anything she could to help.

"It's pretty irregular, I guess I don't have to tell you. I'll need to run it by the chief."

"Yes, of course. Whatever you need me to do, whoever you need to clear it with, I understand."

"I think one of the detectives is going to stand in," Harper said. "Bruce Stillman, he's a good guy. I've worked with him a couple of times before. Maybe one of the CSIs too. Looks like this is turning into a real party."

Gin's heart sank. So much for trying to get ahead of the investigation. Still, maybe it was better for the detectives to be present if she was able to discern anything important.

"Also, I think it's probably best if you just observe," Harper went on.

"I have no problem with that."

"Were you really a Boettcher Fellow at U of C?"

Gin felt the blush rise in her cheeks. Few people would know—or care—that she'd been awarded the honorary fellowship after her second year of medical school. There was only one person who would have shared that information—which told her that Ducky had called ahead, paving the way for her. "I'm afraid so," she said, hoping she didn't sound arrogant.

"Damn. Well, I'm looking forward to meeting you, Dr. Sullivan."

"Please, just call me Gin."

"Okay, Gin, and I hope you'll call me Stephen. We'll do this first thing tomorrow, so come in at nine thirty. You need directions?"

"No, I'll be fine. See you tomorrow."

Gin hung up and realized that she had been staring at a basket mounded with dirty laundry. The dryer was still warm, and she decided to fold the clean laundry and start another load.

It was while she was sprinkling the detergent on the clothes that she spotted the folded paper peeking out of the pocket of her mother's slacks.

M—

I BLAME MYSELF FOR NEVER TELLING YOU BEFORE THAT I'M SORRY. AND NOW I'M AFRAID IT'S TOO LATE. BUT KNOW THAT YOU ARE IN MY HEART.

The words were written in a blocky, masculine hand on a plain sheet of unlined white paper. There was no signature.

"M" was for Madeleine, presumably. But who had written the note? And what were they sorry for?

15

Traffic had slowed to a crawl due to construction as Gin headed into Pittsburgh the next morning. Luckily, she'd allowed plenty of time, telling Madeleine she was going to visit a friend from college. For once, Madeleine didn't pepper her with questions; she seemed distracted as she left for her office.

The Allegheny County Medical Examiner's office was housed in an unremarkable low-slung beige building tucked next to the interstate in downtown Pittsburgh. The most redeeming aspect of its location was its proximity to the Strip District, several blocks of gourmet supply shops and outdoor food markets, though Gin had no appetite for exploring today.

Gin showed her identification and was buzzed back to the morgue, where a tall, rangy, balding man waited next to a distinguished-looking older gentleman, both of them in scrubs.

"Gin Sullivan, I presume?"

"Yes, I am," Gin said.

"Stephen Harper," he said, offering his hand. His grip was firm and warm. "Pleased to meet you, and this is Dr. Harvey Chozick, our chief."

"It's a real pleasure to meet you, Dr. Sullivan," Chozick said, taking her hand in both of his. His eyes were a vivid blue behind his thick glasses. "I've read about your work in Srebrenica. If I was twenty years younger, I would have loved to have joined your team myself."

"The pleasure is mine," Gin said with sincerity. "I read your work on immunohistochemistry during my fellowship."

Gin followed the two men to the sink where they washed their hands before putting on disposable surgical caps, masks, and gloves, as well as plastic gowns.

At the door to the morgue, Harper hesitated. "I just wanted to say," he began, ducking his chin. "If it gets too . . . well, I would understand if you needed to step out. Or . . . or anything."

"I appreciate your concern," Gin said. Through the square pane of glass in the door, she could see the two detectives, Stillman and Witt, standing over the steel table on which her sister's remains were laid out, their details indistinct. "But I'll be fine."

Harper held the door for her; next Dr. Chozick followed, Harper taking up the rear. They arrayed themselves around the table, and Gin had her first look at her sister's body.

She was dimly aware of the hushed greetings of the detectives and the tech who had prepped the work area, and she answered automatically, but her attention was riveted to Lily's remains. Nearly all the clothing had been cut away, except for a few small sections that had become fused with the body's tissues. Some of the skin had sloughed free of the bones, revealing the dried and stretched tendons below, the remnants of organ and muscle tissue still clinging to the skeleton. The sealed cooler had kept out the animals and insects that might have disturbed the tissues, but moisture had still made it inside, allowing the putrefaction process to proceed. The body cavities had long ago burst, the tissues liquefied and then eventually dried, leaving behind a blackened and moldering skeleton covered here and there with tight-stretched, leathery skin. The eyes had sunk and disintegrated, and little facial skin was left to stretch over the teeth and jaw.

Only Lily's hair, a mass of unruly blonde tangles, was recognizable.

Harper began with the external examination of the remains, documenting his findings into the digital recorder. He took samples from the teeth, hair, and nails, which would be tested for further clues to Lily's death. The body had already been weighed and x-rayed, the teeth providing positive identification, but examining the metabolites in the teeth would also provide a general indicator of Lily's health at the time of her death.

All that would happen later, though. At the conclusion of the autopsy, samples would also be cut from the bones, to be scrubbed and ground and purified before being spun in a centrifuge to extract microscopic DNA particles. For now, Harper would work from the outside in, examining what he could of what was left behind.

Any last fears Gin had about witnessing this final examination of her sister's body were quelled as she observed Harper at work. She had been trained for this, had repeated these same steps herself hundreds of times before. This body on the steel table was Lily only in the strictest sense of her corporeal existence; everything that had made her the person she was had already vanished, leaving behind a shell of herself that had further morphed into something that had no emotional connection to an ebullient, lively teenage girl.

Harper documented the condition of the skin and the exposed bone and organs. The scalp and facial skin had detached from the skull, and Harper had only to brush decayed matter off the skull to examine it. He pointed to a cracked depression on its otherwise smooth surface. "The fracture extends posteriorly along the midline of the occipital area," he said, measuring carefully. "Fragments appear to be mostly still attached."

It was impossible to say whether the injury could have been survivable, had Lily received prompt attention. Sometimes the swelling of the brain could be relieved and healing could proceed. But Gin had her doubts—to cause a fracture of that magnitude, considerable force would have had to be used.

When Harper was finished with the external exam, he cut through the ribbons of skin that remained on the torso, lifting them out of the way to expose the body cavity. Many of the soft tissues had crumbled away, their softening the result of saponification, the breaking down of fats, and what was left was dry and fragile. Harper picked up the rib cutters, an instrument close in appearance to gardening loppers, and carefully cut through the ribs to gain access to what was left of the internal organs. Then he began to remove her organs.

The heart and lungs were recognizable but shrunken and desiccated. The stomach and intestines were another matter, decomposed long ago along with their contents. Harper pulled the liver, kidneys, and spleen free, but despite the care he took, they crumbled in his hands. Lily's lower organs had decayed to the point that what Harper was removing was little more than dust and hardened clumps.

The uterus had shrunk and hardened, the exterior a reddish color, considerably less decomposed than the other organs. Harper made a careful incision, gently spreading the outer tissues open—and gasped.

"There—there appears to be a . . ." he began, visibly shaken. "It—wow. A fetus. Looks like an intact placenta."

A fetus. Lily had been pregnant.

Gin felt like the ground was giving out beneath her feet. A wave of dizziness gripped her, but at the last second, she stopped herself from falling by grabbing the edge of the steel table.

She looked away from the tiny, withered sac, catching Harper's eyes above his mask. They were compassionate but alarmed. "Are you all right?" he asked.

Pull it together, she ordered herself, swallowing hard. She forced herself to stand straighter, squeezing her fingernails into her palms. The pain steadied her, and she nodded. "Yes. I'm sorry. It was just . . . unexpected."

"What is it? What did you find?" Stillman asked. "Did you just say a fetus?"

Harper explained in as few words as possible, picking up the camera again. "The placental tissue is badly degraded, but I'd like to photograph it before we go further."

Stillman whistled softly. "Holy shit."

Everyone fell silent as Harper carefully detached the withered sac and laid it on the table. He picked up a small pair of scissors and cut it open, spreading the sides. Nestled inside was a tiny, curled fetal skeleton.

Lily's baby.

"Around fifteen to sixteen weeks, I'd say," Harper said softly, picking up the camera again.

"Can DNA tell us who the father is?" Witt asked as Harper worked.

"Most likely yes, if the fetal skeleton provides viable samples," Gin said, trying to keep her voice from shaking. "And of course, if we have a sample of the father's DNA to compare it to. Given the condition of the rest of the tissues, I think it's a strong possibility."

"How can you be sure?" Stillman demanded.

Gin took a deep breath, steadying herself. "When I was in Srebrenica . . . there were others. Pregnant women. We were able to collect viable DNA in most cases."

"Any chance of getting a rush on that?" Stillman asked.

Gin caught Harper's eye roll. Every medical examiner was asked that question regularly, and no matter how often the answer was no, Gin was certain that cops would continue to ask until the day when the backlog of cases finally was winnowed down. Even then, results for a live suspect would always take precedence over a dead victim—and cold-case results waited the longest of all. Despite the increased interest in Lily's case, they would still be waiting weeks, if not months.

"Sorry," Harper said, not bothering to try to sound sincere. "We'll let you know as soon as we find anything."

Once the tiny skeleton had been photographed from every angle, Harper set it gently in a plastic bin and continued with the rest of the examination, which revealed little out of the ordinary. When he was finished, the techs took over and the others filed from the room.

"I really appreciate this," Gin said, as they peeled off gloves and masks and gowns in the anteroom.

"It's no problem." With his mask off, the ring of hair along the back of Harper's head stuck up in a way that was almost comical. "You know . . . I have a sixteen-year-old daughter from my first marriage. Lives with her mom, but I see her whenever I can. It, ah . . . I guess I just wanted you to know you weren't the only one who . . . Not that I can know what you're going through . . ."

As clumsy as Harper's effort to comfort her was, Gin was grateful. Maintaining professional distance meant that there were too few moments like this, when their cases were permitted to be people—sons and daughters, husbands and wives, parents. If it hadn't been her sister on the table, Gin might have suggested that they get a cup of coffee together.

As it was, she needed to be by herself for a while.

Lily had been pregnant, nearly four months, by the looks of it—and she hadn't confided in Gin. Had her sister been planning to keep the baby? Was she in denial that her missed periods meant a pregnancy? Was it possible that she truly didn't know?

According to Pennsylvania state law, Lily would have had to get parental consent for an abortion, since she was under eighteen. An abortion would have been possible through the second trimester—but Gin knew that doctors, especially those in conservative communities, balked when the pregnancy had progressed past twenty weeks. Had Lily been trying to gather the courage to tell their parents as the window slowly closed? Did the father of the child know that time was running out? Was he determined enough to end the pregnancy that he was willing to destroy two lives to make sure it never came to term?

The implications of this new discovery were dizzying, but the worst part was that Lily hadn't told her. That she had borne this terrible secret alone. Her sister had never kept anything from her before. Why this time?

Was it shame at having made a life-altering mistake? Or was Lily reluctant to reveal the identity of the father? If it wasn't Tom . . . was she trying to keep Tom from finding out?

Could it have been Jake?

The possibility hit her in the gut, taking her breath away. Seeing him over the past few days had stirred complicated emotions. Even now, Gin believed that Jake had loved her. And she was certain she'd loved him. If she'd ever doubted it— ever wondered if what she'd felt for him was merely youthful infatuation—seeing him again had erased those doubts. None of the men she'd dated since—including Clay—had stirred anything close to the passion she'd once felt for Jake.

But that didn't make him innocent.

She was walking toward her car when Stillman approached her, striding quickly across the parking lot. With a sinking feeling, Gin realized that he'd been waiting for her outside.

"Oh, hi," she said lightly, hoping to deflect him.

"Dr. Sullivan. I was wondering if you'd mind answering a few more questions for us, in light of what we learned in there."

"My family has been cooperating," she said tersely, eyeing her car a dozen yards away. Further questioning was inevitable; she just didn't feel like doing it now. The news about Lily's pregnancy was weighing heavily on her mind and she'd been thinking a run along the river might settle her. "Maybe I could schedule something with you for later in the week."

"Our offices aren't far away," Stillman said. "Ten minutes tops in traffic. How about we get it done now and save you another trip up here?"

Gin frowned and tried to step around him. "Unfortunately, I'm meeting someone in a half hour, and I need to get on the road or I'll be late."

Dodging the detective wasn't a good idea; evasiveness wouldn't do anything to shore up their confidence in her. She might even be rousing suspicions. But Gin felt dangerously close to breaking down. She needed time to think, to process what the pregnancy meant.

"That's a shame," Stillman said. "On the other hand, your parents were both able to move their schedules around. Detective Witt's on his way over there now."

His eyes were obscured by mirrored sunglasses, despite the fact that thick clouds had blocked the sun. Gin wished she'd put on her own sunglasses; she was certain her apprehension showed on her face.

She didn't want her parents hearing the news of Lily's pregnancy without her. It was going to be a terrible shock, particularly to her father, who had always been naïve when it came to Lily's behavior.

Now she was in a bind: she couldn't go home without giving the lie to her own excuse. But as she endured Stillman's inscrutable gaze, she figured he already knew.

"Well, that's convenient," she said. "I need to stop by there before I meet my friend."

"See?" Stillman said. "It all works out. I'll follow you."

16

Gin kept to the speed limit along the construction-choked stretch of Route 885, fuming every time she glanced in the rearview mirror and spotted Stillman behind her. The polite concern he'd shown her in the autopsy room had evaporated once they were outside, and his manner had become almost antagonistic.

That meant one of two things: either they thought Gin was protecting someone or they suspected her of lying about something.

Being scrutinized in a criminal case wasn't a familiar feeling for Gin.

As a medical examiner, she frequently did not learn the results of the criminal cases that involved the autopsy evidence she provided, even when she testified in court. Her job was simply to assess the cause and means of death and, in the case of murder, provide any information the police needed for their investigations. What followed—arrests, investigations, convictions—was rarely reported back to her. Sure, she could have picked up the phone and made inquiries herself, but with her challenging case load, there simply wasn't time to become invested in the outcome of every case.

Occasionally, she'd see an officer she'd worked with while she was at court or when they stopped by the office, and she'd find out if a killer had been convicted, a manslaughter charge dropped, a victim finally laid to rest. By then, though, she had often already satisfied herself as to the cause and means of the deaths that they investigated, facts that could be reduced, in the best scenarios, to science. As for the rest—motive, the passions that drove killers, the remorse they might have felt—it was beyond the scope of her duties.

As she passed the hulking skeletons of the steel industry rising up from the banks of the Monongahela River in the half-dozen towns between Trumbull and Pittsburgh, Gin had a fleeting impulse to pull off the road and head back to Chicago, back to her life. The routine of her job seemed deeply attractive right now, an easy escape from the questions swirling around her sister's death.

Instead, as she passed the *Welcome to Trumbull, Home of Prayer* sign, she reduced her speed to what felt like a crawl and continued on to her parents' house. She could see Witt's cruiser parked neatly behind her mother's Lexus. She took the last available space in the driveway, behind her father's truck, leaving Stillman to park on the muddy shoulder.

She left the front door open, not bothering to wait for Stillman to catch up. As she entered the living room, she spotted Witt sitting in her father's chair, his notebook on his lap, looking deeply uncomfortable. Richard sat on the couch with his arm around Madeleine, whose face had gone chalky and pale. A single tear streaked her makeup. When she saw Gin, she staggered to her feet.

"Did you know?" she demanded. "Did you know she was pregnant?"

"I just found out today," Gin said, stung. Did her mother really think she could have kept that secret all these years?

"So you saw it for yourself?" Richard's voice was hollow, his eyes desperate. Gin realized he'd been holding out hope it might be a mistake. "There was really a baby?"

"I did, Dad," she said as gently as she could. Stillman entered the room behind her, and she went to her father and hugged him, angry that this painful, private moment should be witnessed by the two detectives.

She took a seat on the sofa next to her parents, leaving the love seat for Stillman. Catching the look that passed between the two detectives, she gritted her teeth and tried to appear calm.

"I was just telling your parents that we won't have the lab results back for a couple of weeks," Witt said.

There was a knock at the door. Gin got up and answered it. Standing outside, holding his hat in his hands, was Lawrence. He'd parked behind Witt's cruiser, his truck blocking the sidewalk.

"I thought I should be here," he said in a low voice. "Witt and Stillman didn't bother issuing an invitation, but Witt called on his way over to let me know about the pregnancy. You all right?"

"I guess," she said, standing aside for him to enter. "It's just a lot to take in."

When Richard saw Lawrence, he buried his head in his hands. "You," he sputtered, his voice muffled. When he looked up again, tears of rage glittered in his eyes. "Why is he even here? That can't be right. Isn't it a conflict of interest? His son is a prime suspect. Doesn't anyone else get that?"

"Mr. Sullivan—" Witt began, but Lawrence made a noise of disgust.

"I want the same thing as you, Richard—to find out who killed your daughter."

"Dad," Gin interjected. "Please, we all need to work together here."

But Lawrence was already backing toward the door, holding up a hand in defeat. "I'll go, but I just ask that you think about what you're saying," he said beseechingly. "When this is over, when we've got the guy who hurt Lily, we're still all going to be living here in this town. We're going to have to find a way to make it work. Madeleine, Richard, we've been friends for thirty years. You *know* me."

"Just go, Lawrence." Madeleine begged. Her hair hung wilted and stringy around her face. "Please. All of you. My husband and I need time to process all this."

"If you think of anything," Witt said, tapping a card that he'd set on the glass coffee table. "Otherwise, we'll be in touch if we find out anything more."

"Thank you," Gin said, ushering them as quickly as she could out the front door. Lawrence was already pulling away from the curb. Once out of her parents' earshot, she rounded on Witt. "The ME could have handled informing them of the pregnancy. Why come here and upset them? You have their statements."

Witt shrugged. "You never know—sometimes new information will jog a memory loose, clarify something that didn't make sense."

Stillman gave her the ghost of a smile. "This is a big case," he said, as though telling her she'd won the lottery. "Media all over it, not to mention departmental politics. We don't have time to be worrying about everyone's *feelings*. Unless they're feeling moved to share something they might have been keeping to themselves." His flinty gray eyes bored into hers.

"Your sister didn't just undergo an immaculate conception. *Somebody* was responsible for knocking her up."

*   *   *

Gin knew it wouldn't be long before her sister's pregnancy was in the news, ratcheting up the stakes for the media. It was up to the detectives how and when to release the information to the press, and how to craft the story. Sometimes key details were held back, for a variety of reasons—trying to draw out suspects, or control public outcry, or simply respect the privacy of the bereaved—and sometimes they were strategically leaked.

Still, the murder cases she'd been involved with had taught her that news tended to find its way out, even when investigators tried to keep a lid on it. The temptation to leak information—for money, notoriety, or darker, personal reasons—was simply too great in a complex investigation involving too many people at too many levels.

That meant she had only a brief window of time to try to figure out whose baby Lily had been carrying before the entire town was in an uproar.

When Lily had gone missing, Tom was among the first people questioned, since they'd been dating for six overheated months. But Tom had an alibi; Spencer had been teaching him how to drive a stick shift out in the parking lot of the shuttered Montgomery Ward's that night. Two days later, when Jake finally admitted that he had been with Lily that afternoon, Lawrence had stepped aside and let Lloyd question Jake; he'd even taken the extra step of notifying the county police and inviting them to take over. The county police had declined, since they only got involved in homicide, large-scale narcotics cases, weapons trafficking—problems requiring their greater resources and firepower. Missing persons cases, especially those involving teens, which were far more common than anyone cared to admit, rarely got their attention.

The last that Gin knew, Tom had been working in management at the medical center, a job it had been widely assumed that his father had helped him get. She took a chance and tried the general number for the center. An operator directed her call.

"Records, this is Tom Parker speaking."

His voice was both familiar and subtly changed. Deeper, perhaps; or maybe it was just the strangeness of hearing his terse, professional greeting. Tom had always been the joker of the group, the type to ham it up; it had been a thorn in his father's side that Tom never took anything seriously.

"Tom, this is Gin. Virginia Sullivan. I hope I'm not interrupting anything."

"Gin! Oh hey, I'm so glad you called. I didn't get to spend much time with you on Saturday."

He'd come to the memorial with Christine and her kids, but then disappeared in the throng of mourners. Gin had caught only brief glimpses of him, always with a wineglass in his hand.

"Thank you so much for coming," she responded carefully. "It meant so much to me and my family."

"Of course. It was . . . hard."

His voice wobbled on the last syllable, catching Gin by surprise. He'd seemed unfazed, even cheerful at the service; was it possible he'd been covering up his own grief? Gin had long ago concluded that Tom and Lily's romance would have soon come to a natural end, especially since Lily had begun spending more time with Jake. Neither of them had the maturity for a lasting relationship.

"It was hard for me, too." She waited a beat, trying to find the words to put him at ease. "I was wondering . . . Christine invited me to Olive's party, and I'm looking forward to it. But we won't have any time to ourselves there either—"

"I'm not even going to be able to attend," Tom said. "I've got a work thing."

"Well, then, all the more reason . . . I guess I just hoped we could get together to talk. Just you and me. Now that Lily's been found, I have more questions than ever. I'm just trying to make sense of it all, you know?"

"Do I ever," Tom said. "I've barely slept since they found her. I have nightmares—I've been remembering all these little things from back then."

He sounded genuinely tormented, which made Gin feel a little guilty for her subterfuge. "Could you meet for a drink after work today?"

Tom laughed, a humorless, empty sound. "Hell, I could meet you for a drink right now. In the summer on Fridays, this place empties out early. It's just me and the crickets around here."

Gin doubted he was telling the truth. Spencer had put in long hours, including many weekends, for as long as Gin had known him. According to her parents, the medical center was busier than ever. She wondered how Spencer would feel about his son skipping out early, but she wasn't about to let the opportunity slip by.

"I could stand to get out of the house myself," she said. "Is there somewhere we can go that's quiet?" She trusted that he would read between her words and understand that she meant somewhere where they wouldn't be seen—and gossiped about.

"Tell you what, how about the club?" Tom suggested. "It's pretty dead in the afternoon. We'll clear out by the time the dinner crowd comes in."

"Sure," Gin said, though she was less than thrilled with the choice. The Bella Vista Country Club, which wasn't in Trumbull itself but rather fifteen minutes to the west of town, was a beautiful old rambling stone structure built nearly a century ago for wealthy residents of Pittsburgh who owned country estates. Her parents belonged, as did Spencer Parker and a few other well-heeled families who hadn't fled town when the steel industry hit hard times, but most of its members came from more affluent addresses than Trumbull. Even some Pittsburgh residents made the drive for the lush greens and the atmosphere of old money—something Gin had gotten more than enough of back when her mother's aspirations were more social than political.

At least she could count on Jake not being there; the son of a local cop wouldn't make the cut, even if he wasn't despised by an entire town. Besides, she couldn't imagine Jake enjoying the manicured course or the staid, fussy clubhouse—with his hands rough from physical labor, his year-round burnished tan, and most of all, his disdain for the trappings of wealth.

"I can be there in half an hour. Just need to answer a couple e-mails. That work for you?"

"Absolutely," Gin said, already gathering her purse and keys. She'd be at the club in fifteen minutes, but waiting in the bar until the appointed time sounded better than waiting in her parents' echoing old house full of too many ghosts.

17

It was closer to forty-five minutes before Tom came through the swinging doors of the club's lounge, blinking from the sun. He was wearing a button-down blue shirt with the cuffs rolled back over his wrists; his tie was loosened. Even with these modifications, he managed to give off the same air of good-natured, indolent privilege that had allowed him to coast through adolescence with barely a scratch.

"So glad we decided to do this," he said, brushing Gin's cheek with a perfunctory kiss. She thought she detected a note of liquor on his minty breath, but maybe it was just the slightly musty bar smell.

The elderly bartender tottered his way down to them. He had a thin scrim of silvery hair and wore a bow tie and a short-sleeved white shirt. Gin, who'd been dragged to Christmas open houses and summer dances here as a child, thought it might be the same man who'd been tending bar twenty years ago.

"What can I get you folks today?" he rasped in a smoker's wrecked voice.

"Tell you what, I think I'll have a martini," Tom said. "Ketel One, olives, very dry."

"Just a club soda," Gin said—and then changed her mind. "No, on second thought, make that a glass of wine. Maybe a pinot blanc?"

"I got a nice chardonnay," the bartender said. "From California, I think, I gotta check."

"The chardonnay's fine," Gin amended, hoping it hadn't been sitting open for too long; this was still a mixed-drink crowd. Like Trumbull, it was stuck in the decrepit aftermath of its heyday, when its wealthy members had bellied up to the bar with their wives clad in fur and diamonds. Today, the only other patrons were a pair of elderly women sipping pink drinks by the window and a man with a shock of gray hair ringing his scalp who looked like he was taking a nap at the other end of the bar.

"So," Tom said. "How are you and your folks holding up?"

"Oh, about like you'd expect," Gin said. "You know my mom—as long as she's busy, she's fine. And Dad tends to disappear a lot when he's not at work. I found him weeding his carrot patch in the middle of the afternoon the other day."

Their drinks arrived, and Tom gave his an experimental sip, smacking his lips. Gin took a sip of her own drink and found it about what she expected: stale and cheap. Still, it went down easy.

"Sounds like *my* dad—drowning his feelings in work. I hope you don't mind that he didn't come. He doesn't do very well with memorials."

Gin was surprised by the tenderness in Tom's voice; ordinarily he butted heads with his father. But the twins' mother had died in childbirth, and according to her parents, Spencer had never recovered from that loss. No wonder a memorial would be difficult for him.

"Listen, Tom, I've been thinking a lot about that day, when Lily disappeared." Gin spoke carefully.

"Me too. I mean, the water tower! We were there just about every day that summer. You ever think—I mean, it could have been any of us who got killed. It could have been you, anyway, or Christine."

As he spoke, he played with a loose button on his shirt, twisting it idly. Tom had never been a deep thinker, and this observation was typically insensitive. But Gin nodded along.

"I've gone over it again and again, trying to think who might have gone there that day," Gin said. "I mean, we hardly ever saw anyone up there. People tended to stay down near the creek or on the paved trails, remember? No one came up by the tower unless they knew about the old fly ash trails, and they were hidden pretty well by the trees."

Fly ash, the powdery gray residue left over from burning coal at the power plant, had once been hauled up the hills overlooking the river and dumped. By the time Gin was in her teens, the network of trails once used to dispose of the ash was overgrown, used only by kids and the occasional dirt-bike rider.

"Yeah, that's what made it such a good spot," Tom agreed forlornly. "Remember how we used to skinny-dip there? And how Jake fell asleep that one time and we left him and he got so sunburned?"

"He'd worked a double shift," Gin remembered. The joke had been Tom's idea; she'd felt guilty about it, especially when Jake woke up after sundown and had to thumb a ride back to town.

"Yeah. That was Jake. Always working." It wasn't bitterness, exactly, that edged his words. It almost sounded like envy. "I go back sometimes, you know. Once or twice a year. I like to hike up there when it snows, and there's no one around, and you can't even hear the road noise."

"I was wondering . . . about that night. Remember, you said you were driving with your dad?"

"Yeah," Tom said, his tone instantly turning defensive. "He'd just got that BMW M3, remember? He was teaching me to drive a stick."

Gin vaguely remembered the car; Spencer's one ostentatious indulgence was a new luxury automobile every few years. "It's just that I don't remember you ever doing that before. We used to talk about it, remember? How you always said your dad wouldn't let you drive his car after your fender bender? So it's kind of surprising to think you would have done it on a night when Lily wasn't babysitting. When you two could have gotten together."

"She was busy," Tom said. He caught the bartender's eye and signaled for another drink; Gin had barely drunk a quarter of her wine. "Or at least . . . she said she was doing something."

"That's the funny thing," Gin mused. "I've gone over and over it in my head and I just draw a blank. I can't remember her saying where she was going. She was just . . . gone, when I got back from Columbus. I mean, later we figured out that she'd taken those things. The backpack and the clothes."

Watching Tom over her glass of wine as he attacked his fresh drink with zeal, Gin mused that he was anything but strong. He was like one of the buds on her mother's camellia bushes that never bloomed, that remained compacted in its tight ball while all around it the other flowers opened lushly.

Failure to launch, she'd heard some of her colleagues call the phenomenon, bemoaning children who returned home after college or siblings who languished while waiting for inheritances. But Tom, at least, had the resources to limp through life. The job his father found for him kept him in a bare-bones version of the life of privilege that he'd always favored; the rock-bottom cost of living in Trumbull certainly helped. The genes he'd inherited from the mother who'd died giving birth to him had endowed him with stunning blue eyes and good bone structure. From his father he got his athletic ease, the youthful grin—and the faintly arrogant attitude that harkened back to Spencer's own family wealth.

Tom had been a beautiful child, and he was a striking adult, even with the extra weight he was carrying, and if he hadn't been gifted with his sister's quick intelligence, perhaps it had been a good thing. A more introspective man might have judged himself wanting, might have become bitter in the face of failure. But Tom had always been happy to coast on his looks and charisma, even if that meant that he was second fiddle to other, more successful men, that he lived off the largesse of others' toil.

Except . . . what if she'd read him wrong? Then and now? What if the broken capillaries around his nose, the slight paunch around his waist, the trembling hands that he tried to conceal—were indicative of something much darker? Not just a few too many drinks each evening, but a descent into physical and moral lassitude?

"Did you know she was going to meet Jake?" she asked suddenly, the question taking even her by surprise. So much for easing into things.

Tom looked wounded. "Gin, I told everyone then—no. Lily said she had things to do and I let it go at that."

Gin was already shaking her head. "I just don't remember things that way."

"What's that supposed to mean? You weren't there that day. You were off at freshman orientation. I mean, no offense, but I doubt you thought about home at all, you were so eager to get out of Trumbull."

Gin ignored the sting of his unintentional barb. "What I mean is that I can't see you just letting it go. You and Lily—you were inseparable that summer."

"Yeah," Tom said, and then he seemed to wilt a little. He stared into his drink morosely, and then picked it up and downed it. "What do you say, Virginia Jean, want to tie one on? For old times' sake?"

Gin was taken aback. Tom seemed oddly vulnerable, staring at her from under sleepy lids, his mouth—always one of his best features, almost feminine in its shape, but tempered by his chiseled jaw—curved into a hopeful, sad smile.

"You remember my middle name," she said softly.

"Course I do. Come on, you're practically my sister. I mean, remember how your mom used to put us all in the tub together?"

"The bubbles," she said, smiling. "We made beards with them."

Tom laughed with delight. It was, Gin realized with a pang, the happiest she'd seen him since she'd come home, and her heart constricted a little. She had to remind herself that she was here because Tom made a compelling suspect.

"You also told Maribeth Connolly you'd seen me naked," she went on. "You ruined my fourth-grade year."

Tom laughed harder. Did he really not see how cruel he'd been, pointing at her prepubescent body, in her bright-colored tank tops, crowing about having seen her titties? How his bravado had given the other boys license to torment her? Lily was exempt; Lily would stare anybody down, mock them in return.

And even then, there was something between the two of them. Tom and Lily, thick as thieves, Madeleine used to say. When she was only a toddler, he was her self-appointed guardian, the only one who made any attempt to include her while the older girls played. By the time Lily reached grade school, they spent their recess time chasing each other around the jungle gym, despite the difference in their ages.

His laughter died away as he signaled the bartender again. "One for her, too," he said, pointing at Gin's still half-full glass. She didn't even bother to try to stop him.

"Listen," she said. Maybe she could use his inebriation in her favor. "I need to ask you something else. It—it's important to me. Did you know she was pregnant?"

"What? Oh my God, of course not!" Tom said. His shock seemed real. "Jesus, Gin—what do you think I *am*?"

"Look, we were young," Gin said, rushing through the words she'd rehearsed on the drive over. "It would be a lot for anyone to handle. No one could expect you to have known what to do—"

"I didn't know," he said woodenly, his jaw set in a rigid line. "Gin. Come on."

"Had she . . . had she been acting differently with you? I mean, looking back at it, were there signs?"

"How am I supposed to know?" He took a quick, savage pull at his glass. "I mean sure, she got all crazy at that time of the month. You remember. But she was always moody, always unpredictable."

"But before that day. Was there anything that seemed unusual, even for her?"

Tom stared at his glass, worrying his lower lip with his teeth. Finally he shook his head. "Nothing."

Gin took a deep breath. "I don't know how to ask this, Tom . . . but are you sure the baby would have been yours?"

His mouth compressed into a thin, angry line. "I can't believe you're asking me that! I loved her, Gin. I mean—for *real*. Like, more than I've ever loved anyone in my life."

He finished his third drink while staring miserably at her. He set it down and wiped his mouth on his sleeve.

But Gin couldn't help noticing that he didn't answer the question.

* * *

Half an hour later, she was wondering if she ought to ask him for his keys when the swinging doors of the club opened and a man in a sport coat strode purposefully through. It took Gin a second to recognize Spencer: his hair had gone completely white. It was still cut close, and his face was tanned and mostly unlined; he'd obviously kept up his ambitious fitness routine through all these years. And yet, there was something weary and aged about him.

"Virginia," he said, ignoring his son. He clasped her hands in his and squeezed, his face stricken with genuine grief. "I'm sorry I haven't come by sooner. And that I missed the service. Lily . . . has never been far from my thoughts."

"Thank you, Spencer."

"How is your mother holding up?"

"She's doing well. Work, I think, is helping."

"Good. Good. I'm so glad you were able to take some time off from work to be with your folks. Will you be in town for long?"

Behind him, Gin could see that Tom was stewing. He'd pushed his glass covertly away from him, onto the lip of the bar, and he'd tugged at his shirt to straighten it. But resentment came off him in waves, as his father continued to ignore him.

"I'm not sure yet. A couple of weeks, anyway," she hedged.

"I'll have to have you and your folks over for dinner," Spencer said. "Fire up the barbecue."

"That sounds great, Dad," Tom said in a sing-song voice. "I'll bake a pie."

"That's enough, Tom," Spencer said without looking at him.

"One pie would probably be enough, yeah," Tom said. Gin could smell the sweet scent of gin on his breath even three feet away. "Unless Christine and the kids come. What do you think, Dad, should we invite your perfect child? Your beautiful grandchildren?"

"Tom, save it," Spencer said, turning on him. "Gin's lost her *sister*. Try for one minute to show a little respect. Not everything is about you."

The expression on Tom's face was as if he'd been slapped. Pain flashed in his eyes—deep, searing hurt. And Gin had a glimpse of a side of him that he kept buried underneath his glib exterior.

But was his hurt due to his father's treatment of him? Or was the loss of Lily as fresh for him now as it was for Gin? Or . . . was there something entirely different going on?

Tom dug in his wallet and threw a handful of bills on the bar. "Looks like I've got another engagement," he muttered. "Sorry, Gin. We'll have to do this again soon."

"Sorry, Virginia," Spencer echoed, placing a hand on her arm. "Let's catch up more. I'll talk to Richard about dinner."

He exchanged a nod with the bartender, giving Gin the impression this wasn't the first time he'd come looking for Tom here.

Tom clambered off his barstool and pulled Gin close in a drunken hug. "I'm just glad you're here," he whispered. "What a fucking shit show this is."

Then he trailed his father out of the bar, holding his head high with the stilted dignity that only the drunk can pull off.

"Anything else for you, Miss?" the bartender asked, his hand hovering near her nearly empty first drink.

"Actually, I think I'm finished," Gin said, reaching for her purse. Then she decided she had nothing to lose. Someone had summoned Spencer to pick up his out-of-control son, and she doubted it was the elderly ladies by the window. Spencer had influence in this town, and to pull strings behind the scenes, she guessed he was making it worth someone's while.

"Do the Parkers come here often? I mean, Tom specifically— is he a regular?"

"I wouldn't know, Miss," the bartender said coldly, reminding Gin of one of the rules of small-town life that she had forgotten: everyone's business was everyone else's—unless you had something on them. In the blighted ruins of the steel empire, the few who held onto wealth and power could do exactly what they wanted, whenever and wherever they wanted, while the ones whom fortune passed over looked the other way.

*   *   *

By the time Gin exited the country-club grounds, the first raindrops were splattering the windshield. Her phone chimed an incoming text, and she pulled onto the shoulder of the road to check it.

The text was from Madeleine.

Stuck in meeting. Dad will fix dinner.

Gin rested her head on her hands, leaning on the steering wheel. She wasn't up for an evening with her father; his lugubrious moods were contagious, and it became an effort to talk to him. And she doubted that her mother's meeting was all that urgent, despite the looming mayoral election.

It struck her as impossibly sad, that the event that might have drawn another family closer in their grief seemed to have had the opposite effect on hers. Each of them seeking comfort in work, moving away from each other instead of together, helpless to find the threads that could connect them.

She couldn't go home yet. But if not home, then where?

A memory came to her, of bringing Jake here to the very club she'd just left. The women's group had hosted a party every spring for the graduating seniors; the graduates took turns approaching the podium set up in the dining room and announcing where they'd be attending college in the fall, to the enthusiastic applause of women who still remembered the glory days when steel production kept the river bustling with barges and the smokestacks going night and day. Gin supposed that tradition had died along with the expiring economy, now that half the graduating class would be lucky to go to community college and even luckier to find employment when they were finished, but that night, she'd invited Jake to come along and he'd dutifully put on a tie and too-big jacket he'd borrowed from his father. She'd always wondered if he'd noticed the way the ladies' eyes narrowed when he announced he was going to study engineering in college. When they murmured to each other that he'd received a full scholarship, it wasn't meant to be a compliment.

Jake. So many memories of him in this town, and each one seemed to tear the scab a bit further from the emotions she'd struggled to bury.

She had to admit that the long-ago attraction between them hadn't disappeared. When she was with him, a part of her responded as though no time had passed, as though he was still the lover she couldn't wait to return to.

But surely that was just a chemical reaction, nostalgia sifted through the sieve of sexual yearning. It didn't make him innocent. It didn't even mean that she knew him well, after all this time. He could be thinking anything behind those familiar, beautiful eyes.

She dug in her purse for the scrap of paper with Jake's number on it and stared at the numerals, her emotions warring. She could use that attraction, along with their shared history, to try to learn more—to get him to reveal anything he'd kept secret. Maybe it was underhanded, maybe it was unethical, but she'd be doing it for Lily.

She dialed before she could change her mind.

"It's me," she said when he answered. And then she wished she'd planned what to say, because all that came to her was the pounding of her own heart.

"Gin." A pause. "I'm glad you called. I need—I would like a chance to explain some things."

"That would be . . . all right." Could she sound any more stilted?

"Tell you what. Come over for dinner. I'm cooking."

18

G in knew that Jake had built a home high above Trumbull, on the wooded ridge that looked out over the river valley. After he had given up his scholarship and gone to Edinboro University instead (only a hundred and fifty miles away, with low in-state tuition), he'd come home during his senior year when Lawrence had his heart attack. Jake had finished his degree by correspondence and skipped the graduation ceremony, and then he'd gone to work for an old friend of his father's who owned a construction business, one of the few men in town still willing to give him the benefit of the doubt. By the following year, Jake had bought a piece of land with views of the river, the belching smokestacks, and the lush green summer foliage.

Gin had heard that he'd eventually built on that land. He'd done all the work himself, over the course of years; whether that had been his choice or a means of economizing, she didn't know. But as she pulled into the drive, she realized that she already recognized the home that Jake had built for himself: it was the one he'd once promised her he would build for the two of them someday, before Lily died, when they still had the luxury of naïve dreams of a shared future.

Jake had planned to be a mechanical engineer because he was fascinated by the building of things, by creating something functional that was also beautiful. He'd sketched for her, one day while they lay under a canopy of leafy branches by the water tower, a vision for a house that was shaped like a sort of prow, widening to anchor itself into the slope behind it, like a rowboat that had gotten stuck in a reedy shore. The reality exceeded the promise of the sketch: the home's clean lines and curved wood siding made it look both contemporary and evocative of another time and place, where men labored to build enormous seagoing vessels at the very edge of foreign continents, where vast blue seas invited adventure. The setting sun lit the wide panes of glass looking out over the river in pink and gold.

As Gin walked up the path, the front door opened. Jake stood at the threshold, a glass of red wine held loosely in his hand, watching her. A dog poked its snout shyly around his legs, some sort of hound mix with a wildly wagging tail.

"Your house . . ." Gin said when she reached the top step. "It's beautiful."

"Thanks." Jake touched her arm lightly, leading her inside. "It's kept me busy. Don't mind Jett—though I should warn you that if you give her any attention, you'll never be rid of her."

Gin crouched and offered her hand to the dog, who sniffed enthusiastically and then laid her soft muzzle on Gin's palm, her eyes rolling up in delight. The fur on her face was shot with silver and her eyes were cloudy, but despite her advanced years, she seemed healthy, her coat glossy and her gait steady. When Gin stood, Jett leaned against her legs.

Inside, the same reddish-brown wood had been used for the trim, including curving window ledges, moldings, and baseboards. Gin had no idea what species of wood Jake had used, but its beautiful grain invited touch. The furnishings were simple but elegant; large leather chairs flanked a blue sofa, and found objects—rocks with veins of crystal, curiously knotted driftwood, old metal gears with rusted teeth—sat atop the coffee table. An entire wall was weighted down with floor-to-ceiling bookshelves containing hundreds of books.

Gin pointed to the trim around the doorframe. "Did you do all of this yourself?"

"Yes." No elaboration, just a faint note of pride in his voice. "Can I get you something to drink? I've got a Syrah open."

"Okay, but . . . look, Jake, I'm only hear to talk—"

"It's just a meal," he said. "You've got to eat."

She didn't press it further. Her first sip of the glass he handed her was an entirely different experience from the wine she'd had at the bar: cool, complex, almost peppery. "This is delicious."

"It's from South Africa. I seem to have developed a taste for it. One of my few expensive habits, I'm afraid." He said it in the same self-effacing tone he'd employed to deflect her compliments about the house.

"You've always lived alone," Gin said, what she hoped was a neutral entrée into a conversation that might reveal more.

"For all you know, I've moved in a different woman every week," Jake said with a smile. "That's what the town gossips would have you believe, anyway."

"That must be hard."

Jake shrugged. "You get used to it. I guess in a way, I'm almost glad people have treated me like dirt all these years. Now that the worst has happened, and everyone's pointing their fingers at me again, at least I'm used to it. No way it's going to break me now."

He bent to open the oven and check on whatever was cooking, wonderful savory aromas wafting into the room. "The worst is what Dad has to go through," he continued. "For me, I don't mind—I'm really hoping this time they'll find out who did it and exonerate me. But I feel like Dad has to go through the humiliation twice, once for me and once for himself."

Gin thought of her father's drunken fury, the spittle flying from his lips, the muttered curses. "I never thought about how hard it would be for your dad to keep control of the police department, going through something like that."

"People called for his resignation. A few of them brought it up to the city council. Apparently it got pretty heated." Jake shrugged. "It was a long time ago."

Gin wondered if her parents had gone to that meeting, if her father had been among those demanding that Lawrence step down. "How did he end up holding onto his job?"

"Not sure," Jake said tersely. "Wouldn't be surprised if he just outlasted all his critics. Say what you will about Dad—he's tough."

"Mmm," Gin said noncommittally. She wasn't sure how to steer the conversation back to the events of the night Lily had gone missing. "Whatever you're making smells delicious," she said, stalling.

"It's guy food. I hope you don't mind," Jake said. "Heavy on the meat and carbs. One of my bachelor tricks—I make a lot, freeze the leftovers, and pull them out when I've had a long day."

Gin couldn't help but laugh. "That actually sounds amazing. Everyone at work is following a different trendy diet, and between all the things people say they can't eat, we can't go out as a group anymore—there's either no gluten-free options or nothing vegetarian or raw or paleo on the menu. And as for me, I still haven't learned to cook."

Jake grinned. "It's really not that hard, Gin. Hell, half of what's on TV is how to cook."

"Maybe I ought to have Mom teach me while I'm home. Put this time to good use."

"Are you going to be here for a while?"

"I—I don't know." What was she supposed to say? That she was waiting for the lab to return the results that might put the lie to everything she had once believed about him? That ever since she'd come back to town, she lay awake in her childhood bed remembering the way he'd once kissed her— and then trying to imagine him strangling the life from her sister?

That she was already wondering how she could ever go back to her life in Chicago, with her soulless apartment and distant colleagues, her Netflix evenings and dead houseplants, her pleasant-enough dates with Clay and the punishing trail runs that were the only time she felt completely alive?

"How about you show me around?" she said, forcing those thoughts away. "Give me the grand tour?"

Jake took her through the house, pointing out all the custom work he'd done, while Jett followed them. He had chosen each board for the cabinets to make the most of the hickory's grain. He'd built the cupboards under the stairs himself, each drawer gliding perfectly along its rails. He'd come up with a gray-water system that recycled water directly downslope into his garden.

He was pointing out the different varieties of vegetables in the raised beds he'd built when the skies opened, the misty drizzle turning instantly to fat, splattering drops. Jake seized her hand and they ran, laughing, back to the house, where Jett had plopped down to watch them from the porch. Along the way, Gin's hair escaped its elastic, spilling over her shoulders in damp waves.

"Oh, no," she said, when they were safely under the eaves. She ran her fingers self-consciously through her hair. "It goes crazy in the humidity. You have no idea how much of my life I spend flat-ironing it into submission."

"A waste of time," Jake murmured. He reached for a curl that spiraled down over her face, gently pushing it behind her ear. "I always loved it best like this."

"You're lying," Gin protested, caught up short by the electric sensation of his fingertips on her skin. He'd never said anything about her hair, not when she'd spent countless hours struggling to tame it with her blow-dryer while Lily read her quizzes from *Seventeen*, calling questions into the Jack-and-Jill bathroom to determine which Disney princess she most resembled.

"Remember that time we hiked up in the Laurel Highlands?"

"Oh my God, we almost killed each other," Gin gasped. "I was drenched with sweat when we got to the top, after you promised it was an easy trail."

"It *was* an easy trail. Would have been, anyway, if it hadn't hit a hundred that day."

"And if I'd worn something practical instead of those platform sandals."

"Why on earth did you do that, anyway?"

"To impress you," Gin admitted. She'd told him she misunderstood the plan, but the truth was that she'd held her hiking boots in her hands for several moments that morning, weighing comfort against style. For Jake, she'd always chosen style.

"Gin. I was wearing an old T-shirt and shorts that probably hadn't been washed in a week." His smile was teasing now. "I feel like I ought to apologize. I just thought you were naturally beautiful all the time."

"Surely you've had a woman explain that to you by now."

"Oh, yeah." He shook his head ruefully. "If I've learned nothing else in the last two decades, it's that if you want a woman to be ready at seven, you get out of her way at six."

"Is there . . ." Gin tried to find the right words while keeping her tone light. "Are you seeing anyone special now?"

"Special?" He raised an eyebrow quizzically. "That feels like a loaded question. A good way for me to get into trouble. How about this—every woman I've dated is special, especially those willing to put up with me. But no, other than a few friends I see from time to time, the only female I'm steady with is Jett."

Which meant he had friends with benefits, Gin translated. She wondered how many of the women were really happy with the arrangement. Was it evidence of callousness, of self-involvement? The hallmark of a man who didn't care about the feelings of the women he was with?

"What about you?"

"Oh, I—yes. There's someone in Chicago." The admission felt hollow. "He's an attorney. Our schedules don't leave a whole lot of time to get together, so it's . . . it's fairly casual."

"Ah. Lucky guy." Jake's smile seemed genuine, even if there was a tightness to his voice. He turned to go into the house, but at the door he hesitated. "Gin . . . do you think you'll settle down? Get married, have kids, all of that?"

She'd heard that question a thousand times, from everyone from her colleagues to her college friends to, on the rare occasions when they talked, Christine. Her parents were the only ones who never asked; she had always wondered if it was too painful for them to consider the possibility, knowing that Lily would never have those things, would never be a wife or mother.

"I don't know," she said honestly. "There's this part of me that's always—I mean, this is going to sound crazy, I know. It's not a conscious thing, but, emotionally, it's like Lily's always on my mind, how we'll never do the things we talked about. We were going to be each other's maid of honor." She watched him carefully, remembering how they'd planned her entire wedding ceremony—Jake was going to wear a charcoal-gray tux; the bridesmaids, including Lily and Christine and two friends from school, would be in aquamarine. "She was going to have all girls, she always said. She even had their names picked out: Jessie, Callie, and Nellie. I mean, it all seemed so real then, and now it seems so naïve. None of that probably would have happened—but with her gone, it doesn't seem possible that any of it can."

"That's . . ." Jake shook his head. "I hate to admit this, but when it all happened, I was so caught up in trying to defend myself that I don't think I ever fully processed that she was really gone. That happened slowly. I mean, when you and Christine and Tom all left that fall, I suddenly realized I'd lost all of you. Everything. Not just Lily and you, but . . . and it was like some switch got turned, the way I looked at everything. The future most of all. It's true that I gave up my scholarship because I couldn't bear the thought of running into you. But I also just quit caring. What did it matter where I went, when I couldn't be near any of you? I got through school on auto-pilot, and then Dad's heart attack . . . and I guess I just figured that was how it was going to be. Me and him, and if people came around in town, great, and if not, fuck them."

"But you became a legend in your own time," Gin said, wishing she had some crystal ball that could reveal whether Jake was being honest or was attempting to manipulate her with his words. "Mom always manages to sneak in a report when we talk—how your business is growing, how you've been seen with one woman or another."

"Your mom was always kind to me," Jake said. "I tried to stay out of your dad's way but . . . it meant a lot to me. That she didn't just assume that the rumors were true."

"I'm . . . glad, that she could be there for you," she said, the words forced. "But I—"

"Don't say it," he said. He touched a fingertip to her lips, caressing them lightly, his touch searing. "Please. Just let it go for tonight. One night."

He knew. Even without her voicing her doubts, her suspicions, he knew.

For a moment, they stood suspended in the net of their emotions. All it would take was a single step forward. A hand on his arm. His name, spoken with the weight of the longing she still felt. The promise of a kiss was so real that it was as if she was already losing herself in his arms.

But there was a very real chance that he had stolen something precious from her. That even if he hadn't taken her sister's life, he at least knew more about her death than he was letting on. She crossed her arms and stepped away from him.

"Look, Gin—there's one more thing," Jake said. "I probably should have mentioned it earlier, but . . . well, Dad wants to talk to you again."

Gin was rocketed back to reality. Surely Lawrence would step down soon. It might be natural for him to want to clear his son's name before he did. But how far was he willing to go to protect Jake?

She'd come here hoping to determine once and for all whether Jake was guilty or innocent. That hadn't happened. She hadn't posed the right questions that might have sussed out the truth. It was hard to resist being distracted by the attraction between them. Talking to Jake was easy—natural in a way that it never was with Clay or anyone else.

If only *that* were a sign of innocence.

Gin didn't doubt that Lawrence believed in his son. He was gambling his reputation, his career, to prove it. But if Jake was going to go down, Gin didn't want to see the old man go with him.

"Jake. I'm not sure it would be . . . appropriate. Me speaking to him. I mean, when he came over the other day, I felt like he was trying to run interference with the detectives. Surely there's some conflict of interest? I mean, is he even going to be able to stay on the investigation if . . ."

"If I'm arrested?" Jake's eyes had gone opaque, his voice hard. "It's okay, Gin, you can say it. It's not like I haven't thought about it a dozen times. When Dad told me about Lily's pregnancy, I was almost glad, because I know the DNA test will prove I'm not the father. But then I realized that people will go right on suspecting me anyway, no matter what."

Gin swallowed, processing his words. Jake wasn't afraid of the DNA test. That had to prove something—but what?

"And then I started hoping that, by some miracle, they found evidence in the cooler," he went on. "The problem is, there's probably my DNA on the cooler. Not to mention the rest of you—Tom and Christine, too."

"Your dad said they haven't officially questioned you yet."

"No. Stillman wants me to come in tomorrow morning."

"Are you going to tell them about the cooler?"

"Yes." His gaze didn't waver. "It'll be worse for me, I imagine, if I don't."

"Then . . . that's why Lawrence wants to talk to me? After they interview you?"

"If I were a betting man, I'd say so. Look . . ." He ran a frustrated hand through his hair. "It would almost be easier if Dad wasn't involved. He wants so much to protect me but—I mean, I'm thirty-six years old. I've weathered the suspicions of this town for half my life. If I'm officially accused, so be it. Eventually, something's going to prove me innocent."

"But—what if no further evidence surfaces?"

He didn't say anything for a long time. He must have known what she was really asking—she could read the disappointment in his eyes. He had hoped she'd finally believe him, she realized. Had still hoped his word would be enough.

"I'll deal with that when the time comes," Jake said, turning away from her. "Dad said to let you know he'll be at home Friday morning. He's not going in to the office until after lunch."

The night, along with all its fragile promise, was over.

19

Sleep didn't come easily in her parents' house.

Gin read one of her mother's paperbacks until the wee hours, going over the same pages again and again while waiting for fatigue to overtake her. She finally gave up and turned out the light. The night plodded on, punctuated by nightmares and waking spells, and when a thin, dreary dawn arrived, she was exhausted.

She lay in bed until she heard both her parents leave. Then she got up and drank the coffee her mother had left, not bothering to microwave it. She showered and dressed in her last clean outfit, noting that she'd either have to do laundry or go shopping. She dotted on concealer in an attempt to cover up the dark circles under her eyes, but when that didn't work, she gave up and settled for just a quick swipe of mascara.

Driving to Lawrence's house, she avoided the downtown streets, not wishing to be reminded of their deterioration. Even when she was young, many of the shops had been boarded up; now, there were only two stores still open, and they were both the sort of places that sold more beer and cigarettes than anything else.

Instead, she drove up into the streets lined with what had once been company housing, square little structures built for the families of the men who came to work in the processing plant. Now, very few of the residents worked in the remaining active plants along the river. In fact, very few of the residents worked at all.

Still, there were people outside enjoying the weather. Young mothers bounced babies on their laps in the shade while children played in the street. Old men walked slowly down the sidewalks, hunched low in their clothes, stopping to chat with anyone they knew.

What about these people, the ones who lived at the heart of the town because they couldn't afford to move to its edges? Who also bore the opprobrium of what was left of the middle class? Did any of them believe Jake Crosby had killed her sister? Did any of them care?

When she got to Lawrence's house, his cruiser was in the driveway, but he didn't come to the door when she knocked. She tried twice, and then gave the door a tentative shove. It opened, and she walked into the house.

"Lawrence?" she called. "Lawrence, it's me. Virginia Sullivan."

A rinsed plate and cup lay next to the sink; the morning paper was neatly refolded on the kitchen table. She walked through the living room, letting her gaze linger on the photos of Jake in his baseball uniform, Jake's high school graduation photo, a candid shot of Jake and Lawrence on a wooden dock, Lawrence holding a good-sized trout.

She paused at the door of his study, a place she'd never ventured as a teen. The walls were lined with shelves sagging with the weight of detective novels and biographies and books about the civil war, an old passion of Lawrence's.

Her gaze fell on a shoe lying askew on the rug near Lawrence's oak desk.

Except it wasn't just a shoe. It was attached to a leg. Lawrence's leg. She took two steps into the room and saw that he was lying at an unnatural angle, crumpled on the floor, his eyes staring at nothing and his head resting in a pool of inky black. What was left of it, anyway. Most of his forehead was gone.

And in his hand, a gun.

20

I t wasn't the first time Gin had been in an interrogation room in the tiny Trumbull Police department.

Two days after Lily went missing, she'd been ushered into the same room with her parents. Lawrence and Lloyd had dragged chairs in from the conference room. An officer from the county was present, though later that day he would tell Lawrence the case didn't merit their participation. Lawrence had given her an apologetic smile and offered her a soda. Her mother had squeezed her hand so hard she thought it might bruise.

She hadn't had much to say that day. She'd returned the day before from freshman orientation, sure that her parents had gotten it wrong, that she'd walk into the house and hear Lily's voice calling down the stairs to greet her. Instead, she stumbled to answer the police officers' questions about her sister's routines and habits, her friends, Tom. It hadn't yet come to light that Jake had been with Lily that afternoon; that would come the next day when the witness made her statement. The witness recognized Lily from when she'd had her appendix out—it was pure serendipity that she'd been the nurse who cared for Lily post-op. She wasn't as certain about Jake, but it turned out not to matter, since he admitted readily to having been with her.

But none of them had known that yet. Lawrence had been the one to ask most of the questions, with Lloyd nodding along earnestly and the county officer looking bored and checking his watch, making it clear that he thought a teen runaway was a waste of his time. Had Lily's habits changed recently, Lawrence asked gently. Had she argued with anyone? Skipped school? Seemed depressed or frightened?

No, no, no, no. Gin grew increasingly upset as the questioning progressed. Up until then, everyone had said there was nothing to worry about. Even her parents, who tried to convince each other that Lily would come walking in the door any second, who'd told Gin not to get ahead of herself.

But Lawrence's kindness seemed like a clue. The way her parents' expressions seemed frozen in place, another clue. The dawning realization that they'd already had the same conversation, already answered the same questions.

They had all failed to help.

Now all these years later, sitting across from Witt and Stillman, she felt just as helpless. And she couldn't stop thinking about the fact that, back then, Lawrence had been the one sitting across from her—and now he was dead.

She answered the detectives' questions as succinctly as she could, trying to stifle both annoyance and fear that they were treating her like a suspect. She described arriving at the house, calling for Lawrence, then discovering him in the study. She submitted to a cheek swab and fingerprinting. Now she was ready to leave, but the detectives were still asking questions, mostly repeating themselves.

"So you have no idea what he wanted to talk to you about today?" Stillman asked. He had a habit of twisting one of the loops on his belt, worrying the fabric between finger and thumb.

"I assume it was about Lily. He knew I sat in on the autopsy; I assumed he had questions about that."

"I'm still not really clear on how you came to be present at the autopsy," Witt said. Gin couldn't tell if his scowl had anything to do with her or whether it was his perpetual expression.

"I offered to help because of my extensive experience with decomp cases," Gin said. "It's really not all that unusual for an ME's office to reach out when specialized expertise is needed." Two partial truths—she couldn't remember a similar situation at Cook County, and she was pretty sure Ducky would have raised his eyebrows if a victim's relative asked to sit in.

"I know we've had decomp cases before," Witt said. "I've testified in one or two myself. I don't remember them having to bring in any outside experts."

"As I said, I offered. It wasn't a comment on the county medical examiners' skills."

"This was your thing with the Red Cross," Stillman said skeptically.

"Yes," Gin said, irritated by his choice of words. "The 'thing' where a team of volunteer forensic pathologists recovered the remains of victims of war crimes during the Bosnia conflict. The 'thing' where I worked in a mass grave . . . that *thing*."

Any attempt to shame him over his word choice went unnoticed. "Help me understand why someone like you would do that," Stillman went on. "Did they pay you?"

"I—it's not—" Gin stuttered. "It's not relevant, and it has no bearing on my sister's death, but many of my colleagues from all over the country have participated. We do it for the families—in hopes that they'll get a sense of peace over having their loved ones' remains returned to them. And our testimony is used in international court as well."

Stillman shrugged, and Gin silently fumed. But she hadn't told him the entire truth. Because the truth brought her shame. When the opportunity came along, she'd taken it—not out of a strong desire to do good, but because she had stopped feeling anything. Had become increasingly numb, at her job and in the leftover hours when she was essentially just waiting for it to be time to go back to work.

She'd hoped that seeing the evidence of the atrocities first-hand might jar her back into living. That the emptiness inside her might be assuaged when she saw how much worse the lives of people in war-torn countries were. That, perhaps, she'd be *guilted* into appreciating her blessings.

"So these mass graves, they held bodies that had been buried as long as Lily?" Witt asked, in a gentler tone than his partner.

"Yes."

"I guess I can see why they'd want your input," Witt said. Gin was grateful, even if he was only pretending to be sympathetic. "And were you able to offer any insight that they didn't reach themselves?"

"Yes and no." Images of her sister's body, images she'd given herself permission to forget, crowded her mind. The tiny skeleton nestled in its sac. The filament of an umbilical cord that had connected it to Lily. "I'm sure that Dr. Harper would have reached the same conclusions. I may have helped him arrive there more quickly."

"But the baby," Stillman said. "Any chance he would have missed that? I mean, *I* saw it, and I wouldn't have known what it was."

"With our specialized training, it would have been hard for him to overlook." *As long as he'd opened the uterus,* she thought. *As long as it hadn't disintegrated from handling like some of the other organs.*

"Is it possible," Witt asked, "that there was anything you saw that you didn't report? Or that you reported only to Lawrence Crosby?"

"Absolutely not," Gin said. "Don't you think I'm desperate to know who did this?"

"It's kind of an odd coincidence, though," Stillman said. "Crosby killing himself the day you were supposed to talk to him."

"If he actually killed himself," Witt interrupted. "Here's the thing. We're bringing Jake in this afternoon. Under the circumstances, we had asked Lawrence to step aside. We told him we'd keep him posted and that if he had anything to add, to go ahead and let us know, but for all intents and purposes, he was off the case. Now given that, it makes me wonder about the timing. I mean, maybe he found something on his own . . . something he didn't share with us.

"I have some ideas," Witt continued. "One, *someone* may have been afraid he would reveal something he had been keeping to himself. Or two, they thought he was about to find out something they wanted kept secret."

"Like who killed your sister." Stillman was smirking now, giving up any pretense of sympathy.

"Look," Gin said. "Lawrence was . . . I was very close to him, at one time. If you're trying to imply that I might have wanted him dead . . ."

"Just one possibility!" Stillman held up his hands in a "no harm, no foul" gesture. "We've got to look at everyone in your sister's life, especially those who might have had some reason to be upset with her."

"And how does that include me?" Gin had a pretty good idea, but she was going to make them spell it out. She had worked with enough detectives on enough cases that she was familiar with the techniques they used to get people to open up, not just to confess but to reveal more than they intended.

They were making it hard for her to remember that they all had the same goal: to identify Lily's killer. Besides, she was tired . . . so tired. Despite the difficulty she'd had sleeping last night, now she felt like climbing into bed and staying there.

"Jake Crosby was your boyfriend." Stillman ticked his points off on his fingers. "Jake was secretly seeing your sister. Jake knocked her up. You found out."

"Even if that were true," Gin said stiffly, "there's still the problem of who killed her. I trust you've reviewed my alibi—the fact that I was two hours away at a college orientation."

"Yeah, I read that," Stillman said skeptically. "Of course, it wasn't a murder investigation then, so I'm sure they just took your word for it."

Gin was dumbfounded. "That's—that's crazy. There are photos of me at the orientation. Counselors who knew I was there. The other kids. There's no way I could have faked that."

"Even so, you could have found out about Jake and your sister, you could have been angry, you could have talked about it with other people. Maybe convinced someone else to harm her."

Witt cleared his throat. "Funny thing about people who remember her disappearance. At first they want to tell you how devastated the whole town is about her death. But dig a little deeper, and quite a few people characterized Lily as moody and temperamental. A Mr. Viafore said he often heard you two fighting. Others suggested you envied her."

"Tom Parker gave conflicting statements," Stillman said. "At first he said Lily got along with all of you. Later he said she fought with you and with his sister."

"Look," Gin said. "We were typical sisters. Just kids, in some ways. We fought over the usual things, but we were also really close. I was devastated when she disappeared. And again when I learned that her body had been found. I don't know what else to tell you about our relationship."

She paused, wondering if she was about to make a mistake. But holding back seemed like the greater risk. "I do, however, have something I would like to say about the cooler."

The detectives exchanged glances.

"I think it's possible that it was ours."

"Your family's?"

"No . . . the five of us kids. Me and Lily, the Parker twins, and Jake. Jake got it from a friend of his dad's, and we kept it hidden up by the creek that summer to keep our lunch in."

"Why would you want it?" Witt asked.

"It was free," Gin admitted. "Our parents didn't know everything we did up there, and they wouldn't have approved. We used to stop by the gas station and buy beer and sandwiches and sodas and ice. Sometimes we brought food from home. With the cooler, we could stay out there all day."

"You weren't worried someone would steal it?"

"Not really. It's huge, too big for one person to carry off without difficulty. Plus it was in pretty bad shape—you've seen it. Lawrence's friend was just going to take it to the dump if we hadn't taken it. If someone stole it, it wouldn't have been much of a loss."

"Why didn't you say anything about this sooner?"

"I don't really know. I guess I thought someone else already had. I just—I thought you should know before the test results come back. I'm sure all of our fingerprints are on there."

"Christ," Witt said, sighing. "That's just great."

"If we're done, I need to get going," Gin said. "I need to help make arrangements for Lawrence." She had meant it as a dig, a reminder that the man who'd died would be mourned. It was an impulse she'd seen many times from the other side of the desk: the family members she talked to wanting to explain all the ways their loved one would be missed.

"I suppose you'll be a big help to Jake," Stillman said, standing.

Gin didn't bother responding, aware she was being baited.

"You'll be in town for a while, right?" Witt said. "We'd like to be able to get ahold of you until we figure this all out."

"I'll be here."

21

Gin assumed that the Trumbull patrolman who'd responded had gone to notify Jake in person once the scene was secured and the county detectives arrived. She wondered if he'd found Jake on the job, if Jake had had to learn of his father's death in front of his crew at some half-finished construction site, or whether he'd had privacy to absorb the shock.

His house was on her way home . . . sort of. Well, not really; it was a detour of several miles, but checking on him would be the decent thing to do. She owed him that.

No matter how often she'd entertained doubts about Jake and Lily, or if he'd had anything to do with her death, no one would ever convince her that Jake could have harmed his own father. The two men had been exceptionally close; unlike other adolescents, Jake never railed against his father, never rebelled. And he'd given up his dreams of leaving Trumbull to work in a big city, just to be close to Lawrence after his heart attack.

Jake didn't kill his father.

Lawrence's death had to be connected in some way to the investigation into Lily's death. Gin knew this reasoning wasn't entirely solid, but she felt it in her blood.

If Lawrence's killer had wanted him dead because he was too close to the truth, and that person wasn't Jake . . . did that make Jake innocent?

It wasn't an argument that would stand up in court, but this had never been about a legal judgment, at least not to Gin.

It was too much to contemplate all at once. As Gin took the turn that led to Jake's, she tried to redirect her thoughts to practical issues, to finding some way to help. Jake had once had an aunt somewhere, Lawrence's sister. Gin wondered if she was still alive. There were relatives on his mother's side, but Jake had never known them. He might be completely alone now.

Pulling up in front of the house, Gin wondered if she was making a mistake. The elegant building looked leaden in the gloomy weather, the roof almost disappearing against the slate-gray sky, the flowerbeds flattened from the rains. The drapes were pulled shut, and the wind chimes hanging from the eave sounded a few doleful notes.

She knocked, suddenly anxious about what she would say.

Jake opened the door and regarded her stoically. He didn't look surprised to see her. "Come on in. I've been thinking of having a drink. You can be my excuse."

Nothing looked out of place in the spacious main room, but the mood had palpably changed. Even Jett barely lifted her soft muzzle from her paws, thumping the floor with her tail before sighing and resuming her nap.

Gin took a seat at the table where the food Jake had prepared had gone uneaten only the other night. He brought a crystal decanter half filled with amber liquid to the table, along with a couple of jelly glasses, and raised his eyebrow questioningly.

"Just a little," Gin said.

He obliged, handing her a glass containing a half inch of the stuff. She took a sip and nearly spit it out.

"Not everyone likes scotch," Jake observed mildly.

"I don't often drink it," Gin admitted. "In fact I think this is the first time I've tried it. Is this . . . typical?"

Jake gave her a faint grin. "If you're asking if I'm serving you the cheap stuff, don't worry. That bottle cost me almost a hundred bucks. I don't drink it often, so when I do, I make it count."

"I'd say you used to drink me under the table, except we never had a table," Gin said. The second sip wasn't quite as jarring.

"Yeah, I put away quite a few PBRs out of that cooler," Jake said.

"But now . . . ?"

"After Dad's heart attack, when he was convalescing, I let it get out of control for a while. Gave me the idea I might need to keep an eye on my habits." After a moment, he added, "Now that he's gone, I've been sitting here thinking about what else I can give up. Some sort of atonement, I guess."

"I'm so, so sorry," Gin said. "I don't even know what to say. Where to begin."

"He lived a good life," Jake said. "Not everyone gets to the age of sixty-eight while still getting in a round of golf or a trip to the lake every week. I mean, that's what I've been telling myself."

"Is there . . . anyone you should call? Other family?"

"Nope." Matter-of-factly. "Just me. And I suppose that's my fault—Dad probably wouldn't have minded if I'd given him a grandkid or two. Even a girlfriend who stuck around long enough to be introduced."

"Can I ask you a question?" Gin said uncertainly.

"Sure."

"When you told your dad you were giving up your scholarship, did he try to talk you out of it?"

"Nah. You know Dad—he always trusted me to make my own decisions. The only thing that bothered him . . ." His voice trailed off, and he stared out the window.

"What?"

"You, actually. I was so . . . angry with you, that you could ever believe I hurt Lily."

Gin winced. The words were nothing she hadn't suspected, but the pain they reflected was almost overwhelming.

"Dad kept trying to tell me you were coping any way you could. Looking back on it . . . but we were all new to it then. We didn't know how to behave, what was called for. Dad just told me that if I let you go without a fight, I'd regret it."

The unasked question—*Did you?*—hung between them. Gin inhaled the smoky, acrid scent of the scotch. Its beautiful shade reminded her of her mother's bottle of perfume, something Lily was always getting into trouble for using when they were little. Lily had loved to spritz it on her wrists and inhale deeply. "Everything should smell like this," she'd declared, when she was only eight or nine.

"Dad didn't kill himself," Jake said suddenly. "It's ridiculous. Anyone who knew him . . ."

"Jake, I think Witt and Stillman have something, more evidence. I don't know, they were leaning on me pretty hard. I feel like they were holding something back."

"But there's not a lot of incentive for them to shift over to investigating Dad's death," Jake fumed. "Especially if they've already concluded it's a suicide. The media's focused on Lily. The department's going to want to clear that as soon as they can."

"But what if it's connected? I mean, it has to be. Whoever killed Lily . . ."

Jake let his head fall into his hands. "I hate to say it, Gin, but I'm starting to think they may never find out who did it. It could have been someone just passing through town."

"The hitchhiker that witnesses saw."

"They never found the guy. I thought most people finally figured he didn't exist."

"Except he could have gone anywhere. Especially if he was guilty . . . or he could be dead himself now." Gin turned the possibility over in her head, tried to contemplate a life in which she never had an answer, never knew what had happened to her sister. It didn't feel real.

"And that's got me thinking we might never know what happened to Dad, either. Everything's . . . everything's so fucked up."

"But they're investigating. It's too early to give up," Gin protested.

"I wish I had your confidence in the county police, but I think they'll take the easy way out. With the evidence pointing to Dad taking his own life, why would they dig deeper?" He took a sip of his own glass of scotch. "I don't know how to make them see how crazy it is to think Dad would do something like that. I mean, even if he decided to kill himself, he never would have done it there, in his house. Or with a gun . . . I mean there's so much wrong with this picture, but it's nothing I can *prove*." Jake gave her fingers a squeeze and withdrew his hand. "That's why I want to ask you to find out what happened."

"Me?"

"Yeah. Look, I know it's a lot to ask, but I can't exactly do anything in this town without drawing attention to myself. Half the people around here think I'm a murderer. And you . . . well, I mean, no offense, but you've done a pretty good job of disappearing from everyone's radar."

"I—yes. That's fair." Gin took a breath and exhaled slowly, sensing that the tide between them had turned. The doubt she felt had vanished the moment she saw Lawrence lying on the floor. Now Jake was asking for her help, and it felt right to give it—if she could. "Jake, I'll do what I can, but you know I'm just an ME. Despite the way we're portrayed on TV, my job doesn't really involve much investigation beyond the actual body."

"They'll do an autopsy on Dad," Jake said. "There's got to be something there. Some sort of proof."

Gin was shaking her head ruefully. "Again, I'm afraid a lot of what's on TV doesn't really hold up in the lab. If there's something irregular with the wound, or residue on his fingers, something simple like that, they'll find it. And beyond that . . . well, there's a lot of room for interpretation."

"Look, you managed to attend Lily's autopsy. Isn't there any chance—"

"I'll see what I can do," she promised. "But Stephen Harper may not even have caught the case, and I don't think I can try to get any of the other staff to talk to me. It would just be too irregular."

"Just try, Gin. I know I have no right to ask . . ." Now, finally, his voice broke. He quickly mastered it, clearing his throat and looking away, but Gin couldn't help but break a little herself.

Jake had always been the strong one. That's how she'd consoled herself, all those late nights in college when missing him had become almost more than she could bear, made worse by the knowledge that she had been the one to push him away, had been the one who gave in to doubt.

At least he'd been strong enough to endure. Not just Lily's death, but Gin's betrayal.

Now, looking at the man he'd become, she had to face a truth she'd learned in the intervening years.

No one was that strong. Not even Jake.

* * *

Gin was almost back at her parents' house when her phone rang. She pulled over to check the caller ID, denying to herself that it was Jake's name she hoped to see.

It was an unfamiliar number with a Trumbull area code. Feeling the now-familiar pang of fear that more bad news was coming, she answered. "Hello?"

"Gin?"

"Christine?" It took only one syllable for Gin to be able to recognize the voice of the woman who had once been her best friend, after Lily.

"Oh, I'm glad I caught you. I heard about Lawrence. I can't even believe it. I know you were close to him . . . I'm sorry."

"Yes." Gin tried to swallow the lump that formed in her throat, hearing Christine speak of him in the past tense. "It's awful."

"I would totally understand if you didn't want to come to the party tonight, in light of the circumstances, but—well, I hope you will. Olive's mentioned you several times. I think she took a real shine to you."

"Of course," Gin said, grateful for the distraction, though given everything that had happened already today, the party had completely slipped her mind. "I wouldn't miss it."

"Oh, I'm glad. I've got my hands full with last-minute details—the bakery lost the cupcake order and my house-cleaner canceled on me this week, and I had a meeting come up at work that I can't get out of this afternoon. I'm going to have to dash back here to make it before people start to arrive."

Gin had a flash of inspiration. "Can I help? I could pick the kids up at school and bring them home so you can be here for your guests."

"Oh, I—that's—that's very generous," Christine said hesitantly. "But truly unnecessary."

"But it would be a perfect chance for me to get to know them better," Gin said, warming to the idea. "Plus I'd love to see the old school. It's been ages."

"Be prepared for some changes," Christine said. "The pool's gone, and they put up a performing-arts building. Look,

I hate to ask you to take time away from your folks. I know they need you right now."

"But my parents will both be at work. It's really no problem."

"Well . . . all right. I'll call the school and let them know you'll be coming. I'd ask Tom to do it, but he and Dad are down in DC at a conference through the weekend."

"Let me help at the party, too," Gin said impulsively. "I didn't realize you were doing everything yourself."

"The fate of the single mother," Christine said. "I invited Brandon, but naturally he already committed to doing something with Glenda the Good Witch."

"Glenda . . . ?"

"Sorry, I really shouldn't call her that—one of these days I'm going to slip and say it in front of the kids. She's just so very insincere, and she has all this long highlighted hair. As if having an affair with my husband wasn't enough—it's like she wants everyone to think she had no choice but to rescue him from my clutches. *Sorry.*"

"Christine, really, you don't have to apologize. I think you're allowed to hate your ex." Gin guiltily realized she'd never even met him; after missing their wedding, she'd felt too sheepish to call on her brief visits home.

"Listen, if you want, stay around after the party. I'll open a bottle of wine and we can catch up."

"I'd love to," Gin said.

As she hung up, the pleasure of talking to an old friend was tinged with guilt. Christine was just one more person Gin had abruptly cut from her life.

22

A little after three, Gin was in the carpool line at the school, a new innovation since she had attended Trumbull Elementary all those years ago. Back then, everyone walked to school except for a few kids who lived out in the country east of town and rode the bus. Now there was a line of minivans and SUVs stretching past the new building and around the corner.

Tucked into her purse, wrapped in pink tissue and tied with a silky bow, was a gift that Gin was worried Olive wouldn't like. Most thirteen-year-old girls would probably be thrilled with the birthstone necklace, but Olive appeared to be a tomboy; maybe she didn't even like jewelry.

As Gin worried about the gift, she spotted Olive's bright yellow ponytail, bobbing as she raced across the school's front lawn, chasing a boy who was holding something tucked against his chest. She tackled him just short of the sidewalk and they both tumbled onto the pavement, Olive landing on her knees holding her prize aloft: she had taken a book from the boy. Gin grinned, seeing so much of her sister in the exchange; if Olive was anything like Lily, she'd been the aggressor, but the boy would get the blame.

When Olive spotted Gin, she dropped the book on the ground and ran over, pulling Austen out of a group of his friends on the way. "Shotgun!" she yelled before yanking open the passenger door and plopping in the seat. Austen, relegated to the back, gave a brief howl of protest. "Hi, Miss Sullivan," he added.

"Call me Gin."

"Thanks for picking us up, Gin," Olive said. "Otherwise we would have had to *walk*."

"Your mom and I used to walk every day," Gin said, easing her car carefully past the kids and moms. "Believe it or not, we survived."

"Did your mother really take care of my mom and Uncle Tom? Mom says it was like you guys were all one family."

"When we were young, yes," Gin said. "I don't remember much, because we were so little. After my sister Lily was born, your grandpa hired someone to help when he could, but your mom and your uncle still came over quite a bit."

"It's like you were sisters," Olive marveled. "I wish I had a sister instead of Austen."

"Hey!" he protested from the backseat, over the beeping of whatever game he was playing on his phone.

Olive continued to chatter all the way home. Gin couldn't help her growing fondness for the girl, who was every bit as high-spirited as Lily had been. Times had changed; Olive seemed to have turned her personality to her advantage, unlike Lily, whose behavior provoked teachers and her friends' parents to implore her to settle down. To "act like a lady," in Madeleine's words. *Good for Christine*, Gin thought, *allowing her daughter to be herself without censure.*

Olive directed Gin to a neat ranch-style house on a manicured lot. They went in the side door, where the kids deposited their shoes and backpacks in cubbies designated for that purpose.

Christine was in the kitchen, arranging cupcakes on a tiered stand. Balloons and streamers were the only notes of color in an elegant beige and chrome kitchen. A buffet of sandwiches, chips, and fruit was laid out on the table.

"Have all the kids go to the backyard," Christine said. "Olive, answer the door when people come and please remember to thank them for coming to your party. Austen, do not touch anything until everyone is here, do you hear me?"

"But I'm starving!" Austen protested. Christine handed him a polished apple from a pottery bowl.

"Make do."

With the kids out of the kitchen, Christine took off her apron and hung it from a hook by the refrigerator. She was wearing tailored black pants and a silk blouse, looking polished and professional. Next to her, Gin felt underdressed in her shorts and tank top.

"I've got to go shopping," Gin said. "I'm completely out of clothes, but Mom'll kill me if I interrupt her laundry routine, and I can't bring myself to wash a load that isn't full."

"Does that mean you're staying longer?" Christine said. Gin couldn't tell if she was pleased at the prospect.

The doorbell rang before she could answer, and soon the house was filled with kids and their parents. Neighbors mostly, according to Christine, who greeted each warmly while directing the kids outside to where she'd set up games. Soon, the kids were playing Red Rover while the adults clustered near the refreshments.

Gin recognized only a couple of names, but all the guests knew her parents and expressed their condolences for Lily. She thanked them and stayed to the edges, helping with the food and an occasional child who needed a Band-Aid or a bathroom, which was how she overheard the discussion veering to Lawrence's death. She'd forgotten how quickly news moved through a small town.

"Well, I don't approve of suicide, but that man's been through hell." A woman's voice. Gin was around the corner, trying to find the napkins Christine had sent her to look for in the linen closet. She froze, riveted. "I mean, come on, with what his son put him through? What he did to that poor girl?"

"That's awful, Jean," another woman said.

"Maybe. But that doesn't make Jake innocent. I mean, there's something wrong with a guy who drives forty minutes to shop for groceries."

"So, just because he doesn't like to associate with you, that makes him guilty?" a man interjected. "Maybe he's just picky. Seems like there've been plenty of other women willing to overlook his shopping habits."

A crying child interrupted the talk, his mother taking him outside to settle an argument, and conversation moved on to other things. Gin continued to help, and answered the door to find her own parents holding a brightly wrapped gift. She covered her surprise; after all, she should have assumed that they had remained close to Christine.

Later, after the cupcakes and ice cream were served, the adults repaired to the living room, drinking wine while the children watched a movie upstairs.

Lawrence's name probably wouldn't have come up again, if it weren't for Richard. "Your mother tells me Jake's going to hold Lawrence's service as soon as they release the body," he said to Gin rather abruptly. She could smell the wine on his breath. The small circle fell silent; she could feel everyone's attention shift to her father.

"Richard," Madeleine muttered warningly.

Christine looked to Gin, her eyebrows raised. Gin had a bad feeling about where the conversation was headed. She didn't trust her father to stay silent about his dislike of Jake, even in the face of Lawrence's death.

"Dad, please," she said quietly.

"No, come on. All I said was that I hear the service is going to be soon."

"We can talk about that later," Madeleine said tightly. She was on her second glass of wine; Gin wondered if she should bundle both of her parents into her car and take them home, and come back for their car tomorrow.

"Lawrence's passing is such a loss to the town," one of the other guests said diplomatically, after an awkward beat had passed. "He was the heart and soul of the police department."

"I'll never forget the time he brought Anthony home at three in the morning after he got drunk after a football game," one of the mothers said. "I credit him for keeping our boys out of trouble."

Conversation turned to reminiscences about the many kind acts Lawrence had performed, on and off the job.

"I guess Lawrence was a regular hero," Richard mumbled, slopping more wine into his glass from the bottle on the table. "Although if he were all *that* good, he would have found my daughter's killer years ago."

"Richard, I'm leaving if you don't stop," Madeleine said. Then to the others, "I'm sorry. We're both a little tense right now."

The other guests were quick to reassure her, and Richard seemed mollified, apologizing for his remarks. *At least Lawrence was well regarded*, Gin thought. He'd be remembered fondly.

"I have to thank you all for your kindness," Madeleine said, dabbing at the corners of her eyes with a tissue. "I think we've been through every emotion there is at this point—from grief, of course, to . . . But no matter what we are dealing with as a family, I'm going to have to make a statement as deputy mayor. We can't have people going after each other's throats over something that happened so long ago. This town doesn't need that. I trust the police to do their job, and I'm going to hold a press conference Monday morning saying so."

There was a moment of shocked silence at Madeleine's announcement. Richard got angrily to his feet, knocking over a vase full of colorful carnations. Water pooled on the coffee table, and several guests scrambled to mop it up with paper napkins.

"Madeleine, this is hardly the place——"

"These are our *friends*, Richard," her mother said firmly, though a tremor at the corner of her mouth gave her away.

"Mom," Gin muttered, leaning close, "please, save this discussion for later."

"I don't want to discuss it. I've made up my mind."

"Without asking the rest of us? Me and Dad?" *And Jake*, she thought—Jake, whose father had been dead less than twenty-four hours. "Please reconsider."

Tears rimmed Madeleine's carefully made-up eyes, and the other guests appeared both embarrassed and riveted, busying themselves with cleaning up the mess. Richard seemed to be on the verge of leaving, until Christine came into the room carrying a tray of cupcakes.

"Okay, the kids have stuffed themselves and now—what happened?" she said, surveying the ruined flowers, Richard's stony expression. The guests looked at each other.

"I was just saying that I'm going to hold a press conference at city hall," Madeleine said, recovering her voice.

"Nothing's decided yet," Gin interjected. She had to find a way to stop her mother; she couldn't bear the thought of the latest developments becoming prime-time fodder, throwing more controversy into the investigation and possibly hampering its progress.

"Maybe it's a good idea," Christine said carefully, setting the platter down and sitting next to Madeleine on the couch. She took the older woman's hand. "I can't imagine how hard this must be, but keeping it out in front of the public eye—that's got to be a good thing. Keeping up the pressure on whoever killed Lily."

"It might even get national attention," one of the men said. "That'll force them to keep on it until they solve it."

"I've always said they stopped looking for the hitchhiker too soon," his wife agreed.

Gin stood and took her father's arm. "We should probably go, Dad," she said, trying to keep her fury in check. "You coming, Mom, or should I drive Dad home?"

"I don't need to be driven anywhere," Richard snapped. "I think I'll walk."

Madeleine rose with a sigh, but before she could detach herself from the group, Gin ushered both her parents out of earshot.

"Listen," she said in a low voice, "this is Olive's party. A thirteen-year-old girl is out there with her friends trying to celebrate her birthday. Do you really want to turn this into a circus?"

Madeleine's defiant gaze dropped a little; Richard wiped his hand over his face. Her parents were falling apart in front of her. Gin wasn't sure how much more either of them could take.

"You're right, sweetheart," Richard said in a heavy voice. "We should go."

"I didn't mean any harm," Madeleine said woodenly. "Everyone is going to hear what I have to say on Monday anyway."

Her parents huddled together while Gin made their excuses, thanking Christine and apologizing to the guests. Gin decided she would wait until another time to speak to Olive, rather than interrupting her among her friends.

Christine drew her into the kitchen. "I'm so sorry," she said. "Maybe I should have just canceled the party."

"No, no. Olive deserves to have things as normal as possible. None of this is the kids' fault."

"It's no one's fault, Gin," Christine said, folding her into a brisk hug. Gin could smell her hairspray, feel the crisp starch in her cotton shirt. "No one but whoever killed Lily."

"I'm beginning to wonder if it would have been better if she'd never been found," Gin confessed. She'd seen the stress an unsolved case could put on a family—both in her years at

Cook County and remembering back to the aftermath of Lily's disappearance. But knowing the truth about Lily had brought little peace so far. "I don't know if my parents can go through this again."

"Your mom is tough," Christine said, pulling away. "And your dad—he's just trying to help. Dealing with things in his own way. My dad's the same way, he has a hard time coping with his emotions, so they end up coming out at the worst possible time."

For a moment, both women were silent, Gin thinking about their fathers' friendship, a decades-old bond that had grown more tenuous over time, an echo of the distance that had asserted itself between Gin and the others. The loss of Lily had altered so many things about their lives. It made her profoundly sad.

"Please tell Olive I enjoyed myself," Gin said. "Maybe I could take the kids out for ice cream or something while I'm here."

"That would be great," Christine said. "And I'd love to get together, too. Just us."

As Gin herded her parents to the cars, she flashed back to other occasions in the distant past, the end of long evenings when the two families parted. Christine and Gin doing their best to exclude Lily, Tom tormenting all three girls. Spencer waving from the door, always seeming a little melancholy. Gin had never understood why he didn't remarry, didn't find a new mother for her friends. Only now did she see that relationships were far more complicated than she'd ever imagined then.

"See you back at the house, Virginia," her father said, as he got into the passenger seat of Madeleine's Lexus.

But when Gin turned the key in her own ignition, she let the SUV idle for a moment, thinking about the road to Jake's place, about the beautiful home and the broken man who lived there.

23

Gin and her parents spent Sunday together, by tacit agreement avoiding talking about anything significant. After church and brunch downtown, Richard left for his garden, and Madeleine and Gin played tennis at the club. Gin appreciated that her parents were making an effort to back away from the case, as she had requested, but by the time dinner was over, she was exhausted from the effort of staying politely detached.

When she was finally alone in her room, she checked her e-mail and discovered a message from Stephen Harper. "This won't be released until we've got a definitive COD, but I thought you'd want to see the preliminary findings. Call when you've read it."

He'd attached Lawrence's preliminary autopsy results. Gin scanned the report carefully. Then she read it again, focusing on the images of the entrance and exit wounds and the drawings and measurements made during the examination.

With a growing sense of unease, she dialed Harper's home number. He picked up almost immediately.

"Gin. Thanks for calling back."

"I suppose you've already noticed this, but the bullet trajectory doesn't support suicide," Gin said without preamble.

"Yes. I noticed that, too. I was thinking he could have managed it if he'd had something to support his arm, or if he'd raised his elbow as high as possible while standing, but I agree—it would have been awkward."

"Maybe," Gin said doubtfully, "but I think it's far more likely that someone else pulled the trigger. The entrance wound is clean and there is no residue on his fingers. And there's another thing . . . I saw you noted the peri- and myocarditis."

"Yeah, it was considerable for a man with no other signs of incipient heart failure—"

"But what if it was chemically caused? Say by a chemotherapeutic agent—they're known to cause cardiotoxicity. Couldn't he have been injected with something?"

"I don't know . . . I guess so. It seems like a reach, though. Cardiotoxicity usually builds over time at therapeutic doses . . ."

"But not always," Gin said excitedly. "And not if someone deliberately injected him. What are we looking at for a turnaround on the tox?"

"Probably over six weeks, at the moment—but I can give you some good news there, at least. Harvey was getting a lot of pressure from Captain Wheeler on this one, and somehow we came up with funds to send it out."

"Out—you mean, outside the county lab?"

"Yes, there's a private company we've used a few times. They bumped it to the top of the queue. We'll still be waiting at least a week for some of the tests, but the preliminary screen just came in. I've just started going through it, and I'll bring it up this afternoon at rounds, but I wonder if you'd mind looking it over to see what jumps out at you."

"I'd be more than happy to," Gin exclaimed. "Would you mind e-mailing it to me?"

"Already typing."

She squeezed her eyes shut for a moment. "Stephen," she said softly. "I don't really know how to thank you."

"How about I thank you? We're really short-staffed. People don't quit dying just because my colleagues go on summer vacation. And we're getting a lot of pressure on this one, as you might imagine."

After hanging up, Gin refreshed her e-mail over and over until the report arrived, then scanned it anxiously. A pattern of details began to emerge the second time through, and she checked it once more and dialed Stephen back.

"Suppression of protein synthesis," she said when he answered. "And elevated calcium homeostasis. There had to be an anthracycline present in the blood."

"That's the conclusion I reached, too," Harper said. "But other than the swelling, there was no evidence of long term cardiotoxicity—"

"Which we'd only expect to see if he was being treated for cancer," Gin said. "That wasn't the case here. And that suggests an extraordinary dose of an anthracycline must have been present."

"A potentially fatal dose in this case—"

"Though it wouldn't have mattered. As long as he was already unconscious, there is no way he could have shot himself."

Someone else had pulled the trigger. Someone else had wanted Lawrence dead.

"We'll know in a few days," Harper says. "I'm guessing Doxorubicin. Meanwhile, I'll call Stillman, but I can't give him anything official."

"I appreciate that."

"But listen, that isn't all. Harvey rushed the DNA, too. We had it tested against all the samples from the investigation, as well as CODIS."

"And?" Gin's heart thudded from the suspense.

"This won't be public yet, but there was no match. The father of the baby wasn't anyone that they took samples from. Of course, they'll be expanding the pool as the investigation continues."

Gin blinked, and let out the breath she had been holding. Seventeen years ago they hadn't taken any DNA samples, because the cops were convinced Lily had simply run away. But once Lily's body had been found, they'd taken samples from the entire family—and Jake, frontrunner among suspects.

Jake wasn't the father of the baby.

"I—I appreciate the call, and all the information," Gin said shakily.

"Of course. I'm sure we'll speak again soon—and I'll be in touch if I learn anything more that might be useful."

Gin managed a rote good-bye, even though her mind was now swirling with thoughts. Jake hadn't fathered Lily's child. Someone had killed Jake's father. Gin's remaining doubts about Jake disintegrated and vanished.

Stillman and Witt were bound to take DNA from Tom now, whether he liked it or not. Surely, that would at least clear up the identity of the baby's father. But what if it didn't? Who else could possibly have been such an intimate part of Lily's life, without Gin knowing? No match had been found in the database, but that only proved that the father hadn't been convicted before. That left countless possibilities.

But maybe they were getting closer to the truth.

* * *

In the morning, Gin took a long run, showered, and still managed to arrive at the press conference ten minutes before it was due to start. She'd dressed in a simple shift she'd borrowed from her mother's closet and twisted her hair into a knot at the nape of her neck. Her sunglasses completed what she hoped was an adequate disguise, but she took the precaution of tucking a book in her handbag to disappear behind and the gift which, in the confusion of the party's end, she'd forgotten to leave. If anyone stopped her to talk, she'd just explain that she had to leave to deliver the gift to Christine's house.

But she had another motive, and as she scanned the small crowd gathered to watch the media set up in front of the steps, Madeleine directing her staff from the podium she had moved to the base, she saw that she was in luck. Jake was leaning against a tree near the street, his arms crossed over his chest.

Despite his mirrored sunglasses, no one could miss Jake's familiar scowl and ramrod straight posture, and people were giving him a clear berth. He either didn't notice the many glances directed his way or genuinely didn't care. Half the crowd probably had already convicted him in their minds by now, Gin thought, and the rest might if Richard had a chance to speak.

She'd tried both her parents' phone numbers but neither picked up. Gin couldn't share the results of the toxicology report with them anyway; Harper had already committed a breach of protocol by speculating on the findings with her.

She didn't dare disrupt an investigation that might finally lead to her sister's killer, even for the sake of her parents. But there was one man who deserved to hear the news from her.

She edged over to where he was standing but was blocked by a group of office workers who'd taken a break to come see what the media attention was all about. Before Gin could make her way around them, her mother's voice rang out over the crowd.

"Welcome, everyone." Her mother was flanked on one side by the mayor, an elderly woman Gin barely recognized, and on the other by the city manager. Neither looked very comfortable, and Gin wondered how much political capital her mother was burning through to make this happen. But Madeleine had planned her remarks with care, and as she began by thanking the town for its unflagging support during all the years that Lily had been missing, her voice was clear and unwavering.

Gin took advantage of the crowd's focus on her mother to dodge behind the back of the group, slipping between parked cars until she got to Jake. He turned his head slightly to indicate he'd seen her, but said nothing.

"Listen," she said, leaning close and keeping her voice down, "I need to tell you something, but I can't give you any details now."

That got his attention. "Is everything all right?"

"Everything's fine. And I wouldn't come to you now, not with everything that's going on—but I thought you should know, unofficially. Please don't talk to anyone about this until they release the results, but—they were able to test the infant DNA. You've been cleared—there wasn't a match."

She couldn't see his eyes behind the mirrored lenses, but she caught the tightening of his jaw, the tiny tic at the corner of his mouth.

"Gin," he said heavily. "You're not telling me anything that I didn't already know. Or anything I haven't already said."

She bowed her head, aware that it wasn't enough. That she owed him an apology for not believing him. But there wasn't time for that now; maybe there never would be a way to cross the divide she'd created. "But now everyone will know."

"And can you guarantee that's going to change things?" he said, his voice low and angry. "At least your mother appears to have accepted me back into the fold. Guess I can go celebrate." Then he turned and stalked away from her, toward his old green truck that was parked down the street, before she could tell him the rest, including the contradictions in the tox report.

Gin couldn't chase after him without drawing attention to herself, so she turned her attention back to her mother in time to hear her say, "—the support of our friends and family as our community searches for answers. As many of you know, Richard and I have been friends with the Crosbys and Parkers since our children were barely toddlers. I believe I speak for all of us when I say that we join you in our belief in the law enforcement agencies of our county and town to bring justice not just to my daughter's killer, but to anyone who would presume to bring hatred and violence to Trumbull, Pennsylvania. This is our town, and we stand together to defend it against all evils."

At that point, she gave a slight nod to the front of the audience, and several figures broke from the crowd and ascended the steps to crowd in between Madeleine and the other council members. Gin was briefly surprised to see that the men her mother had asked to join her in front of the cameras were the detectives, Stillman and Witt. But it made sense; Madeleine was the master of the expedient gesture. Gin was sure she'd turned them into the allies that she needed now.

As Detective Stillman took the microphone and embarked on the careful description of the case using the evasive speech with which Gin was all too familiar from the many press conferences she had been a part of, she scanned the crowd again, and finally found Spencer standing with Christine near the front. He had his hand on Austen's shoulder, but Olive was nowhere to be seen.

She waited until Stillman finished his brief statement and handed the microphone back to her mother, who politely turned down the many shouted questions and ended the press conference. Then Gin made her way to Spencer.

"Oh Virginia, there you are," he said. He looked exhausted, the color in his tanned face faded, gray smudges under his eyes. "I was hoping I would see you here. I'm so sorry we had to be away for all of this. Christine tells me you were able to make it to Olive's party."

"She's an adorable girl," Gin said. "You must be so proud of her."

"Oh, I am. Listen, I'll talk to your father later, but I want you all to know that I want to help with the investigation in any way I can."

"Thank you," Gin said automatically. "I—I know my parents appreciate your support."

"I'd better get back," he said, squeezing her arm lightly. "Half the office is here; we've left the place pretty short-staffed."

"Of course," Gin said. "Christine, will you say hi to the kids for me?"

"Yes, I'd be happy to. Olive would be here, too, but she has a violin lesson. And . . . you know, I wasn't sure it was the best idea for her to be here. She has such a vivid imagination."

Gin almost asked where Tom was, but thought better of it. Maybe he'd stayed back because of what Spencer had already mentioned—too many of the staff were already here. Maybe it was too difficult for him to revisit the past. Maybe he was already starting his happy hour . . .

It dawned on Gin that, as the onlookers lingered while the media packed up their gear, it would be a perfect time to talk to him, if she could get to the surgery center while everyone else was away. She didn't want it to get back to the detectives that she was making inquiries.

She walked briskly, cutting through the park and taking a shortcut she remembered from her childhood, going through the lobby of an old bank that had been converted to offices to reach the surgery center from the back entrance. She found the directory near the elevators and located Tom's office number. When she got there, he was talking on the phone, turned away from her in his leather chair, gazing out his window overlooking the green valley and the smokestacks rising above it. She waited until he hung up to slip into the office, closing the door behind her.

Tom glanced up at her, and for a moment, a strange series of emotions flitted across his face. Had she been wrong about him? All those years when she'd thought Tom had grieved with the rest of them, when she thought his deterioration was because he missed not just Lily but—as she herself did, as she believed Christine did even if she never put it into words— missed the way their lives had been, before. The summer Lily disappeared had been when everything changed, when they were no longer children, any of them, and no longer family. Because that's what Gin had always believed them to be, the four of them, raised by her mother in shared naps and baths and hand-me-downs. Even the romance between Tom and Lily had seemed like a sweet drama, first love as extended child- hood, a way for them both to experiment much like Christine and Gin had once married off their Barbies to all the matching Kens. No one had ever taken it very seriously.

No one but her mother, Gin corrected herself. Madeleine had been firmly—almost forcibly—set against Lily and Tom's romance. At first she'd forbidden it outright, but after an unusually tense discussion with Richard, who'd pointed out that it would be next to impossible to enforce a ban on a boy whom she herself had helped raise, Madeleine had settled for strict limits on the time Lily was allowed to spend with Tom, as well as rigid supervision. Which, of course—Lily being Lily—she quickly found ways to circumvent.

"Hey, Gin," Tom said glumly. "Isn't your mom doing a press conference?"

"It's over. It made me think, though, that I ought to come and talk to you."

"Yeah, sorry about the other day. At the club. I, ah . . ." He gave an unconvincing little laugh. "Had a lot on my mind."

Gin looked at him more closely. His skin had an oily sheen over a gray pallor. He looked ill, his eyes glassy, his hair lank. His fingers twitched nervously at the pressed crease of his trousers.

"No, sure, of course. It's just . . . listen. I've been consulting with the ME's office."

"Christ." Tom picked up the Red Bull can in front of him and crumpled it in his fist. "You, too? I'm surprised that hasn't made it around town yet—everything else has. I mean, shit—a baby . . ."

"It—must be a lot to absorb," Gin said cautiously. Trying to read his emotional state was like trying to detect patterns in a thunderstorm, his body tense with the anxiety he was only partially successful in hiding.

"Yeah, and now those detectives want me to come in and give a DNA sample. And not just to prove paternity, either. They think they might be able to match it with some tissue they got from the cooler."

"Don't you think that's a good idea?" she said. "I was thinking that I should, too."

"But we all used that cooler. They could find anything."

"That's why I'm thinking we should do it. Then they can exclude any matches, and focus on anything else they find."

"What, like fingerprints from old Lloyd?"

"Him or—or whoever put her in there."

Tom was already shaking his head. "No thanks. Not until they come after me with a subpoena."

"But why? If you've got nothing to hide—"

"I *don't*," he said forcibly. "I'm so sick of people pretending I'm not really a suspect. Even Dad, he's offered his attorney to talk to me." He made air quotes with his fingers: "Just to 'get a feel for things.' Do you know how it feels to have your own father believe you're capable of killing someone, and he won't even say it to your face?"

"I'm sure that's not it," Gin said, though she wasn't, not at all. "Besides, it would take all of a few minutes to give a sample, and you'd never even have to discuss it with Spencer."

Tom laughed hollowly. "Seriously? Considering everything else that's been leaked already . . . you don't think he'd find out?"

Gin tried to get her bearings in the rapidly shifting landscape of Tom's possible culpability. His reluctance to be tested could be an indication that he had something to hide . . . or perhaps something much simpler.

"Tom . . ." she ventured. "It seems like things between you and Spencer are . . ."

"Shit. They've gone to shit." He spat the words, but the pain in his eyes was clear. "He's not even my boss—technically— but that hasn't stopped him from threatening to can me, just because I came in hungover a couple times. Or have me canned. Or whatever."

"But surely he would understand that what happened so long ago, when we were all just kids . . ." Gin struggled to find the words to reassure Tom that she was on his side—and to ignore the pangs of guilt from knowing that she was only being partially honest with him. "That just because you spent a lot of time with her doesn't mean . . ."

"That I'm a killer?" Tom laughed bitterly. "Doesn't matter. If Dad would stop and think for one minute, he'd *know* I would never have hurt her. I loved her. But that's not what he cares about. It's all about how it *reflects on the family.*"

These last words were spoken in a perfect imitation of Spencer's cultured baritone voice, so real that Gin had to stop herself for looking for him in the room. "But with the baby, I mean that complicates things—it seems to me that makes it all the more important that you cooperate."

"I've been thinking, though," Tom said, reaching for the minifridge under a corner of his desk and getting out another energy drink. Even leaning down to open the fridge seemed to be a huge effort, his face flushing and his hands trembling as he popped the top. "What if Lily didn't know it herself? That she was pregnant?"

"Tom. She was between fifteen and sixteen weeks along. She would have missed her period several times. There's no way she didn't know."

"But if, I don't know, she was in denial or something. Or not regular. I mean, you'd know that, wouldn't you? Being her sister?"

"We . . . weren't close that way," Gin said, hating to admit it. Other sisters talked about everything under the sun. Other sisters probably got their period together, borrowed tampons from each other, complained about cramps and bloating to each other.

But not Gin and Lily. They'd loved each other deeply— Gin had always loved her sister best among all her friends, had never questioned that their bond was the tightest—but there were things they simply never talked about.

"She told me." He blinked, looked away. Perspiration gathered along his brow and he jiggled his leg nervously. "Sometimes. If it was that time of the month."

Gin didn't want to think about those conversations any more than she wanted to think of Tom and Lily together, making love, or their young approximation of love.

"But you were . . . intimate. And you didn't use protection?" She phrased it as a question rather than a statement, though she was sure she already knew the answer. Lily would be the sort to believe that nothing bad could ever happen to her, and Tom would be careless, as he was in most things.

"What do you think?" Tom asked. Then his features compressed into a scowl and he added something unintelligible.

"I'm sorry, what did you say?"

His gaze arced past her and up to the ceiling and he pushed away from the desk. His hand flew up and then crashed down on the edge of the desk in front of him and he made a sound that, this time, was definitely not a word.

Gin's concern abruptly turned to horror when she realized she was witnessing the start of a grand mal seizure. Tom's limbs began to flail and he crashed to the floor as his muscles went through rhythmic contractions, and she quickly knelt down to clear the floor of anything that might injure him, moving the desk chair, waste basket, and a planter out of the way. She checked her watch to time the seizure, then rolled Tom gently to his side and grabbed a throw pillow from the couch opposite his desk and put it under his head. By the time she estimated that two minutes had elapsed, the jerking of his body was already starting to subside.

Gin waited until Tom seemed to be past the worst of it to yell out into the warren of offices, thinking it would be quicker than calling. "Tom Parker is having a seizure, can you please send a cart?"

A woman stuck her head in the door, took a look at Tom lying on the floor, and immediately disappeared.

"Tom," Gin said urgently, taking his hand. "Let me know if you can hear me. It's me, Virginia Sullivan, and we are in your office."

He rolled his head back and forth a couple of time, staring first at the ceiling and then at her, but he said nothing. His eyes fluttered half closed, and he made a gasping sound, foamy spittle bubbling at his mouth, but didn't seem to see her. She eased him back into a comfortable position on his side, and he didn't resist.

She continued to speak quietly to Tom, knowing he might not be able to hear her for several more minutes, until he regained full consciousness. She checked his pulse and breathing and wondered if she should make sure that help had been called, when a team appeared at the door with a cart.

"He suffered a seizure," she said, getting out of their way.

"Was this his first?"

"I don't know."

"What medications is he taking?"

"I don't know, I'm not—we're not—"

"He's Spencer Parker's son," one of the first EMTs said. "We should get him down here."

"I'll try to find him," Gin said, and she raced for the door, taking one last look over her shoulder. They were starting oxygen, fitting a mask in place. She knew there was little else to be done at this point, at least until they had more information about what had caused the seizure.

Tom had never suffered a seizure as a child, so that ruled out a number of possibilities. But Gin had a sinking feeling she knew what had been behind this one.

24

By the time Gin got back to Tom's office, unable to find Spencer, he had come around, and was seated in a wheelchair, about to be taken up to a room. "Please, don't tell Dad," he said. "Or Christine. I want to handle this myself."

"Can I . . . can we talk later?"

Tom shrugged, looking defeated. "Sure. They're taking me up to six. There's a waiting room there. I'm not sure how long I'll be, though."

Gin decided she'd wait for a while, since she didn't have anything else pressing to do. While she waited, she tried to reach Madeleine, but her phone went straight to voice mail, as it did while she was in meetings.

It was a good hour after Tom was taken upstairs before a nurse came into the waiting room and told Gin she could go in. Tom was sitting up in bed with an IV drip, looking pale and exhausted. There were purple circles under his eyes, and his skin sagged around his jaw, but he still managed to look almost boyish in the hospital gown, his hair askew.

"So I guess you probably figured out I've been having some trouble," Tom said awkwardly.

"You mean with substance abuse. That's what caused the seizure, wasn't it? An abrupt withdrawal?"

Tom raised his eyebrows, then winced, suggesting he was having a postseizure headache. "That's so not a sexy phrase. Abuse—I didn't abuse anything. I smoked it, snorted it, railed it . . ." This time his attempt at a laugh made little headway. "Then I discovered benzos. Nice and neat. Easy enough to get, too, if you know the right people at the dispensary."

Gin grimaced. She would have guessed benzodiazepine—known as "benzos"—or barbiturates, given Tom's probable access to prescription medications, though abruptly quitting other drugs could also cause seizures. "Have you been using for a long time?"

"Off and on. Funny thing is, I finally quit. After they found Lily. I just . . . I mean, I guess I'd always hoped she'd gone somewhere, pursued her dream, lived the life she used to talk about. I mean, I knew it was crazy . . . but she was *Lily*, you know? And then when I realized that she hadn't gone anywhere at all— that her life . . ." His voice thickened with tears, and he cleared his throat. "She would have hated what I, the way I've become. And I thought, I mean I know it kind of sounds stupid . . . but I thought maybe this was a sign I should step up and do the things I always told her I would. Shit. *Shit.*"

He grabbed a handful of tissues from the box beside the bed and ground them against his face.

"You went cold turkey?"

"Yeah, I haven't had anything stronger than a few drinks and a hell of a lot of caffeine since then. And believe it or not, I was going to try to quit drinking, too. I just didn't think I could do it all at once." He looked so contrite that Gin felt herself softening toward him, and had to force herself to hold onto her resolve.

"Have you had other seizures?"

"No. It was only after you started asking me all those questions, on top of those damn detectives practically coming out and saying they thought I did it. That I killed her." His gaze dropped to the sheet covering his body. "That I ever could have hurt her."

"Tom!" Christine burst through the door, Olive trailing in her wake, looking frightened. "Oh my God, what happened?"

Tom looked accusingly at Gin, not answering his sister. Gin shrugged: after failing to locate Spencer, she had done as Tom asked, and told no one that he had been admitted.

But everyone in the hospital knew Spencer Parker, who had served as its chief administrator for many years. Someone had made a courtesy call, whether to Christine or to Spencer, it didn't matter. Gin was surprised that Spencer hadn't already appeared, but maybe he was trying to respect his son's wishes, at least for now.

But for Christine, his twin, there were no such boundaries. Never had been.

"Want to tell her, Gin?" Tom said in an exaggerated attempt at cheer. "Or shall I? Me? Okay, well then, sister dear, I am very sorry to break it to you that your brother is a drug addict."

Christine gasped, her eyes going wide. She put her hand on Olive's shoulder and steered her out the door. "Go sit in the waiting room," she said in a no-nonsense voice, and the girl complied, looking frightened.

"He had a seizure," Gin said, as succinctly as she could, once Olive was out of earshot. "It was probably caused by abruptly withdrawing from regular benzodiazepine use. The days ahead are going to be rough ones, but the good news is that Tom should be able to make a complete recovery."

"Benzo . . . what?" Christine echoed, looking from one of them to the other. "Is that a prescription drug? Tom, please tell me this isn't true."

"It's true," he said, almost defiantly. "I'm a full-on addict. I finally found something I'm good at."

"The benzodiazepines are psychoactive drugs like Valium and Xanax," Gin explained.

"Oh, but that's just the tip of my little iceberg," Tom muttered. "I'm a full-service junkie."

Christine whirled on Gin. "What are you doing here anyway? This is a private—a family matter!"

"Aw, hell, Christine, Gin *is* family," Tom protested. "Look, don't take this out on her. I got here on my own steam. She tried to help me, sis. She was there when it happened."

At first shocked by Christine's anger, Gin quickly realized that Christine was mostly afraid, and was lashing out because she didn't know what else to do. Christine had always acted as her brother's front line, his protector.

"Christine, it's going to be all right," Gin said gently. "Tom has already made the most important step, which is to choose sobriety. There are very effective programs to help him and—"

"None of that is any of your business." Christine looked more furious than mollified. "And what were you doing coming here and talking to him anyway? Trying to make it look like he killed Lily?"

"*What*? No, I—" Gin broke off as Christine grabbed her arm and tried to pull her out of the room.

"What about you, Chris?" Tom said, recovering his strength a little. "You sure got here quick. Just in the area? Or are you over here with Olive again, pretending everything's fine?"

"Olive? Is something wrong with Olive?" Gin asked.

"No, no, she's fine, we just had a follow-up visit on a minor matter." Christine gathered herself, patting down her hair and taking a deep breath. "Look, Gin, I'm sorry if I overreacted, but you can't—I mean I know these are hard days, horrible, for you. For all of us. But people can't go around making accusations with nothing, with no reason." Her fury had morphed into something that looked a lot like panic. She was twisting her hands and shrinking into herself, and her appearance had lost some of its polish. A few errant strands of her pale blonde hair had escaped its precise style and hung over her eyes, and her blouse had come partially untucked from her pants.

"Christine, I promise you, I wasn't accusing anyone of anything," Gin said. But was that true? Was she all too anxious to pin the murder on someone—anyone—other than Jake? "I just thought I'd come and visit Tom here."

It was a lame excuse and it earned her a suspicious reception. "Well, if you don't mind, I'd like to speak to him for a moment in private," Christine said.

Gin excused herself and walked back down the hallway through the administrative wing. At the atrium where the surgery center connected with the rest of the hospital, skylights opened onto a fountain with comfortable seating and colorful art. Olive was sitting on one of the benches, writing in a notebook.

"Hi, Olive."

The girl looked up, breaking into a tentative smile when she saw her. "Gin! What are you doing here?"

"Just visiting with your uncle, as a matter of fact."

"Is he really a drug addict?"

Gin hesitated, trying to find the right words to soothe the girl while still observing her mother's request not to interfere.

"It appears that your uncle has been abusing prescription medications. The good news is that he is determined to get healthy, and I can promise you that if he enters into treatment, he will get better."

Olive was silent, biting her lip as she considered what Gin had said. Eventually she nodded.

"You and Uncle Tom used to be friends, right?"

"I think we're still friends," Gin said, hoping that was true. "Your mom and your uncle are . . . important to me."

"You want to sit with me? Mom said she'd only be a few minutes."

"Sure," Gin said, taking a seat next to the girl. "This is a good coincidence, actually. I forgot to give you your birthday gift the other day, and then I saw your mom and forgot again, and I've been carrying it around in my purse."

"You didn't have to get me anything!" Olive protested. But her face shone with delight as she accepted the package.

Gin noticed that the notebook Olive held in her lap held drawings, not words. The drawing the girl had been working on was a copy of the painting hanging on the wall; it featured a boat bobbing in a harbor.

"Wow, that's really good," she said. "I had no idea you were an artist."

"Oh, I'm not, really," Olive said, blushing and flipping the notebook closed. "It's just something I do for fun."

Gin sensed that pushing her further would only embarrass the girl, despite her obvious talent. She watched her tear the wrapping off the gift.

"It's beautiful!" Olive exclaimed, lifting the lid off the white box to reveal the necklace nestled inside.

"You and my sister have the same birthstone," Gin confided. "Alexandrite. I think it's so pretty because it seems to change color in the light. Would you like me to put it on you?"

"Oh yes, please." She leaned forward and Gin fastened the delicate chain around her neck. "I love it!" The girl threw her arms around Gin in an impulsive hug.

"You know, you remind me of Lily," Gin said, gathering the wrappings and ribbon to throw away.

"I've seen pictures. She was so pretty."

"So are you!"

"Ugh, God, no, I'm completely breaking out." Olive grimaced and pointed to a thin line of redness near her hairline. To Gin, it looked like standard adolescent skin issues, but she remembered how cataclysmic a breakout could seem at her age. "And it's on my legs, too. Mom's taking me to the dermatologist."

"Oh, is that why you're here today?"

"Well, actually it's because I've been having these stomach pains. Really bad, like I've had to come home from school a few times."

Christine came walking down the hall before Olive could elaborate. Stomach pains could be so many things—cramps, a change in diet, anxiety. How did mothers do it? Gin knew that she and Lily had given her mother plenty to worry about when they were teens.

"Mom, look what Gin gave me for my birthday!" Olive jumped up and held out the pendant, twisting it so that it flashed purple and teal in the light.

"It's lovely," Christine said. She caught Gin's gaze and held it for a moment, smiling uncertainly. "Gin, you've been so thoughtful, and I'm sorry for. . . . But Olive and I need to get going if we're going to make it to our appointment."

"We're seeing a specialist," Olive said. "He's like one of the best in the state for—"

"That's enough," Christine said firmly. "Let's let Gin get back to her day, shall we?"

"Has she been having the stomach pains for long?"

Christine's head snapped back up. "Pains?"

"I was telling her about how I had to stay out of school last week, Mom."

"Oh, you know kids," Christine said lightly. "If it's not one thing with them . . . Austen keeps falling off his skateboard and opening up the exact same cut on his knee. I don't think it's ever going to heal."

"Maybe they'll have to amputate," Olive giggled.

The pair walked down the hall, arm in arm, and Gin walked slowly toward the exit to the parking lot.

She had the distinct impression that Christine had been trying to change the subject.

25

G in was getting into her car when someone called her name. She looked up to see Christine running toward her. She was alone.

"I'm glad I caught you," she said. "I just dropped Olive off at the waiting room."

"I'm sorry she's not feeling well," Gin said carefully.

"She's fine. Look, I want to talk to you about Tom, though. I'm sorry for the way I came at you in there, but, well, I'd like to ask you not to talk to him anymore."

"Not *talk* to him?" Gin frowned. "Listen, Christine, if you have any doubts about his addiction—"

"I know he drinks." Christine clutched the strap of her purse so hard her knuckles went white. "And I know he's had a problem with drugs. But he's working on that. He's going to go to meetings."

"That's . . . a great start," Gin said. She'd been around the families of overdose victims enough to know that denial could run very deep in loved ones. "But he's going to need a lot of support and compassion while he's recovering—benzodiazepine withdrawal has to be managed with care, because it has some dangerous side effects and it can last a long time."

"I appreciate that, but it really is something we'd like to keep in the family."

"You know . . ." Gin said carefully, aware that she might well be pushing Christine further away. "Addiction is a disease that affects the entire family. You might want to explore treatment for yourself too, especially if you'll be seeing a lot of Tom in recovery."

"I don't need a lecture." Gin was dismayed by the abrupt change in Christine's mood, the hostility in her voice. "What I need is for you to stay away from my family."

"I—I don't understand."

"I've seen what you're doing," Christine said. "You show up here and start accusing people. I mean, I'm just devastated about Lily. We all are. But you won't convince people my brother killed her—at least, not if I can help it."

"I'm not trying to convince anyone of anything," Gin protested. "I just want to know what happened to her. I happen to have some specialized skills that could be useful to the investigation, and they've invited me to participate."

"As a *doctor*," Christine retorted. "Not a detective."

"Sometimes the lines blur," Gin said, bewildered by her friend's defensiveness. "For instance, my medical training helped me to deduce that Lawrence actually died of heart failure, not a gunshot wound."

Christine looked at her blankly. "I don't understand. He was shot in the head. That had to be fatal."

"It would have been, if he was still alive. But at autopsy, the medical examiner found evidence of a fresh thrombus and plaque rupture in the coronary arteries. In laymen's terms, that means that the artery was blocked, and the heart wasn't receiving oxygenated blood," Gin explained. "Lawrence was likely in a coma when he was shot, but in any event, he couldn't have pulled that trigger himself. He was *murdered*, Christine. It wasn't a suicide."

If she'd hoped to shock Christine into confiding something, it seemed to have the opposite effect. Christine merely shrugged. "Maybe he had a heart attack just as he was pulling the trigger."

"Unlikely, but I suppose possible. It is much more likely that its failure was caused by a drug overdose, and if that's the case, it'll show up in the tox screen."

"I can't imagine why anyone would want to hurt Lawrence," Christine said tightly. "But it doesn't make any sense to connect his death to Lily's. The county officers had already taken over the case. Lawrence was being kept in the loop just to be polite, from what I hear."

"That doesn't mean he didn't know things," Gin insisted. "Things someone wanted kept secret."

"Like who, Jake?" Christine shook her head sympathetically. "It must be hard to come back here and see him doing so well for himself. Especially given the way things ended between you two. Knowing you might have stayed together, if only . . . things had been different."

"That's not—"

"Look, Gin, I've been divorced almost two years now. I know it's no picnic being single at our age. At least I've got my kids. I can only imagine that you're painfully aware of your biological clock. And seeing Jake . . . well, it must bring up all kind of complicated feelings. But that doesn't mean you should put emotion before reason."

Gin had never seen Christine like this, so deliberately cruel. It was true that they hadn't been typical best friends—there had always been some distance between them—but Gin had always assumed that was because the sisters' bond was so tight, there wasn't much room left over for another girl. And Christine had Tom, her own best friend in addition to being her twin.

"You don't have to believe me," Gin said, the tremor in her voice betraying the hurt she felt. "But I am truly only trying to find out who killed Lily. Jake told the police where he was and what he was doing that day. So did I. And my parents, and Tom. But what about you? Can you even remember what you were doing that afternoon?"

"Of course." Christine glared. "It's not like you were the only one affected by her death. I remember everything about that time. I've asked myself a million times why I didn't come by that day to see if Lily wanted to go to Rengel's, especially since you were away at orientation."

Rengel's was a corner drug store that sold candy and sodas. Gin had driven by it the other day and been saddened to see it shuttered. Back then, they'd often gone to buy licorice vines and Fanta and sit in the park next door, talking.

"What did you do instead?"

"Worked on my scrapbook," Christine said. "I was adding all the photos from senior year and graduation. My dad told Lawrence all this back then. He came home early that day because he'd had a dentist appointment, and we were in the house together from four o'clock on, until he and Jake went out to practice driving the stick shift that night. It's all in the notes."

Gin vaguely remembered those details from the investigation so long ago. Lawrence had asked the question from every direction: what had the girls been up to in the days leading up to her disappearance? Was she sure they hadn't talked on the phone that night? Now she understood that he was trying to find evidence that Lily had been planning to run away.

"Listen," Christine said. "If what you're saying is true, and someone gave Lawrence a drug to induce a heart attack, I assume it was some sort of controlled substance, right? Something you couldn't get unless you were a doctor?"

"Or someone with a lot of authority in the hospital," Gin shot back. "Like Tom. Or your dad, for that matter."

Christine laughed. "Oh, that's rich. It's not enough to accuse my brother, you have to go after Dad, too?"

"I'm not accusing anyone of—"

"When the only physician in our families is actually *your* dad." She smirked. "How easy would it have been for him to get his hands on that drug? And then go see his old friend Lawrence, the one who bungled the search for his daughter all those years ago? I mean, *I* certainly wouldn't believe your dad could be capable of anything like that, but you have to see it from a cop's perspective. Means and motive, isn't that what they say?"

"That's ridiculous."

"Maybe." Christine hitched up her bag on her shoulder and turned to go. "It's what happens, though, when people go around accusing others without evidence. The whole thing turns into a giant mess. People get hurt."

Gin watched her walk back toward the hospital, wondering how things had gone so terribly wrong.

26

That night, Gin waited until the dishes were done and her mother had gone up to her room, and then knocked on the door of her father's study.

He seemed surprised, but invited her in. Gin couldn't remember a time either she or her mother had ever dared to interrupt him when he was working. It wasn't that she was afraid of angering him, exactly, though he'd made clear his preference not to be disturbed; it was that Richard Sullivan at work was wholly absorbed, his entire focus on what was in front of him, and Gin instinctively knew it would take considerable effort to find that focus again if interrupted.

Lily, of course, had barged in whenever she felt like it. Lily could never remember rules like that; she was a creature of her impulses, and hence people tended to forgive her.

"Dad." Gin took in the neat desk, the lowered blinds, the pipe resting in its onyx stand, a thin curl of fragrant smoke wafting toward the ceiling. Richard had given up actually smoking the thing long ago, but he liked to light it now and then and contented himself with the secondhand smoke, a pleasure even as a pale shadow of itself.

"Hi, honey. How was your day?" he asked, as though she was back in high school again, as though he were waiting to find out how she did on her English paper or that they'd got new music in Concert Band.

"I'm okay, I guess. I saw Mom's press conference today. I thought she did well."

"Oh, yes." Richard removed his glasses and polished them on his shirt, frowning. "But I didn't see you there. Did you come by yourself?"

"Yes, I stood near the back . . . Dad, listen, something's bothering me."

He looked instantly wary. "Yes?"

She prepared to tell him what she'd learned from Stephen Harper, chagrined that she'd now shared confidential information with several people. A measure of how much she was willing to sacrifice for the sake of the truth, perhaps. But also, she didn't believe any of those people would talk. Tom, Jake, Christine, now her dad—each of them had their own complex web of connection to the case.

Connection . . . or culpability?

She took a deep breath. "At Lawrence's autopsy, the pathologist found evidence of heart failure. Thrombosis caused by recent plaque rupture in otherwise healthy arteries. If that's true, you know that there was no way he shot himself—he would never have been able to pull the trigger."

She watched her father carefully, but his only reaction was a slight frown and a shake of his head. "God help him."

"Dad—I have to ask you. Please. I know how you feel about Jake. I know how badly you need to feel like Lily's killer has paid."

"So you want to know if I killed Lawrence?" He shook his head, the lines on his brow deepening. "Absolutely not. Virginia, I haven't hurt anyone, sought revenge, or interfered with the case. I give you my solemn vow."

That was it, then, wasn't it? As far as Gin knew, her father had never lied to her. His inflexible ethics were a matter of occasional teasing in the family; Madeleine sometimes became frustrated at what she termed his "rigidity."

And yet, something continued to bother Gin, on a level too deep for her to put her finger on. Things between her parents had been strained, and Gin thought it was more than the terrible revelation about Lily.

"You were his physician," she pressed. "You know they're going to want to talk to you."

"I'll talk to them," Richard said curtly. "They won't see my records, however. Patient confidentiality is a serious matter."

"They can subpoena you, Dad."

"Let them." Richard leaned back in his chair and crossed his arms. "Until then, I know my rights very well."

"Would you let me look at them, at least?" Gin tried. "If there's something there that would raise an eyebrow, it would be better for us to be prepared."

He was already shaking his head. "Virginia, I am very well aware that you are among the best in your field. Your mother and I couldn't be any prouder of your accomplishments. But the fact remains that your patients, for lack of a better word, are dead. When it comes to interpreting the information in my patients' records, I must insist that I am the best authority."

He wasn't going to let her see anything. Gin wasn't surprised, but she wished her father would change his mind. Doing so would allow her to clear at least one of the layers of doubt that seemed to be enshrouding everyone she had ever cared about.

As she gently closed the door to her father's office, he was already bending over his blotter again, the pool of golden light cast by his desk lamp accentuating his wrinkles and making him look older than his years.

Another dead end, at least for now. Gin stood motionless in the hallway, listening to the faint creaking of the old house's foundation, wondering where to turn next.

And realizing there was only one person she wanted to talk to as the threads of the investigation knotted ever more tightly.

* * *

Shortly after midnight, Gin was standing at the end of her parents' driveway, a breeze off the river lifting the ends of her hair from her shoulders. For the umpteenth time since calling Jake earlier in the evening, Gin wondered if she was making a mistake. She'd made the call with no agenda other than to talk through the latest development—but Jake had other ideas. The way he had outlined his plan, there was no risk to either of them, no risk of getting caught. But even if that was true, she was still betraying her father's trust.

She'd dressed in a sundress she'd found in her closet. It was at least a decade old, a spaghetti-strapped cotton shift in shades of emerald green and turquoise, and it was perfect for the humid, warm night.

Headlights bounced toward her on the uneven pavement. Gin hopped in the passenger seat of Jake's truck, and he made a wide U-turn at the end of the street.

"Thanks for picking me up," she said.

"Well, the way I see it, I owe you." He sounded only slightly less irritated than he had when she called him after talking to her father. "You didn't have to share with me what you learned about Dad's autopsy. And you definitely didn't have to agree to help me break into your father's office."

It was only her certainty of her father's innocence that led her to agree. But what if that trust was misplaced? It was almost too wrenching to consider.

They rode in silence out past the town limits, up onto a sloping, wooded stretch of land where only a few cabins lined the fire road. Jake drove carefully on the switchbacks until they were nearly at the top, then parked next to a simple wood-sided cabin. A light glowed golden through the windows.

A man came out onto the porch, holding a mug in his hands. Jake let the engine idle, and Gin rolled down her window and called to the elderly retired policeman. "Lloyd?"

"None other. That you, princess?"

She moved over on the bench seat, her hip touching Jake's, making room. Lloyd set his coffee mug on the porch railing, picked up a small gym bag, and clambered in next to her. "You sure are a pretty sight."

"Careful, Lloyd, I think she's covered by worksite harassment rules now," Jake said.

Lloyd just laughed. "Good thing I'm retired, then. How long's it been, sweetheart?"

Gin squeezed his hand and smiled. "Too long, and I'm to blame. I'm sorry I've been out of touch."

"Ah, well, I've been busy, too. There's only so many hours in the day to throw money into the lake."

"That piece of junk still afloat?" Jake inquired drily.

"Hey, buddy boy, I'll race my boat against this tin-can truck any day."

The two men bantered most of the way to the hospital, and Gin was grateful for the levity. She knew that Lloyd, who had been Lawrence's partner for many years before Lawrence was promoted to chief, would do anything to help solve his friend's murder.

She, however, was about to betray her father's trust in the most serious way imaginable. If he ever found out she'd broken into his office, she would fear his anger more than any legal consequences.

"Pull around back there, son," Lloyd said, directing them on a fire road that led behind the hospital to where the dumpsters were located. "Now remember, I don't want to know exactly what you're looking for. All I'm going to do is get you in without showing up on the security feed. After that it's up to you."

Jake looked at Gin significantly. "What did you tell him?"

Gin had given Lloyd few details, mindful that she'd already told too many people about the evidence of damage to Lawrence's heart. "Only that the records may contain information that will clear Dad from suspicion in Lawrence's death," she said, which was more or less true. If Lawrence had already been diagnosed with recent heart damage, it would weaken her theory. "He won't release them because of patient confidentiality rules, but I feel like his future is more important than any rule right now."

"Or, your father's records might implicate him. One way or the other, we're going to find out." Jake got out of the truck, slamming the door.

Lloyd whistled softly. "Never seen that boy so worked up. Not for years, anyway. Gin, I can't believe your father did anything like this."

"Me either. Lloyd, I really appreciate your help. I just can't afford to come under scrutiny, and Dad absolutely cannot know I was here."

They got out of the truck and followed Jake to a cluster of willow trees on a landscaped berm. At the bottom of the slope was a small, plain metal door on the south wall of the hospital. Above were windows to patient rooms, but nearly all of them had the drapes closed.

Lloyd explained, "Reason I picked this door is, it's only got one camera on it. I'm betting that door's only there for legal egress. You can see there hasn't been much foot traffic." He shone a small flashlight down on the concrete pad outside the door. It was covered in leaves. "This won't take but a minute, but don't follow until I signal, hear?"

He pulled the hood of his sweatshirt up over his head, covering his face, suddenly transforming himself from an old man to a figure who could be anyone, and handed Jake his keys.

"That there's a laser," he said, pointing to the key chain. "Cost me twenty bucks. Now you can buy 'em for half that. Anyway, you need to keep it focused on that camera lens. See, bolted over the door?"

"Yes, I see. That'll disable it?"

"Well, enough so nobody's watching me, anyway." He picked up his gym bag and started down the hill. Jake pointed the beam at the lens, and Lloyd gave him a thumbs up. He took something out of his bag and knelt in front of the door.

"What's he doing?"

"Well, whatever that thing is, it looks an awful lot like a cordless drill."

They watched in silence for several moments. Lloyd returned the object to his bag and got to his feet slowly, massaging his joints, and came back up the hill.

"I'll take over," he said, taking the laser from Jake. "Once you get in, I'll shut it off until you get back. With any luck, no one's noticed yet. This might not even be on the main feed."

"What did you do?"

Lloyd shrugged. "Just drilled it out, is all. It was a simple deadbolt. One thing I learned from being a cop—you don't really have to be all that smart to commit ninety percent of the crimes I investigated. It's just lucky that most crooks are stupid."

"Wish us luck," Gin said.

"Aw, hell, you kids won't need it."

Jake followed Gin down the slope. She could smell the burnt oil scent of the drilled metal, and when she tried the knob, the door swung open effortlessly. Inside, she switched on the flashlight Lloyd had given her. They were in some sort of basement utility room. At the far end, she could see light seeping under the door.

She held her breath as she tried the knob. Another deadbolt, which she easily turned—and then they were standing in a windowless hall.

She chose a direction at random and walked quickly, Jake following silently. They arrived at a set of stairs and took it up to the main floor. No one saw them as they entered the hall and studied a sign showing directions to various departments.

"This way," Gin said, quickly calculating the fastest route to the physician's offices.

There was always the chance they would run into another physician, but she was counting on the late hour to keep the wing empty, and as they reached the first of the offices, she was gratified to see that they were all darkened. It didn't take long to reach her father's office.

"Well, here goes," she said, taking her father's keys from her pocket and stifling a stab of guilt over having lifted them from the hook once she was sure he had gone to bed.

Inside, the office looked the same as it always had. Walnut desk and expensive ergonomic chair. Beige sofa and small conference table. Computer, shut down for the night. Filing cabinet, bland mass-produced art, single houseplant nurtured by the office manager. Photos of her and her mother arranged on the credenza.

Gin had seen her father write prescriptions at home many times. An eye infection, a bout of strep, her mother's occasional UTIs—like many physicians, he wrote the occasional scrip for family and friends. Unlike others, however, he kept scrupulous records. She'd seen him save the duplicate sheet from the prescription pad, and once, in his office, he showed her where he kept them. At the end of the year, he stored them with his other important documents.

Digital prescribing was beginning to catch on elsewhere in the world, but in the United States it was still rare, and Gin breathed a sigh of relief as she got the black cardboard file box from the shelf behind her father's desk and lifted the lid. The square of paper on top was dated just today.

She paged through the sheets, squinting at her father's near-illegible handwriting. A dozen pages in, she found what she was looking for.

For a moment she just stared at the prescription, her heart thudding, heat blooming behind her eyes. *It couldn't be . . .* She just couldn't believe it.

On June 2nd, Dr. Richard Sullivan had prescribed 400 mg of Doxorubicin. The name of the patient was illegible. But a pharmacist wouldn't be blamed for overlooking that, as Doxorubicin, a medication used in cancer treatment, wasn't commonly abused and wouldn't raise red flags.

It *was* regulated, however, to make sure that a patient didn't exceed cumulative thresholds, because of the likelihood of heart damage—specifically, the buildup of dangerous plaque in the arteries.

If Gin remembered correctly, 400 mg was almost the lifetime limit. And taken all at once, the results could be disastrous: heart failure immediately, or in the hours or days following, even if the patient had no other history of heart problems.

She read the damning words three times, then finally looked up. Jake already knew; she could see it in his eyes.

"That's what killed Dad, isn't it."

"This doesn't necessarily mean—"

"Gin. When you got to town, you basically accused me of killing your sister. So don't act like I don't have the right to draw my own conclusions," he said angrily. "Look. Your father has blamed me ever since Lily disappeared. I've never understood why until just now. It's because he was the one who killed her."

"What?"

"I'm such an idiot." He looked like he wanted to smash something, fists clenched at his sides.

"Even if this was what killed Lawrence—even if, for some unfathomable reason, my father wanted your dad dead—how can you say that means he killed his own *daughter*? That's insane."

"You don't understand. She came to me that week. She wanted to talk."

"Your famous 'brotherly' conversations," Gin snapped, immediately regretting her sarcasm. "The ones you conveniently forgot to tell anyone about until there was proof you were with her that night."

Jake went still. "I thought we were past that," he muttered. "If you still think—if you have even the least suspicion that I killed her, then I'm walking away right now."

She could hear his breathing, harsh and ragged in the dim, silent building. Shame mixed with anger and other emotions she couldn't untangle. "No," she finally said tightly. "I don't . . . think that."

"Then listen to me. Call those talks whatever you want, but Lily had something she wanted to get off her mind. Only she never quite got around to telling me what it was."

"Convenient—"

"Damn it, Gin, listen to me. She said that she'd started to question the meaning of family. Frankly I had no idea what she was talking about. Hell, I was eighteen, I probably wasn't a very good listener. I think I told her to just have faith that it would all work out." He shook his head in disgust. "I may have been the reason she never came out with it. But don't you get it—whatever she was going to reveal caused her a lot of agony, or she wouldn't have taken so long to work up to it."

"You're accusing my father of—of—" Gin couldn't bring herself to say it. The unspeakable thing that Jake was saying her father had done to Lily.

"I'm not saying he necessarily molested her," he said. "But whatever it was, he obviously wanted it covered up, and the shame was overwhelming her. I'm sorry, Gin, but look—I mean, it makes sense, doesn't it? She'd finally gotten the nerve up to tell—maybe threatened him that she would tell—and if she'd had a little more time, maybe she would have. But he stopped her. Silenced her for good. And then what better way to protect himself than to accuse someone else—someone who already had a strike against him. He knew that people would jump to conclusions if they knew Lily was spending time with a guy who wasn't her boyfriend. He *used* me. And when my dad figured it out, Richard had to make sure he didn't tell, either."

The bitterness in Jake's voice chilled Gin almost as much as his accusation. "My father has never—*never*—done anything like what you're suggesting," she protested hoarsely.

Jake raised an eyebrow. "How do you know? People misjudge each other all the time. I thought I knew Lily, but she never could bring herself to trust me enough to tell me. I thought I knew you, but you—"

He didn't finish the thought. Didn't have to.

"My father submitted his DNA, along with everyone else. He gave his statement; he had an alibi." She replaced the lid to the box and put it back on the shelf and headed for the door, not bothering to make sure Jake was following.

They returned the way they'd come. Gin had left the door to the utility room slightly ajar, and she breathed a sigh of relief to find it still open. They were out in the warm night air in moments.

"Everything go okay?" Lloyd asked, snapping off the laser and pocketing his keys.

"We got what we needed," Jake said in a clipped voice.

Lloyd didn't ask questions on the way back. He undoubtedly sensed the tension between the two of them and chose not to intervene. Or, maybe he didn't want to get involved, didn't want to risk being called out of retirement for more than a single night's cloak-and-dagger adventure. Breaking into the hospital had been an adrenaline rush for the old guy. It had been exciting for Gin, too—right up until the moment they unearthed the damning evidence.

"Keep me posted," was all Lloyd said when they reached his cabin, and he got out of the truck and hobbled slowly up to his front door. Jake waited until the elderly man was inside before putting his truck in reverse.

The drive home was silent. When they reached her house, Gin couldn't stand it anymore. "Look. I'll agree not to rush to judgment—on anything. I just ask that you do the same."

"You've got to be kidding. This might lead to confirming who killed your sister. Everything we're doing, in the end it's for Lily—we owe it to her. We need to tell the detectives what we found."

"No. Please. For one thing, we could both go to jail for what we just did."

"I doubt that. You can just tell them what you suspect, without saying how you know, and they'll subpoena your dad's records."

"It doesn't work quite like that," Gin objected; the ME's office had been turned down many times when asking for the freedom to search people's property for clues to their death. "There's no guarantee they'll find sufficient cause. Look. Let me talk to my dad, let me give him a chance to explain why he prescribed the Doxorubicin. I'm sure there's an innocent explanation."

"Yeah, I'm sure there's a lot of call for chemotherapy drugs during joint replacements."

"Jake. I promise. If I'm not satisfied with the answers Dad gives me, I'll share the information with the investigation."

"And give him time to destroy his records? No way."

"I'll—I'll deny being here with you tonight."

"That's fine. I'll just leave an anonymous tip."

"Jake." Gin could feel tears threatening—but whether they were over Jake's refusal to cooperate, or his terrible accusation, she wasn't sure. "Please. Just give me one day."

"It's late, Gin," he said wearily. "You'd better get some sleep."

She hesitated, remembering dozens of times that he had dropped her off in this very spot, in this truck, so long ago.

At last she opened the door and got out. The winds had turned; the humidity had lifted from the air. The breeze coming off the water now was cool and carried with it the ripe scent of decay.

She opened her mouth to say something, one last plea for Jake to reconsider, but he reached across the bench seat and shut the door. He didn't look at her as he drove away.

*　*　*

Gin slept poorly, tossing and turning until the sky was beginning to lighten. Eventually, she drifted into a heavy, dreamless stupor. When she woke, she was shocked to see that it was almost noon.

She pulled on her running gear and took a route through the streets rising up into the hills above town. Many years ago, when the steel industry was in its infancy, men came to towns like Trumbull from all over the country, seeking their fortunes. The steel companies erected housing, churches, stores, taverns. Now all that was left was their skeletons, their overgrown, burnt down, boarded-up shells, populated with the unfortunate and desperate.

Eventually Gin reached the newer neighborhoods above town, tidy ranch houses with wind chimes and vegetable patches, and ran along the ridge, watching smoke rising from a cola-processing plant twenty miles away. Her lungs burned and her muscles ached, and she realized how much she'd missed her regular runs. She emptied her mind of everything but her senses, and focused on the smell of fresh-cut grass, the sound of birds calling to each other, the river lazily looping through the valley far below.

When her phone rang, she almost ignored it; this was the first time she'd felt like herself since returning to Trumbull. But then she remembered that it could be Jake—coming to his senses and agreeing to give her the time she needed, or else letting her know he'd decided to contact the detectives despite her pleas.

But the call wasn't from Jake. It was from her mother.

"Hello?" she said, out of breath.

"Please come home, Gin," Madeleine gasped, her voice thick with emotion. "They've arrested your father."

27

Gin ran hard all the way home, taking the most direct route through town. She tried not to get ahead of herself, tried to remember that there could be a dozen good reasons why her father had ordered the drug, and now he would be forced to reveal them. Even now, he was probably explaining it to the officers; he might even be on his way home.

There was no way her quiet, gentle father had murdered anyone. Gin would stake her life on it.

When she finally got to her street, she could see two cars parked in front of her parents' house: behind a sober, dark sedan, she recognized Christine's red minivan. And there, standing on the porch, in a filmy skirt that grazed her knees, was Christine, flanked by her kids.

What was she doing here? And why on earth would she bring Olive and Austen with her? Gin sprinted the rest of the way, but she still reached the house after all three had gone inside. She had to pause on the porch for several moments to catch her breath, doubled over with her hands on her knees. When she finally straightened, her tank top was matted to her skin with sweat, and her hair had escaped its elastic.

There was nothing she could do about her appearance now; she pushed open the door and went inside.

Christine was standing at the counter, stirring the contents of a mug so vigorously that liquid slopped onto the tile. Austen drew on a piece of paper, chattering about some game involving a sorcerer. And Spencer stood in the middle of the room, his phone pressed to his ear.

Spencer saw her first. He gave her a flash of a smile so brief it was more like an involuntary grimace, held up a "just a moment" finger, and walked into the hall, no doubt so he could hear his conversation better.

"Hey, everyone," Gin said.

Christine turned at the sound of her voice, a worried expression on her face. "Gin. God. I'm—when I heard the cops had come by . . ."

Gin knew that Christine was trying to apologize. It had never been her strong suit; her pride had kept her on the offensive since they were kids. Her clumsy attempt didn't diminish the knot of resentment inside Gin—if anything, it made it worse to remember the way Christine had spoken to her just yesterday, the anger she'd directed at her when Gin had only been trying to help Tom.

"We came right over. Well, Dad got here first. He's on the phone with his lawyer now."

A lawyer. Yes. They needed one, didn't they? Gin's thoughts immediately went to Madeleine: in a crisis, her mother was the strong one—her mother had *always* been the strong one, but it had taken the loss of her daughter to make everyone see it.

"Where the hell is Mom?" she demanded, aware that her voice had taken on a shrill tone.

Her gaze fell on Olive, whose mouth was bunched up in a small, worried smile, and immediately Gin regretted the way she'd spoken. She wondered if Olive was aware of the tension between her and Christine. She would make it up to Olive, when they got this latest crisis under control.

"Madeleine's on her way," Christine said. "She was trying get them to let her see Richard, but I don't think she had any luck."

"It was my fault." Gin blurted it out before she could consider the ramifications: she couldn't confess to having looked at his files without also admitting that she and Jake had broken into his office. And while she was ready to defend her own actions, she couldn't throw Jake under the bus.

"It's no one's fault," Christine said.

Gin wanted desperately to believe her. But how to explain her father's signature on the prescription? Could he have made a mistake and specified the wrong drug? But that wouldn't explain how it got into Lawrence's system—if indeed the tox screen identified it.

Spencer walked back into the kitchen. "Paulson says he can meet with Richard later today. He cleared his calendar."

"Who's Paulson?" Madeleine came walking into the kitchen on the heels of the conversation. Her outfit was as polished as ever, her linen skirt grazing her knees, her creamy blouse accented at her throat with the pearls Richard had given her to celebrate the birth of their first child. But her face clearly reflected the full weight of recent events: the lines around her mouth were deeply etched, and there were dark depressions under her eyes.

"He's a criminal defense attorney in Pittsburgh," Spencer said. "He came highly recommended by Ed Chee—remember, the lawyer who reviews contracts for the center. Good guy."

"How is Dad? Did you talk to him?"

"Yes, they let him call me. He sounded all right. Calm." Madeleine sat in one of the chairs pulled up to the kitchen table, her body slumping forward in an uncharacteristic lapse of correct posture. "They're treating him well, at least. He knows almost everyone there."

"When can we see him?"

"He wasn't sure. Visiting hours are over already for today, but maybe we can try tomorrow."

Madeleine looked so fragile that Gin bit back further questions. "Olive, do you want to help me for a sec?" she asked, going to the cupboard where she knew her mother kept snacks. She got down a package of Oreos and a serving plate, and Olive got to work arranging the cookies.

Gin approached Christine, who was standing nervously in the door to the dining room. "Listen, Christine, I appreciate you coming here."

"Oh God, I'm such an idiot," Christine blurted, handing the mug of cloudy liquid close to her body. "I'm so upset, I can't even make tea. I think the leaves all escaped the strainer."

"It looks . . . well, I was going to say it looks fine," Gin said, and then suddenly the two of them were trying not to laugh, turning their backs to the serious conversation taking place behind them at the table.

"How did any of this happen?" Christine said suddenly, the laughter dying on her lips. "All any of us ever wanted to do was just—just grow up. In this little town. Nothing bad was ever supposed to happen here, that's why Dad moved here."

"I know," Gin murmured. "I know. It's all—"

"Dad will help Richard all he can," Christine promised. "He's good at this stuff, he's had to represent the surgery center on a few lawsuits over the years."

"But Chrissy, this would be a criminal case," Gin said, easily slipping into the nickname that no one but the two families had ever used. "Not civil."

"Still . . ." Christine gave a little shudder. "I can't even hear that word associated with your dad. It just doesn't make any sense."

Gin understood what she meant. Her father was a fastidious follower of rules, a believer in order; he'd never incurred so much as a library fine.

But someone had to be brought to justice for the deaths of two people. The people of Trumbull were going to demand it, and Gin had been ready to lead the charge—right up until the moment the evidence started leading back to her own family.

* * *

Gin sat on a canvas bag she'd taken from her car under the long shadow of the water tower, tipping a Pixie Stick against her lips, tasting the sweet-tart candy she hadn't had in years.

Once Madeleine had arrived, she'd turned into a whirlwind of efficiency, but there was nothing else to be done until the discussion with the attorney. Once Spencer and Christine and the kids left, Gin had needed to get away. She'd stopped to fill up at the gas station at the edge of town and, spying her one-time favorite treats near the register, bought the Pixie Sticks and a can of Fanta, which lay unopened on the ground next to her.

Two other vehicles were parked at the Bear Creek trailhead when she arrived: an old, rusted-out pickup and an equally decrepit sedan. Gin guessed that their owners were either fishing downstream where the creek widened before joining the river or tending illegal marijuana plots that were obscured by the dense woods. She didn't particularly care about either, as long as they gave her privacy today. She just needed a place to be alone and think about everything that had happened.

Which was why, when she heard someone's footfalls crunching along the nearly hidden trail leading up to the water tower, her heart sank. She was set to gather her things and move on, when the hiker came through the trees near the far end of the clearing.

Jake.

He was dressed in faded jeans and a T-shirt so old Gin thought she remembered it, a soft green that had once been more vibrant. He was wearing work boots that had been liberally used and abused, and a workaday steel watch. All in all, he looked more like one of his crew members than the head of a successful construction business.

When he saw her, he stopped and shook his head. "You'll have to get a little more creative if you want to dodge me," he said.

"How did you even know I was here?"

"Saw you pulling out of the gas station going east. Wasn't really that tough. You were either headed here or on to the East Coast, and even if it was the latter, I might have considered joining you."

His tone had been joking, but there was a hard kernel of bitter truth underneath his words. What was there to hold Jake here, now that Lawrence was gone? Why should he stay behind in a town that reviled him—especially now that he'd given the police a new direction to search?

"Well, I came here to be alone," Gin said icily.

"Yeah. Sorry." And he *did* sound sorry, but that only somehow increased Gin's anger at him.

"You didn't even wait one day. That's all I asked you for."

Jake lowered himself to the ground, leaving space between them. "You're right. I didn't. Look, Gin . . . I truly am sorry, more than you could possibly know. I hate putting you or your family under scrutiny—and I never imagined they'd just arrest him like that. But you have to understand—the truth *matters*. I mean, you of all people know that. I don't want your dad to be guilty—please know that. I desperately hope there's a good explanation for what he did. But . . ." He looked out over the river, squinting against the late afternoon sun. "After all this time, I'm not letting this thing go unsolved if there's any way I can help it."

Gin felt something loosen inside her. Jake was right, and that only made it worse. She couldn't blame him for needing to know the truth, even if that meant jeopardizing her father's freedom. But it was just one more thing standing between them, one more painful piece of evidence that whatever they'd once shared was gone forever.

They were silent for a long time, listening to the water rushing over the stones where they had lain in the sun so many years ago. Occasionally a distant grinding of gears or honking horn was a reminder of what lay beyond the wooded trail, the people going about their lives, eking out an existence from the decaying town.

"Gonna drink that?" Jake finally asked, after the sun had descended into the trees and the heat of the day had given way to cooling breezes.

Gin handed him the soda. "I haven't had one of those in so long. I can't even remember the last time."

Jake popped the can open, took a long sip, and handed it to Gin. It tasted wonderful, and she exhaled with pleasure, releasing some of her pent-up anxiety. "Do I have an orange mustache now?"

She'd been joking, but his gaze on her mouth was anything but amused. For a moment, she thought he was going to wipe the dappling of soda off her lips with his thumb, and the anticipation of his touch was electric.

Instead he took the can back and stared out at the wooded, sloping descent to the creek. "So are you meeting a secret lover?"

"No, I just . . . I guess I feel close to Lily here. Not because this was where she's been all those years, but because we spent so much time here. Good times."

"I know. I'd hate to admit how many times I've come here myself over the years. Just to skip stones into the water or watch the sunrise, if I wake up and can't get back to sleep."

So he had it, too. The insomnia. Gin wondered if it followed everyone who'd lost someone the way they had, with no closure, no explanation. From time to time, in the shadow place between wakefulness and restless sleep, she sensed Lily's presence, not so much a ghost but a memory that spanned all the years they'd lived together. Lily as a baby and a child and an adolescent, her memory a sweet ache.

"Gin, I want to apologize. If I hadn't pushed you to break into the surgery center, your dad wouldn't be under suspicion now."

"Do you believe him now? That he didn't have anything to do with your dad's death?"

"I do, which is maybe stupid of me." He sighed. "If I'd gone with my gut from the start, I'd never have had any doubts. This whole investigation has knocked me off my moorings."

As it would anyone, Gin thought. Being accused by everyone you've ever known . . . she couldn't imagine. She'd done the cowardly thing, not only by leaving for college mere weeks after Lily had disappeared, but by staying away for the next two decades. And now that she was back, she saw her absence for what it was: a retreat based on fear of facing the emotions she had buried deep.

"Everything's . . . I mean, I came home prepared, or at least telling myself I was prepared, to deal with Lily's body being found. To get some closure after all these years." She sighed and ran a hand through her unruly curls. "I even thought, somehow, it might be good for me to help try to figure out who killed her. But I never imagined I'd be put in a position to have to defend my dad from a murder charge. Ever since I got here, I feel like things just keep getting worse."

"Gin, none of that is your fault. And I know it's hard but . . . you can't give up now. I mean, Dad had to be close to figuring this all out. The fact that he wanted to talk to you—he must have found something. Something critical to the case."

"But why me? Why not just tell the county police?"

"I don't know. I've asked myself that a hundred times. Dad and Lloyd worked with the county guys a lot in the past. Other than the usual intradepartmental friction, I don't think they ever minded. Dad knew Stillman from some other case and said he admired his work."

"Then it had to be something he didn't want them to know," Gin said, the dread growing inside her. "Something personal about one of us . . . oh God, what if it really was about Dad?"

But she just couldn't see a way for it to be true. If Richard had ever been driven to an act of violence, he wouldn't try to cover it up. It wasn't a defense that could ever be used to convince a jury, but there were men in this world who were simply incapable of dissembling, and Richard was one of them.

"Unless . . . he was protecting someone else."

"What?"

"Sorry, I was just thinking out loud. If Dad wrote that prescription for someone else . . . not knowing what they were going to use it for, not knowing it would cost Lawrence his life. But now he feels like he can't reveal their identity . . . oh, Jake, I don't know, that's probably crazy thinking."

"No, no, it's okay, you're just brainstorming. I do that myself. I've probably sat here and thought about every damn person in this town at one time or another, and wondered if they could have had some grudge against Lily. If they could have wanted to hurt her."

"I always tried to convince myself it was a stranger. Somehow . . . it was easier that way." Gin blinked, holding back the threat of tears. "I used to feel so guilty about that. I mean, I tried so hard to keep believing she might come back . . . but every year it got harder."

"That must have been awful."

She merely nodded. "Awful" didn't begin to describe what those years had been. Unable to confess her deepest fears to her parents, to add to their pain. She'd lost Jake, her best friend as well as her first love. She'd drifted apart from Christine and Tom and her other friends in Trumbull, and told no one in her new life about her past. Her name was common enough that people rarely connected her to the news story. When, on very rare occasions, she confided in people, they seemed to sense how painful the subject was, and didn't bring it up again.

"Gin . . . I know I don't have the right to tell you what to do. But I think you need to see this through." His hand covered hers. "Stay. Work with me on this. We don't have to tell anyone, but you and I are closer to this case than anyone besides your parents. We've got the most to lose."

His and Richard's reputations, and possibly their freedom. The stakes didn't get any higher.

"Look, I didn't count on Stillman and Witt moving so fast on that tip," Jake admitted. "I think it's a sign of how desperate they are to get some closure on this. My fear is that, in their haste, they might come to the wrong conclusion."

"And they don't have a lot of incentive to clear Dad," Gin agreed. "I certainly hope Paulson's as good as Spencer seems to think."

"Let him and your mom handle that. You and I can spend our time better, I think."

"You sound like you already have a plan," Gin said.

"Not really."

After a moment, Gin said, "Well, maybe I do. Do you remember Rose Red?"

28

"Sorry, sorry, just throw that on the floor," Rose "Red" Applegate said an hour later, pushing papers and fast-food bags off one of the extra chairs in her tiny office while Gin cleared the other. Then Red served them the fresh coffee she'd brewed in the ancient Mr. Coffee that sat on top of a filing cabinet.

"Love what you've done with the place, Red," Jake said drily, causing the sixty-something woman to throw back her head and laugh. "You really ought to invite *House Beautiful* in here for a photo shoot."

"Gotta love you Crosbys," she said. "Your dad was one of the only guys in town to stick up for me back when I first got this job. Hell of a guy, and the world's a sorrier place without him." She raised her mug solemnly and the three of them shared a silent toast.

Red's appointment to the medical center's security staff a decade earlier had been controversial, not just because she was publicly out as a gay woman long before small-town America was comfortable with it, but also because she was a recovering alcoholic. But Lawrence had given her his unflagging support, eventually convincing others to evaluate her on the basis of her performance, rather than the local gossip. And he'd called her "Rose Red" with affection rather than derision, taking the power out of the snub—her partner, Linda White, even named her business Snow White Interiors. Without Lawrence's support, the couple might never have been accepted into the social fabric of the town.

"You look good, Red," Gin said. The woman was lean and fit in her uniform, the drab gray shirt a sharp contrast to the vibrant, close-cropped red hair whose color probably came from a bottle now. "Thank you so much for agreeing to talk to us."

"You know this is off the record," she said. "I don't need folks thinking I'm trying to insinuate myself into this case. And if the county cops come around, I'm going to have to tell them everything I tell you."

"Understood."

"Okay. Well, I went over the tapes for the other night after you called me, and I was right. There's no way your dad was here, unless he's got the ability to move through walls. Every entrance to this place is on camera."

"Oh," Gin said, feeling a huge sense of relief—along with guilt over their own efforts to beat the security system.

"*But*," Red held up a finger for emphasis. "Someone else was. That kind of surprised me. Spencer Parker was here at a little before two AM."

"Spencer?" Gin echoed. "You're sure?"

"I wasn't, at first. Here, let me show you."

She swiveled her computer monitor around so they could all see, a difficult feat on a desk covered with photos of her and Linda's many nieces and nephews as well as an impressive collection of paper cups from the area's restaurants.

"Okay, look here," Red said, pressing play on the recording as a man entered the back side of the building, looking down at his watch as he came through the door.

"But the video quality is terrible," Gin said. "It could be Spencer, but it could also be a hundred other men."

"Uh huh," Red said, replaying the feed slowly. Each frame revealed a man in poor resolution with his face away from the camera, deftly turning as he entered the building so that it was never fully in view. Even his clothes, a nondescript dark polo shirt and plain khaki pants, could belong to anyone. "Right. No way you could make out an ID on him, almost like he was purposely avoiding the cameras. Except . . ."

She tapped at the keys, and the view switched from the building entrance to a view of the overflow parking lot. The quality of the picture was even worse, since the lot was lit from two tall lights that cast pools on part of the lot while leaving the edges mostly dark, but they saw a car enter in slow motion, head for the far corner, and park. The man who got out of the car did indeed look like Spencer. And the Mercedes emblem on the back of the sedan was recognizable.

As were the characters on the license plate.

"Most folks don't know we got a camera on that lot," Red said. "It only just went in last month, after we had some vandalism on the signage."

"Wait, wait." Thoughts chased each other through Gin's mind. "Spencer came here in the middle of the night, and tried to enter the building undetected—but he's the practice management director! Wouldn't he have known about the camera? Wouldn't he have been the one to approve it?"

"Now that's a good question. Also leads to the one you haven't asked—why I haven't shown this to the police already. Like I said, if they come and ask, I've got no plans to hold back. Thing is, though—I mean, Spencer's more than just my boss." Red's characteristically tough demeanor slipped a little, and she blinked rapidly. "Yes, ordinarily he'd have to green-light a purchase of that size. Cost almost four thousand dollars, not counting installation. But for the last year or two, Spencer's been more interested in the big picture, hasn't wanted to know the details as long as the support departments stay within their numbers. Between me and Rex—he's head of buildings and grounds—we kind of work out the fine print between us and just give Spencer the highlights."

"But Spencer's always micromanaged everything," Gin said, remembering the discussions he and her father always ended up having even on evenings that were supposed to be purely social. It would have been difficult to find two men more devoted to their jobs. "I can't imagine him letting go of the reins like that."

"Me either. Except . . ." Red hesitated. "Listen. It takes an addict to know one sometimes. And I've had my eye on Tom Parker. I think he's a high-speed train wreck waiting to happen, and I think his dad's just about desperate to do anything he can to stop it."

"You're saying that Spencer's been less attentive than usual because Tom's been screwing up?"

Red shrugged. "Hey, I may not be management, but you'd be surprised the kind of stuff I see . . . people tend not to notice someone in a uniform after a while, we just blend into the background. Now I got nothing against Tom, he's always been decent to me. But he's really been struggling lately. Leaving early, stumbling in after two- and three-hour lunches, sleeping at his desk—I see it all."

Gin and Jake exchanged a look.

"Is there any way to see what Spencer did while he was inside?" Jake asked. "Maybe he was here trying to cover up something Tom did. Maybe Tom was on the verge of getting fired."

Red was already shaking her head. "It's impossible to say, we don't have cameras in the office wing other than in the reception area." She shrugged. "Not the way I would have designed it."

Gin blew out a frustrated breath. "So we have no idea what he did once he was here."

"Well, at least I can tell you with ninety-nine percent certainty that your dad wasn't here," Red said. "So whatever happened that night, either Spencer was responsible, or someone else entirely."

"Thanks, Red," Gin said. "Just one other question—who else has keys to Dad's office?"

"No one. Not even the IT guys. Spencer has always insisted, since we have a lot of the old records in hard copy. He even has the physicians' offices cleaned during the day—some of the docs complain about that, but it's the only way to ensure that the custodial staff doesn't have access to the keys."

Gin and Jake stood, carefully sidestepping Red's clutter. "Listen, it's nice to see you back here. If only it were under different circumstances," Red said. "You ever think of moving back for good?"

"I'm pretty settled in Chicago," Gin said, her automatic response whenever anyone asked if she missed her hometown.

But it wasn't really true, was it? Guiltily she realized that Clay hadn't been in touch since their last, stilted conversation—and that she had barely noticed. And besides Clay, there were no neighbors, pets, not even a houseplant to miss her while she was away.

Trumbull had become, for her, a repository of secrets, a landscape of grief. Her parents had become practically strangers to her. And Jake—until this week, Gin had thought that if she never saw him again, it would still be too soon.

"Well, I know we can't compete with the big city," Red said, giving her a lopsided grin. "But this place has its moments."

As they said their good-byes, Gin could feel Jake's eyes on her, and she wondered what he was thinking.

*　*　*

"We need to tell the cops," Gin said. "This should at least cast some doubt on whether my dad wrote that prescription."

"And throw suspicion directly on Spencer," Jake said. "You heard Red, he's been focused on Tom. So far everyone's been jumping to conclusions, myself included. Maybe what we need to do is take a step back and think before we give the police anything that will lead them to go after another innocent person."

"But Jake—" Gin's words caught in her throat. "Dad is in *jail.* I mean, everyone thinks of him as, I don't know, stoic . . . strong and silent. Which he is . . . but I just can't bear to think—he's probably in there with drug dealers and domestic abusers and, and, whatever he is, he isn't—"

"It's going to be all right." Jake interrupted her increasing distress by settling a hand on her shoulder. His palm warmed her through the thin cotton of her shirt. "Gin, listen, you can't focus on that right now. It won't help him."

"But . . ." She took a deep breath. What she was about to say couldn't be taken back. "What if Spencer really was there to get the prescription pad that night? What if he forged Dad's signature and dated it and left the copy so that there wouldn't be a gap when the auditors went through the records at the end of the year?"

Jake frowned. "But the office was secure," he said. "You heard Red. No one can get into the physicians' offices."

Gin was already shaking her head. "Dad and Spencer probably had each other's keys. Back when they were still getting the surgery center off the ground, they were like one person in two bodies. And since Spencer made the rules, he would have been able to make an exception, too—I'm sure he convinced Dad it was a good idea."

"But that was years ago. They grew apart," Jake said. "Even I could see that, after I started hanging around with you guys. And Lily said . . ."

But he stopped, shaking his head.

"Lily said what?"

"Nothing. Never mind."

They had been walking toward Jake's truck, but Gin stopped and grabbed his arm.

"Don't do that, Jake," she snapped. "There is no 'never mind' anymore. Whatever you know, whatever you're thinking, I deserve to know. At least when it comes to Lily."

He regarded her for a long moment and then pulled his arm back—not angrily, but firmly. "You have no idea what it's been like for me," he said quietly. "It's too late to talk about what I *deserve*, but you'll have to understand that I've got a long history of my words being twisted and thrown back at me."

The interviews, the interrogations. The dirty looks and unvoiced suspicions. All those people who wouldn't hire Jake when he started his company, who shunned him even when his father was ill.

"You're right. I can't understand what you went through. And—and I see now that I was a part of it. Turning on you." Gin drew a shuddering breath, those terrible lonely under-graduate years now looking completely different in her memory as she considered what Jake had been going through. "I owe you a lot more than an apology, Jake, and maybe someday I'll find a way to make it right. But for now, I just need to know what happened to my sister. And you're the only person I can count on to help me. So *please*, tell me what she told you, even if you don't think it matters."

Finally, Jake nodded. "Okay. A couple of weeks before she disappeared, Lily called me and asked if we could talk. I thought maybe it had something to do with you—that she wanted to surprise you with a party for your graduation or something. The first time, I met her outside the gym after school and we walked the track, talking about nothing, about everything. And it seemed like she was leading up to something important, some big secret that was weighing on her

227

mind—only she never got there. It started to get dark and she said she'd better get home, and that was that.

"Only, a couple of days later, she wanted to talk again. Same thing: walking, talking about this and that, but she seemed preoccupied, sad . . . even a little scared, but at the time I couldn't think of a reason why, because it clearly wasn't about you."

"She must have found out she was pregnant," Gin mused. "But why you? Why would she pick you of all people to confide in?"

She had let go of his arm, but Jake put his hands on her shoulders and forced her to look at him. "Gin. Don't."

"Don't what?" she demanded, barely able to stop herself from wrenching free of his grip. There was some dangerous current between them, something bigger even than their disagreement.

"Don't blame yourself. You're way too good at it, but it's got to stop. I think Lily picked me, in a way, *because* of you. I was like a big brother to her, and that would never have happened unless you and I were . . . close."

It made a kind of sense, but Gin was still too raw from learning that her sister had chosen someone else to confide in, to forgive her. "If she had just *told* me. I could have helped her consider her alternatives, I could have listened . . ."

"'Could have' is almost never the right road to take," Jake cautioned. "All we've got is now. The moment in front of us."

He hooked her chin with a finger and forced her to look up at him. His expression was serious, his eyes narrowed, his mouth tightened. But as the moment lengthened, he seemed to relax, the frustration giving way to something else.

He didn't take his hand away. Instead, he traced along the line of her jaw until his fingers brushed against her earlobe, then stroked her hair.

Gin's heart raced with anticipation, the memory of his kisses—so long ago, tender and unartful—mixing with the raw desire of a grown woman. *Jake.* The name she tried to banish from her mind so often, late at night, when she couldn't sleep. The man who was a harder, damaged version of the boy he'd been.

It would be so easy, to close the gap between them, to lift her face to his. To give in to the roaring need that drove their encounters now—at least, for her. But what if he didn't feel the same way? What if, for Jake, this was merely a crossed synapse—a memory mixed with the confusion of the last few days? Would kissing him purge the worst of what had passed between them—or further muddy the terrible truths that Gin was more determined than ever to find?

Reluctantly, awkwardly, she broke away, taking a step back so that his hand fell from her hair. "So what do we do now? I still think we should go straight to the police—"

"We go straight to Spencer." If Jake had been as discomfited as she by the close call with intimacy, he hid it well. "He's probably in the office now."

"Why not let the police handle that? They can get there as fast as we can . . ." She shuddered, trying to banish the lingering memory of his touch and focus instead on changing his mind.

"Because if the police confront him, and he has something to hide, he's sure to shut down. You yourself told me he's worked with lawyers a lot—what's to stop him from clamming up and calling one the minute they walk through his door? At least if we go ourselves, we've got a chance to get him to open up. Especially if this is . . . if he's got some good reason for being there that night. That's all we need to find out, and if we're satisfied he had nothing to do with the prescription or with Dad's death, then we walk away and don't mention it again."

Gin was silent for a moment, turning over his words, realizing that he was right. "Okay. But not just us." She pulled her phone out and tapped a number near the top of the list. "There's one person he never could say no to, and that's my mom. If she's there, I feel like he'll be more likely to tell the truth."

29

While they were waiting for Madeleine, Gin excused herself and walked into the parking lot, out of earshot from both Jake and the knot of people huddled together smoking on their breaks.

She dialed with a heavy heart, knowing she should have done this long ago. Clay picked up on the first ring.

"Is everything all right?" he asked without even saying hello.

"Yes, everything's—it's fine," she said. "I'm sorry I haven't been keeping in touch better. There's been so much going on— but that's not really an excuse."

"Are you . . . is your family . . . are you holding up okay?" he asked awkwardly, tripping over his words.

This was the problem, Gin thought. And it wasn't his fault. They simply had never become close, the way lovers should be. She had held parts of herself back, substituting what she thought he wanted to hear while keeping things light.

And now it was too late.

Not just because she was facing down the hardest days of her life without him, and she suspected that had cemented the distance between them permanently. But because these few days with Jake had reminded her of what real love felt like, with all its attendant passion and frustration and yearning—even if that love was in the past. Or perhaps *because* it was in the past—yet still, almost two decades later, it burned hotter inside her than anything she'd ever felt with Clay.

"I'm all right," she said carefully. "But, I thought we should talk. Coming here has—well, it's brought up all kinds of things for me."

"Gin, you don't have to—"

"No. Please. Let me finish. I've realized that Chicago, for me, has been a form of escape. A way of turning my back on my whole past. But the thing is, you can never really put something like what happened to us behind you. I don't—I can't quite figure out what it means for me, for my future, but I do know that there are a lot of . . . loose ends that I need to tie up here. One way or another."

"Does that mean you're staying?" Clay's voice was kind, and—from the sound of it—neither surprised nor devastated.

"I—I'm not sure. At least for now."

She heard him sigh on the other end. "Gin. I care about you. You know that."

"I do . . ."

"And I hope we always remain friends. I'm here for you—if you need me to come, I'll be there in hours. Anything at all. But it seems to me . . ."

"I'll say it," Gin said gently, reflecting that if she hadn't fallen in love with Clay, at least she had chosen a kind and decent man to spend her otherwise lonely evenings with. "You shouldn't have to. You've been nothing but good to me. You deserve . . . you deserve the best, a woman who will give you all of herself. I'm not, I can't be, that woman. I'll always—" she cleared her throat and swiped at her eyes.

"You're a good woman, Gin," Clay said. "I've always wished I could make you see that in yourself."

* * *

Madeleine pulled up a few moments after Gin had hung up. She and Jake watched her circle until she found a parking space.

"Tell me again why you didn't just come out and tell her?" Jake said.

"Mom's . . . protective," Gin finally said, though it wasn't quite the right word. It was more that, since returning home, Gin had come to understand that her mother couldn't stand to lose much more. The steely resolve that had gotten her so far in local politics was, Gin had realized, actually just a cover for the unresolved grief buried deeply inside her mother.

"You think she'll try to protect *Spencer*?" Jake asked.

"I don't know. I just was afraid that if I told her flat out what we learned from Red, she'd refuse to even consider the possibility."

"So you want to tell her in front of him instead?"

"At least then she'll see for herself how he reacts. And so will we."

"I don't know," Jake said uneasily.

But Madeleine was walking briskly toward them. "Jake!" she said, forcing a smile. "Gin didn't tell me you were here, too."

"Actually, Mom, I wasn't entirely honest when I said I was visiting Tom," Gin said. "He's been released into a rehab clinic already."

"Then—" Madeleine glanced from her to Jake and back. "What were you doing here?"

"Just . . . there's something I wanted to discuss with you and Spencer," Gin said, guiding her mother toward the entrance, knowing she wouldn't question her further in front of Jake. "It shouldn't take long."

"Well, I must say this is all very mysterious," Madeleine said tightly, but she allowed herself to be led to the warren of offices at the back of the wing.

Spencer's door was open, and he was turned away, talking on the phone. When Gin knocked lightly at the door frame, he turned, and—maybe she imagined it—for a fraction of a second, his expression registered dismay before mouthing "come in." While he concluded his call, Gin and Madeleine took the chairs across the desk from him, while Jake remained standing.

"This is an unexpected pleasure," Spencer said. "Especially since I've been negotiating our light-bulb contract all morning. You'd be shocked to know what it costs up front to refit the entire place with CFLs."

"I'm sure I would," Gin said evenly. "Listen, Spencer, I'll get right to the point. You were here late on Wednesday night. That was the night that a prescription was written for Doxorubicin on Dad's prescription pad. We know that Dad wasn't here that night, and you were the only other person who could have gotten into his office, and so . . ."

She let the implication hang in the air. Spencer's face went dark with anger, while her mother looked from Gin to Spencer and back in alarm.

"What are you accusing me of?"

"Nothing. I'm not accusing you of anything, just—"

"What is going *on*, Virginia?" Madeleine demanded. "Where on earth did you get such a notion?"

"I can't say, not right now, but Mom, it's true, okay? Spencer was here that night, and somehow, a prescription for Doxorubicin got written. I'm not saying it's the same drug that ended up killing Lawrence, but you've got to admit that this raises all kinds of red flags."

"But if this is true, why haven't you told the police?" Madeleine asked. "They could clear this up in no time."

"Do I need to call a lawyer, too?" Spencer asked, his voice hollow—but that question seemed to upset Madeleine even more.

"Is this what we're doing now?" she demanded, her voice going high and shrill. "Just accusing everyone in sight of hurting Lawrence because we haven't been able to find who did it? Accusing *Spencer*?" She turned on Jake. "I know Lawrence was your father—and believe me, I know what it feels like to lose someone you love. But that does not give you license to appoint yourself his avenger. Not you *or* my daughter."

"Gin, Madeleine . . . Jake," Spencer said, recovering his composure. "You're right. I was here that night. But it's not what you think. I was in Tom's office. There may be an internal investigation, now that he's in rehab. I . . . I'm not proud of this, but I went to his office because I wanted to make sure that there wasn't anything incriminating there. The drugs he was into . . . well, it's somewhat ironic, under the circumstances, but I'm fairly sure that someone in this center was supplying him. I just don't know who it is. But I would never have any reason to suspect your father. Christ, Virginia, he's the last person in the world I'd ever accuse of anything even slightly unethical."

"Did you find anything in Tom's office?" Jake asked, and Gin could tell he didn't buy Spencer's story. It was subtle—a weight to his voice, nothing anyone else would notice.

"No, just a couple bottles of Aleve and a bag of those cinnamon red-hots he likes." He sighed. "Look, I know my son has a tough road ahead of him, getting a handle on his addiction. I just didn't want to make it more complicated than it already is. For what it's worth, if the investigation leads to a recommendation to fire him, I won't stand in the way. I should have been tougher with Tom a long time ago."

The pain in his voice, the regrets of a father who was impotent to help his child, made Gin question her suspicion of her parents' oldest friend.

But Jake was undeterred. "My dad knew something," he insisted. "Something big enough to get him killed. So you'll forgive me if I don't quite buy your story. I'll need more to go on to convince me that you were only looking out for Tom."

"*Jake*." Madeleine turned to face Jake head-on. "For all these years, I've believed in you. I've never let myself get so caught up in the desperation for answers that I forgot who you were to all of us."

Unlike Dad, Gin thought.

"But now you have to do the same thing. You have to remember who we *are*, all of us, before you start making accusations that could hurt us even more."

"Listen, Madeleine, it's all right——" Spencer tried to interject, but Madeleine ignored him.

"Virginia, I don't know if this is partly your way of trying to protect your father, and I know I've encouraged you to get involved in the investigation. But with everything that's happened, I think it's time to stop trying to interfere and let the police handle this. *All* of it. You'll forgive my cynicism, but after seventeen years of wondering if I'll ever see my daughter again, I've gotten a little jaded where their skills are concerned. Yes, I pray that we find out who killed Lawrence, if indeed it was a murder—and I'm not convinced of that. If it wasn't a suicide, then I hope the killer is prosecuted. But I'm not willing to risk the reputations of one more person I care about to make that happen. We have to live here. You get to go back to Chicago and pretend none of this ever happened, but the rest of us don't."

The speech seemed to have exhausted her, but Gin was stung by her final words. Was that what her parents thought? That she'd run away—from not just her grief, not just Jake, but from them, too?

And worse—was it possible that her mother was right?

"I . . . I need to go," Gin mumbled, getting up and staggering toward the door. Jake was out of his chair in seconds, coming after her.

She'd been pursuing the truth—or so she thought. Instead she'd stirred up a nest of resentments that seemed to have no end.

And the one man who seemed determined not to let her face it alone was the one man who should have hated her most of all.

She raced down the hall, but not so fast that he couldn't catch up.

* * *

"Jesus, Gin, if I concede that you can kick my ass, will you slow down?"

She was halfway to Jake's truck and still deciding if she was going to walk home or let him drive her. But hearing his voice made up her mind. She'd been inconsistent, needy, bristling, and he was still jogging along to keep up with her.

It wasn't the fact that Jake was willing to overlook her flaws, to have faith in her while he searched for the truth. No, it was something much more important, something Gin had lost sight of between the last day the five of them had all been together—five friends bound by blood and friendship—and the day last week when a hollowed shell of herself had pulled into town.

It was the fact that with Jake, she was always herself. She didn't edit, hide, or camouflage any part of her, even the parts that shamed her, the ones that hurt so much. Jake knew her habits, her passions, her rages, and her secret regrets, and right now the comfort of having him near was too hard to resist.

She slowed to a walk. "I could never kick your ass," she said softly. "Every time I came close, you were just letting me."

"Naw. Don't sell yourself short. Those arm-wrestling matches? Totally cleaned the floor with me."

If he was trying to lighten the mood, to lift her spirits, it wasn't working—well, maybe it was working a little. After all, it wasn't a crime to remember those lazy afternoons when wrestling matches turned to make-out sessions, and then— that last summer—when make-out sessions turned to something more, something that seared her in a way she'd never come close to feeling again.

It wasn't a crime to miss him. To wonder what might have been. Was it?

"Listen, what do you say we go see Lloyd?" Jake asked. "If Dad confided in anyone . . ."

"Right." Pushing her emotions away for the moment, she shared the feeling she hadn't been able to shake, that Lloyd had known something that night, something he hadn't told anyone.

"But that doesn't make any sense." Jake opened the passenger door of his truck for her, an unconscious habit, and a gesture that Gin found far more pleasing than she would have cared to admit. When he offered his hand, she allowed him to help her up into the seat, the imprint of his touch staying with her even after he'd closed the door.

"If he'd known something," Jake continued as he started up the truck, "why not just tell us? Instead of taking the risk of helping us break in?"

"Maybe he only suspected," Gin said. "I'm not sure. I'm just hoping that he'll be more willing to open up to us, since nothing else has worked so far."

They drove in silence most of the way. When they reached the rustic cabin, Jake glanced her way. "Am I the good cop or the bad cop?" he asked, an edge to his voice.

Gin felt a rush of dangerous electricity travel through her body. Something had changed between them, and she knew Jake had been feeling it, too. But was now the time to let her guard down—with her father's guilt in question, her mother's brittle composure threatening to crack, the truth about her sister's fate hanging in the balance?

"I don't know," she answered helplessly. "I was just planning to go with the truth."

Jake parked and cut the engine, then turned to look at her, resting his arm along the bench seat so he could brush a strand of her hair behind her ear.

"We'll have to work on that," he said, before turning away.

No one answered the knock on the door, but an old radio sitting on a sawhorse on the side of the house was playing a baseball game. Jake led the way around the house, where they found Lloyd kneeling next to a patio chair with a drill.

"Well, now, look who's here," he said, getting slowly to his feet, holding onto the chair for support.

"What are you working on?" Gin asked.

"Ah, I just made a couple of new armrests for this chair," Lloyd said. Sure enough, the battered old aluminum frame sported beautiful new lacquered hardwood arms. "I don't know why folks can't build anything to last these days. Here, take a load off for a spell."

He insisted that Gin take the newly upgraded chair and dragged its mate close. Jake sat on the stump that served as a chopping block. Gin couldn't help wondering if the old man still split his own firewood, and reflected that there would be a lot fewer heart-attack victims on her table if everyone stayed as active as Lloyd in advanced age.

"You can probably guess that we're here with more questions," she said.

"Yep, I figured it was just a matter of time."

She and Jake filled him in about the exchange with Spencer.

"Lloyd . . ." Jake asked. "Is there anything at all that you can think of, anything Dad might have learned that someone would have been willing to kill him for? Anything he said recently that struck you as unusual, or noteworthy, or . . . ?"

"Well, now," Lloyd said carefully. "Thing is, your dad was just fit to be tied when they connected that cooler to you. He came to me first thing to see if I knew anything about how it got there. I told him everything I knew, which wasn't much." He grimaced. "That didn't sit well with him at all. I guess you know how your dad was. Like a hound that caught a scent, I couldn't say nothing to convince him that they weren't going to be able to pin this on you, Jake."

Gin stole a look at Jake, who was glaring at the ground, his jaw like stone. She knew how much he missed his father.

"Thing I didn't tell you, the other day, he asked me to go up to the records office with him and hunt down the old case records."

"But the county police already had them."

"Not all of them." He took a deep breath. "And that's my fault. See, when Lily didn't turn up all those years ago, it didn't sit right with me, especially when the name everyone was whispering around town was yours, Jake. I didn't tell your dad, because you remember he went through a hard time there, and talking to him was like talking to a post. But I kept her file out, and whenever I had a little time, I'd check unidentified victims all over the surrounding states to make sure there weren't any new cases that might match. Lawrence . . . well, he had to know I was doing it, because I didn't exactly hide it, but we never talked about it."

"Not until last week," Jake said.

"Wait," Gin interrupted. "You had the file out all this time?"

"No, not all of it, and tell the truth, I'd forgotten myself. You remember I retired kind of suddenly after my embolism. Well, Lois just took everything in my office and boxed it up and sent it up to records. I guess she figured there wasn't anything in my desk worth following up on. And it was true, I'd put most of the file back long before then. But I'd kept a copy of Lily's medical records out. I'm sorry to say it, Gin, but I figured this way if there was a need . . . if some Jane Doe turned up in New Jersey or Ohio who seemed like she could be a match, I wanted to be able to confirm quick. I just, I figured your family had been through enough, and if there was ever bad news to deliver, well, I figured it ought to come from me." His mouth went slack. "I'm sorry I couldn't keep that promise to you."

"Oh, Lloyd," Gin said. "I don't even know how to thank you."

"Anyway, Lawrence remembered I'd kept that copy, and since he couldn't ask to see the file without the detectives wondering why, he asked me to help. Took us all morning, but sure enough, we found my boxes." He chuckled unexpectedly. "Lois had even packed up a bottle of Wild Turkey I used to keep in my desk drawer, and I had half a mind to take a nip. But your dad saw something in that file that shut him right up. I asked him every way I could think of to let me in on it, but he just kept saying he needed to check on something. That was his way when he was onto something—wouldn't come out with anything until he was sure. Part of what made him a good cop, a good chief. Anyway, I figured I'd know soon enough. And then . . ."

"Do you still have the records?"

"No, son, and I've been beating myself up for that. Your dad took them and I don't have any idea what he did with them."

Jake leaned forward. "I think I might."

30

"I don't know why I didn't think of this before," Jake said as he led Gin in through the back door of his father's house. The front door was still crisscrossed with yellow tape, and—just to be on the safe side—they had parked around the corner and cut through the woods behind the houses. Despite the fact that the house now belonged to Jake, it wouldn't help their cause for the neighbors to see them snooping through it now.

"That looks like a gun safe," Gin said, tracing a finger along the polished ebony side of the tall cabinet in Lawrence's den.

"That's because it is," Jake said. He stood on the desk chair and felt along the top of the pine shelves built into the opposite wall, coming up with an old tobacco can that rattled when he shook it. "Or was, anyway. Dad was big into repurposing things. Wouldn't keep guns in the house after I was born, other than his service piece, and he locked that in his bedroom safe every night. That left this one free. Used to belong to my grandfather, and"—the door opened on oiled hinges—"I guess Dad couldn't bear to get rid of it."

Inside the cabinet, the support that used to hold the rifle barrels in place had been removed, and shelves installed in its place. Simple file boxes were stacked on the lowest shelves along with bundled receipts and rubber-banded check registers. Jake picked up items and set them down until he came to a small cardboard box with the name "Marnie" written on the side in marker.

He lifted the box flaps and peered inside, then went still.

"What is that?" Gin asked.

"My mom's stuff, I think. I've never seen this in my life."

"Do you want me to open it?" Gin asked hesitantly. As a teen, she'd been clumsy about the subject of Jake's mother, steering clear of it because she couldn't imagine what it would be like lose her own mother so young.

"No. I'm okay." Jake took two smaller white boxes from the carton. Lifting the lid on the first long, rectangular box revealed a strand of pearls. They were luminous even in the dim light of the room, sliding sinuously through his fingers.

"She had those on in her wedding picture," Gin said.

"You remember that?" Jake said, surprised.

"Well, yes." Gin was embarrassed; the picture—the only one of Marnie Crosby in the house—sat on the mantel above the fireplace in the living room, but she had only examined it when Jake was out of the room. Looking for clues to the boy she'd loved. "I *am* a woman, after all. We notice certain things."

"I'm well aware you're a woman." Jake opened the other small, square box. Inside was a dainty platinum ring set with a row of sparkling tiny diamonds.

"Her engagement ring?"

Jake said nothing for a moment, then snapped the box shut and set it back inside the cabinet and resumed searching. Gin wondered what he was feeling, what seeing his mother's things had stirred up for him.

He named the items he found as he went through the documents: titles to home and car, passports, bank statements.

Finally he landed on a sheaf of papers in an old file box. He riffled through the papers, which appeared hastily stuffed in.

"This is it. There's a ton of stuff here . . . mostly medical records, it looks like, and a few other things. Birth certificate. Oh look, first communion . . . report cards."

They sat on the floor, cross-legged, going through the papers. After a few minutes, Jake held up an office visit form and said, "I can't make any sense of this. You people have your own language, not to mention the worst handwriting I've ever seen."

"It's a cliché because it's true," Gin said. "They teach it in medical school and then we hone our illegibility skills during our internship."

Her attempt at humor got only a thin smile from him. Jake's mood had darkened, whether because of seeing his mother's belongings, or sadness over Lawrence, she couldn't tell. "Look," she said, "do you want me to take these and put them in order for you? I can summarize what's here in layman's terms for you."

"That would be great," Jake said. "I need to make a run up to the city. I was supposed to be there this morning, we're pouring a new foundation in East Hills, and the guys are on overtime until I get this resolved. I'll drop you off on the way."

He closed the doors to the cabinet and locked it, dropping the key in the tobacco can and replacing it on the shelf.

At the door to the room, they both took a last look around.

"This is so different from my father's office," Gin said, taking in the dusty trophies from Jake's football days lining the shelf that ran along the wall near the ceiling, the bookshelves full of tattered paperbacks and old encyclopedias, the prize catches mounted and hung in pride of place. Photos of Lawrence and Jake camping, fishing, building a tree house. An ancient television, crocheted afghans folded over the plaid sofa.

This was the domain of a man who was comfortable in his skin, a man whose pleasures were as simple as the code he lived by. A room that invited you in, encouraged you to share what was on your mind. A place where you could be who you really were.

Growing up outside the orbit of Richard's exquisitely cultivated privacy had been hard enough for Gin, with her desire to please, her knowledge that she was the second-favorite.

She'd envied Lily then, bright beauty, shiny treasure, able to command Madeleine's attention so easily. But now she realized how hard it must have been for her sister, who had no tools in her arsenal to attract her father's attention.

Gin touched the fringed edges of an afghan sadly: how might things have been different if Richard had been able to come out of his private domain and interact with the rest of his family? Would Lily have had to act so wild to get his attention? Would she have been so defiant?

Would she still be alive?

"Gin." Jake's voice, so familiar, so dear. "Are you all right?"

"I'm sorry," Gin said, shaking her head. "I just . . . kind of got lost there for a minute. Memories. Too many of them."

She attempted a rueful laugh, but it came out choked. Jake brushed at her cheek where a tear had somehow trailed. He didn't take his hand away.

Standing in the late afternoon sun, dust motes sparkling on the golden beams that entered through the picture window, it could have been twenty years before—the day Jake Crosby first kissed her in a spot not far from where Lily's body had been found. He'd walked there with Gin, her hand in his as natural as breathing, while Tom and Christine argued about some long-forgotten disagreement and Lily flipped through a magazine while lying in the sun. That kiss had been both a surprise and not, because it felt as ordained as if everything in her life had led up to that moment.

This kiss was different. His hand against her face was a question, his steady gaze unflinching. Her lips met his and all the years that had passed, the experiences and disappointments and achievements and near misses and regrets that adulthood brings, steadied what had once been exuberant inexperience. This was different: this was raw, wanting—and dangerous. She wanted more, and she could tell he did, too. She had to have him—or run away from him.

She chose the latter. For a thousand reasons. For the only reason.

"It's just . . ." she whispered.

Jake stepped back, letting his hands fall to his sides. "I know."

They both knew better. But now they also both knew what they had been missing.

*　*　*

When Gin arrived home, she was afraid the close call with Jake was written on her face—that her mother would read both the fervid urgency of their rekindled attraction and Gin's guilt over how close she'd come to giving in to it.

But Madeleine came flying out of the house, keys in hand, and barely slowed.

"Paulson came through. He got your dad out on bail," she called over her shoulder. "I'm going to pick him up!"

She didn't invite Gin to join her, and after only a few seconds of considering getting right back in her car and following, Gin decided to wait. Let her parents have this moment—maybe it would make up for some of the tension between them.

Besides, she wanted time to compose herself before greeting her father, time to wipe all traces of doubt from her manner.

She was wiping down the kitchen counter when they returned, having discovered that her mother had been halfway through assembling dinner when she got Paulson's call, and finished the job while she waited. The aroma of baked chicken and scalloped potatoes filled the house when Madeleine led Richard into the house like a docile goat.

"Virginia," her father said, brushing her cheek with papery lips. He smelled of chemicals and body odor, and his clothes were soiled and wrinkled.

Gin couldn't help it—she threw her arms around her father and held on. Even though she felt him stiffen in her embrace, she couldn't bear to let go for a few moments. Funny how it wasn't when he'd been taken away that it sunk in that they could lose him—but when he returned.

At last she released him, and he shuffled toward the stairs. "You girls eat without me," he mumbled. "I need a shower."

*   *   *

Her father never came back to the table; Madeleine checked on him after they had eaten and reported back that he was "out like a light." She retired upstairs soon after, and Gin finished cleaning up by herself, relishing the quiet of the kitchen, the citrusy scent of her mother's spray cleaner.

At eleven thirty, she was sitting cross-legged in her bedroom, a tumbler of her father's bourbon on her old painted nightstand, the box of papers spread out on the bedspread.

The knock on her door wasn't entirely unexpected. Gin had been playing music on the portable speaker she'd borrowed from the living room, and she knew Madeleine was a light sleeper.

"Sorry, Mom, I'll turn it down," she said.

"Actually, honey . . . may I come in?"

Her voice was so plaintive that Gin felt guilty for not trying to engage her in conversation after dinner.

She got up and opened the door to the room—it still stuck, just as it had all those years ago—and her mother perched on the desk chair while Gin resumed her spot on the bed.

"It's been a long day," Madeleine began. Then she seemed to register what Gin was doing, and a deep crease formed between her brows. "What on earth . . ."

"Mom, why would your medical records have been in the case file from back when Lily went missing?" Gin asked, hoping to avoid having to explain why she had the file.

But she wasn't prepared for her mother's reaction. Madeleine picked up a page from the top of the stack, scanned it, then flipped through several more in increasing agitation. "What on *earth* . . ."

"It's okay, Mom, these are only copies. I haven't done anything illegal, if that's what you're worried about." That was true, wasn't it? After all, Jake was Lawrence's son; the house would be his soon enough, and everything inside it. Even if Lawrence's possession of the files was questionable, Jake hadn't done anything more than stumble on them.

"But why . . . oh, God . . ." Madeleine gathered all the papers into her lap and went through them, as though she was searching for something. When she reached the bottom of the stack, she looked up at Gin over her reading glasses. "That's it? All of it?"

"Yes—"

Madeleine visibly relaxed, her shoulders slumping and her breath leaking out in a slow exhale. "Well, would you like to tell me how you happened to have them in your possession?"

"What were you looking for, just now?"

"Nothing. Just, as I'm sure you're aware, it wouldn't look good if the media knew you had these. What with your father under suspicion."

A stab of guilt shot through Gin. Her mother was right, of course; it would look like she was trying to defend—or cover up—her father's actions. "I'm being careful," she said defensively. "No one knows I have them." Except for Jake. Who didn't count.

"Virginia." Madeleine pushed her reading glasses up on top of her head and sighed. "You are an expert at a lot of things, and I defer to you in all of them. But you are not experienced in the psychology of a small town. Not anymore. You've forgotten how a rumor can grow into an accusation around here—how it can turn into accepted fact no matter how ludicrous, just because it went up and down the gossip chain. Word of mouth means a lot more here than it does in the big city."

"Of course," Gin said tightly, though she seethed at being chastised like a child. "But you're the one who was acting like you thought the box was on fire. Mind telling me what you were looking for?"

"Nothing," Madeleine said, rising from the chair with a dismissive wave, which belied the deep lines on her face. For the first time since Gin arrived, Madeleine's appearance was showing her exhaustion. "Just trying to protect what's left of the family reputation."

"Mom," Gin said, stopping her at the door, filled with remorse at having judged her so harshly. Madeleine was a creature of her upbringing, and emotions didn't come out easily, but that didn't mean they weren't there. Gin had seen other women like her, who remained stoic throughout the identification of their loved one's body, only to fall apart in the parking lot or, as one mother of a cocaine overdose had done, hours after returning home, when she hanged herself in her daughter's bedroom.

What if Madeleine's increasingly erratic behavior was the sign of a breakdown? What if the pressure of maintaining her cool exterior, even in the face of accusations against her husband, had finally broken her?

"This has to be hard on you," Gin said gently. "Have you thought about taking a little time off from work? You know that you need time to grieve, too, right?"

"I've done my grieving," Madeleine said grimly, "and I'm afraid I gave up my right to self-pity a long time ago."

She shut the door behind her.

Gin sat without moving for a while, turning off the music and listening to the sounds of the old house. The foundation creaking, branches tapping against glass, old pipes sighing and popping.

Something was off, and it wasn't just Madeleine's cryptic comment. Gin picked up the stack of papers that her mother had left on the chair and went through them, slowly, one more time, sorting them into three stacks: Lily's medical and dental records, Madeleine's medical records, and a "miscellaneous" pile that included anything unrelated to health.

Then she put her mother's records in order. They went back as far as the eighties, when Lily and Gin would have been babies. Mostly they were routine: pap smears, flu shots, treatment for a variety of routine illnesses. Records from when Madeleine broke her ankle hiking along the creek, and from a lump in her breast that turned out to be benign. Physicals and blood tests every few years with notes about borderline anemia and a mild vitamin D deficiency. A consultation about hormone therapy at the onset of menopause.

Nothing from before the girls were born.

On impulse, Gin dialed Jake's number. He picked up on the first ring.

"Missing me?" he asked, and it was hard to detect irony in his voice. But the electric tension between them earlier in the evening had given way to the pervasive sense that something was off.

"Jake . . . I hate to ask you to do this," she said, and then explained about finding her mother's records. "Do you think you could go back and look through the safe again? See if there's anything we missed?"

"Gin, is there something you're not telling me? Something specific you think I'll find?"

"No. But . . ." She blew out a breath, not sure if she was being irrational. "It's just that Mom's been acting a little strangely. I can't help feeling that she's hiding something."

"You don't think she suspects your father, do you?"

"Oh, no, that's not what I meant. And I don't think she knows who killed Lily, or even suspects—she'd say something, I'm sure of it."

"Then . . ." She could sense Jake choosing his words with care. "If she's hiding something, but it doesn't have anything to do with Lily, are you sure that you really want to know?"

"Yes," Gin said without hesitation. She wanted the truth—no matter what it turned out to be.

31

I t was nearly two o'clock in the morning when Jake texted her:

You up?

She'd been dozing, the papers pushed to the floor, the bourbon tumbler empty. But she'd forgotten to disconnect her phone from the speaker, and the chime of the incoming text woke her.

She sat up in the dark and fumbled for her phone, then typed back.

Yes. Find something?

Jake replied,

Can I come over?

Gin hesitated, her hand poised over the screen. Whatever it was, he wanted to tell her in person. Or . . . was it possible he just wanted to see her?

She shook her head, chastising herself.

OK. I'll meet you out front.

* * *

Jake cut the lights as he coasted toward the end of the street, where Gin was sitting on the guard rail the town put up after some joy riders had gone flying into the field and nearly killed themselves. She knew he was just trying to avoid waking the neighbors, but the moon was so bright, hanging low in the sky, that he could have easily driven the whole way to her house navigating only by its light.

He leaned over and opened her door, and she jumped into the cab.

"This better be good," Gin said, but then she caught his expression.

"Gin." He unbuckled his seat belt, and a sense of foreboding turned into full-on dread as he dug in his shirt pocket for a folded piece of paper. "This is . . . I don't know what it means, but I figured you would."

She stared at the paper but didn't take it. Somehow she knew that once she'd seen it, she could never go back.

"I found it in the gun case, in the ammunition drawer. Dad made a little wooden false back. He never could resist tinkering . . ." He unfolded it carefully. She could make out the neatly labeled columns at the top of the page, the grid of ghostly white blurs against a dark background.

The names on the y-axis.

"Do you know what it is?" Jake asked.

"It's a RFLP," Gin said woodenly in a voice did not sound like her own.

"A . . . 'riflip'? Translate for the idiot, please?"

"Sorry, it stands for Restriction Fragment Length Polymorphism. It's used to follow a DNA sequence as it's passed on to other cells." She paused, the implications of what she was seeing slamming home. "It was the gold standard for paternity testing in the eighties, before they had DNA swab tests."

"And this means . . ."

Gin reached a shaking hand and traced the column of white blurs that were stacked on top of each other. "This is a positive test. Donor A is the parent of Donor B. The margin of error is negligible."

"And Donor A . . ."

Gin closed her eyes, her mind spinning with the implications. ". . . was Spencer Parker, according to this. Spencer was Lily's biological father."

For a moment, the stillness took on the quality of a movie, something Gin was watching from a distance, something that was happening to someone else. The results were incontrovertible, but her mind wouldn't accept them. *Of course* Richard was her sister's father. Lily was her sister. Madeleine was their mother. Dad was their dad.

Spencer Parker had come to the door a hundred, a thousand times when they were small, exhausted from his long day at the surgery center, about to embark on another equally exhausting evening as a single father of twin toddlers . . .

Spencer Parker at her parents' annual Christmas party, ducking out before he'd even finished his first drink, because he needed to "help Santa."

Spencer and Richard in a million boring discussions about the surgery center, always the surgery center, while the kids all rolled their eyes at the dads' shared obsession, mindful that if they dared say anything out loud they'd get a lecture about putting bread on the table and soccer shin guards not growing on trees.

And finally, Spencer and her mother. How many times had Gin seen the two of them together and thought nothing of it? Spencer handing her a platter of burgers at a barbecue. Thanking her for watching the kids. Offering to help with the dishes. Spencer, always polite—to the point of being formal. Stiff, even.

But he wasn't always like that. Only with Madeleine.

"God. How could I be so stupid?"

She let herself fall into Jake's arms, her face against the soft cotton fragrant with the scent of fabric softener and cut grass.

"You weren't stupid," he said, patting her back gently. "There was no reason for you to notice. No reason anyone would have."

"But thinking about it now . . ."

"Gin. Don't go back. Don't beat yourself up. Whatever was between Spencer and your mom, they were the ones who made those decisions. They're the ones who've had to live with the consequences all these years."

"I just can't believe . . . I mean, my mother . . . oh my God. That means Tom and Christine are Lily's half-siblings. And her and Tom . . ."

She opened the door to the truck and half-stepped, half-stumbled onto the ground. She felt nauseous and dizzy, the concentric circles of implications spinning in her mind. Lily had dated her half-brother. Lily had been pregnant. Tom could very well be the father of the baby she'd been carrying.

She staggered through the weeds, over the rise to an over-look with a view of the town beyond. She knelt on the ground, pebbles and stalks poking into her skin. She thought she might be sick, but she hadn't eaten since breakfast, and her body had nothing to give up. Instead she wrapped her arms around herself and rocked, moaning, trying to make sense of the horror that her sister had unknowingly been a part of.

Then Jake was at her side, with his hand on her back, pulling her against him. "Gin. You couldn't have known. No one could have known." He continued murmuring, kissing her hair gently, chastely, holding her close.

When her moans turned to tears, she wrapped her arms around him and held on for dear life.

* * *

When Madeleine came into the kitchen the next morning, Gin was waiting. The coffee was made, and she had managed a shower after a couple of hours of tortured sleep.

"Well, you're up early," Madeleine said crisply, reaching into the cupboard for her commuter mug. "Sleep well?"

Gin ignored the question. "How's Dad?"

Something in her tone must have caught her mother's attention. She turned and stared at Gin, then set the mug down on the counter. "Still asleep. I don't think he managed a wink in that jail. Is something wrong?"

Gin had spent the last hour rehearsing the words she intended to say. But what came out was little more than a strangled gasp. "How could you?"

Later, Gin realized that her tone had given her away, that her mother had guessed. The expression on Madeleine face morphed from mild curiosity to shock to horror to tormented acceptance, and she sank into the chair across from Gin. Her hands trembled on the table.

Gin slid the RFLP across the table. Her mother barely glanced at it.

"Did Spencer know you had the test done?"

"No," Madeleine replied quietly, her voice a dried husk. "No one knew."

"You took a real chance, having it done at the hospital. Weren't you worried Dad would find out?"

Madeleine laughed bitterly. "Your father was the one who explained confidentiality laws to me," she said. "So no, that wasn't one of my concerns at the time."

"But how did you get Spencer's blood?"

Madeleine gave her a ghostly flash of a smile. "That was how I got the idea, actually. It was only a few days after Lily was born. I was sitting with her in the backyard, nursing. Your father was pushing you in the swing, and Spencer let himself in the back gate like always. He'd brought a bottle of champagne." The bitter smile again. "We were both trying too hard to be adult about it. It had been over for a long time by then, and we'd agreed never to speak about it again, even to each other."

"It hadn't been over for that long," Gin snapped, surprised by her own anger.

"Actually, it had. Well over a year. But there was just one time. One crazy, irresponsible night when your father had to go to a conference in Las Vegas, and Spencer got stuck late at the office, and by the time he came to pick up the twins . . ." She shrugged, and her thin shoulders sagged. "I'm deeply ashamed, in case you're wondering."

"Mom, I . . ." Gin had to think of the words. She tried again. "I'm not here to judge you. I'm sorry about the way I started this conversation. I just—there are so many things I don't understand. And I could accept that it's none of my business, but this—"

"Do you think I don't *know* that?" Madeleine's hand shot out and seized the paper. She looked at it quickly and then crumpled it in her fist and pressed it against her face, letting out one huge, keening wail. Then she threw the paper to the floor and savagely rubbed her eyes with her knuckles, smearing her makeup, gulping for air. "I've thought of little else for the last two decades. Your sister would be thirty-four this summer. That tally is always in my head. I know it like I know my own name. I'll know it on my deathbed."

She opened her eyes and stared bleakly at Gin. "I might as well have killed her myself."

"Mom, God no, why on earth would you say that? Do you know who did it?"

She was already shaking her head. "I have ideas, of course. For a while I was so sure that Spencer did something to her.

I couldn't even stand to look at him. And then—God forgive me, but there was a time . . . a very brief time when I was convinced your father found out somehow, that—but he loved Lily more than anything on this earth. We both did."

Even now, even with the horrors unfolding between them, Gin couldn't help but zero in on what her mother had said—and what she hadn't. It was true: Lily had been her parents' treasure. They loved Gin, she knew that, but they could never love her as much as the daughter they'd lost.

"Not Dad. And if not Spencer, who?"

"I don't know. I just don't know. If I did—if I could have been sure—don't you think I would have told someone? I was so certain she was dead, you see, but what kind of mother says something like that? I had to pretend to hold out hope. I had to try to *make* myself hope. And Virginia, let me tell you, that is its own kind of hell. All those candlelight vigils . . . the anniversaries of her disappearance—and your father, always reminding me that we had to keep believing, even while he railed against Jake as though he'd found him with her blood on his hands."

Tears coursed trails through her smudged mascara. "If I ever believed Jake could really have hurt her, I would have killed him myself," she said matter-of-factly. "But I couldn't do that to you and your father. And eventually, life sort of . . . grew back around me. Not the same, of course. But something."

"Mom." Gin reached across the table and took her mother's hand. It seemed so small, so cool. Her nails were perfect, her rings glittered. But the hand lay heavy and immobile in hers. "I don't know what to say. I'm trying to wrap my head around this. But . . . whatever happened, I don't blame you." If it wasn't true, it was close enough that she could pretend. "But you have to see that this changes everything. I mean, all the possibilities. Spencer, Tom—"

"What does it *matter!*" Madeleine yanked her hand back as though she'd touched a hot stove. "She's *dead*. Her baby—our grandchild—is dead. Nothing will bring them back."

"But we have to know—"

"What if it's Jake?" her mother's eyes narrowed, glittering with emotion. "Would you still want to know then? What if he found out somehow, what if he was seeing Lily like everyone said?"

"But if you didn't tell anyone, and the test was confidential—"

"Well, someone found out, now, didn't they?" Madeleine grimaced. "You see, that's the part that your father left out, when he was preaching medical ethics to me. The thing that you can never change. Doctors are people just like the rest of us. So are nurses. So are lab techs. Someone obviously remembered that 'confidential' result. Where did you get it, anyway?"

"It was in Lawrence's things," Gin said quietly.

She watched her mother think it through. "Oh no," she whispered.

"Yes. Lawrence knew, and someone killed him to keep from telling," Gin said. "That's one way to look at it, Mom. But it wouldn't be too good for you, would it?"

Where was this urge to cruelty coming from? As Gin watched her ordinarily imperious mother crumple, as her frosty façade disintegrated until she was every bit as human as anyone else, it wasn't compassion that filled Gin but a faint, reprehensibly smug satisfaction.

Her mother's mistakes had somehow led to Lily's death.

Gin didn't want to blame Madeleine. She wanted to remember that everyone was human, and everyone made mistakes. But the stakes were simply too high. If Lily had lived . . .

So many things would have been different. She and Jake would have gone to Ohio State together.

And Lily would have given birth to Gin's niece or nephew. Gin shuddered as the ugly truth crowded out the image: the baby could well have been the child of Lily's half brother, potentially burdened with genetic issues in addition to being condemned to the inescapable shame of an unthinkable taboo.

Bile rose up fresh inside her. This time, she made it to the bathroom just in time to expel the bitter, foul mess, to hunch heaving on the cold tile floor over the toilet, tears mixing with her own sweat.

She wasn't aware of her mother's presence in the powder room until she was kneeling next to her, wrinkling her linen suit, unmindful of her hosiery on the floor. "Baby," she whispered. "My poor sweetie, just get it out, that's right, poor angel . . ."

She waited patiently, stroking her back, until Gin was done. And then she held Gin close, just like a mother was supposed to do.

32

After Gin had brushed her teeth and changed into clean clothes, she came into the kitchen to find that her mother had poured two cups of coffee and set out a plate of sliced fruit and muffins.

"You need to eat something."

Madeleine was back to herself, for better or worse. And, Gin had to admit, she was right. She helped herself to a muffin.

"Mom, I need to get a few things straight."

"That's fine. And if you feel that it's time to get the detectives up to date with all of this, I'm ready." She took a breath. "I just ask that you let me talk to your father first."

"Mom . . . let's just take this one step at a time, okay?"

"Okay."

"I understand now why you objected to Lily dating Tom."

"That was . . . that was one of the most wrenching things I had to do. I know this sounds naïve, but I just never believed that Lily would be . . . intimate with him. My God, she was only sixteen."

Gin shook her head sadly. She'd seen girls as young as twelve on her table, fetuses born premature to girls barely old enough to menstruate.

"I convinced myself that they would get over it quickly. I mean they were so unsuited to each other. Tom was so . . . well, self-satisfied, I suppose. I mean I loved the twins, you don't raise children in your own home, alongside your own children, without developing a certain . . . attachment to them. But still. I saw even then that he was going to struggle in life. He had it too easy, too early.

"And Lily was nothing like Spencer. That helped. I convinced myself she took after Richard, which . . . well, I guess that shows you my state of mind. But she also reminded me of myself in some ways. And in other ways, she was just—purely, irrepressibly herself. Your father and I used to worry about the choices she would make, but that all seemed so far in the future . . . like her time in Trumbull was safe, protected. The four of you, and then Jake, running around together in a little wolf pack. We thought we were so blessed—right up to the day that Lily came home and told us Tom was now her boyfriend."

"I remember that you tried to forbid it."

"And if your father would have, just once in his life, let me have my way without analyzing it to death—but I couldn't argue with his logic without raising suspicion. And Spencer was so delighted, you see. He convinced Richard it was a terrific idea."

"But didn't Spencer have any idea that she could be his daughter?"

Her mother was already shaking her head. "That night when he came over . . . he said he'd been working late but I could tell he'd been out. He used to do that once in a while—his way of blowing off steam, I guess. It's like what Tom does now, but Spencer always used to keep it under control. He'd go out to some roadhouse over in Archer and have a few drinks. He hid it well, but . . . well, that night he came in the door and the minute I told him the kids were asleep he had me up against the wall."

"Mom," Gin rebuked, dizzy.

"Sorry, but I thought it was important you know. He was drunker than I thought and it was over so fast. I never even got my dress off. Later he didn't even seem to remember." She shrugged. "Maybe he *didn't* remember. The only thing he ever said about it later was that there was no way he should have been driving that night. Which was true . . . but I was in shock, I guess, and I didn't stop him. Soon after that he started seeing a woman from Clairton. And he found a regular sitter, so we saw less of each other."

"Okay. So . . . no one ever said anything, and we grew up . . . and all those years you never told anyone."

"Not a soul."

"Then how did Lawrence suspect?"

"After they found the body, he came to talk to me, he had all his notes from years ago. He kept coming back to the fact that I hadn't wanted Lily to date Tom. I think he was trying to build a case against Tom, especially since Jake was back under suspicion. He thought my objection to Tom had to do with his character, and he kept asking me questions, coming at it from all different directions."

"But you never really suspected Tom, did you?"

"I don't know, honey. Sometimes . . . when I think about how he's always gotten his way, about how he's never done an honest day's work in his life—I'm sorry, but it's true, everyone says so. Men like that are unpredictable."

"Okay. So Lawrence suspected Tom, maybe, or guessed at the truth perhaps—"

"Well, I suppose he must have, otherwise why go hunting for my medical records? That stack he had—he must have paid someone off for the whole set."

"I don't know, Mom. Paying someone would be illegal . . ."

"So maybe he subpoenaed them or, I don't know, flashed his badge and that was enough to convince them. The important

thing is that once he knew, he went to Richard, and Richard—"
She put her hands together, like she was praying. "You know
your father. Honor is very important to him. He could never
have forgiven me, and he would have done anything to keep it
from getting out."

"Mom! You can't mean that you think Dad killed
Lawrence?"

"Yes. That is exactly what I'm saying." Her mother's fists
clenched and her mouth thinned to a hard line: Madeleine at
her most formidable.

"But—"

"Listen to me, Virginia. I have been on this earth for a lot
longer than you have. I have been married for nearly thirty-
eight years. In that time, I've learned that there is very little
any of us wouldn't do when we're put to the test."

"But how could you *live* with him? How could you be in the
same house with him if you thought he—he—" She couldn't
bring herself to say the words, to put "Dad" and "murder" in
the same sentence.

"Considering the truth I kept from him," Madeleine sighed,
"I wasn't really in a position to judge, was I?"

"I can't—that's not—" Gin pushed her chair back from the
table. She'd gotten all she was going to get from her mother,
and she doubted she could change Madeleine's mind now anyway. "Look, promise me one thing."

Madeleine lifted her eyes to gaze miserably at Gin.

"Don't say anything about any of this, not to anyone. Not
Dad, not the cops, not Jake. Okay?"

"All right. For now."

"I'll call you later. I need to do some things."

"Take care of yourself today, sweetheart," Madeleine said,
walking heavily to the stairs. "I think I'll just go freshen up
before I leave."

33

G in parked in the back of an abandoned service station several blocks from the hospital. Yesterday's discussion with Red had heightened her caution: given the revelations of the last twenty-four hours, the fewer people who were tracking her whereabouts, the better.

Walking along the broken sidewalks and littered streets of the least affluent part of town, she couldn't help but consider the metaphor. Trumbull, in the days since her childhood, had fallen precipitously from grace. Not even her mother, perhaps the town's biggest booster, could possibly fail to see the ignominious despair that had been swept in along with poverty and drugs.

And what of herself? The intervening years had changed Gin, too, but her poverty was one of joy, of exuberance, of faith. At eighteen, her life hadn't been perfect—but she'd had a fundamental confidence that life would lead her on a path that would have its share of delights: she'd go to college, marry Jake, have darling children, and live in a pretty house somewhere far away.

Instead, she lived on a hamster wheel of work and sleep. Her investment in her job had become rote as well. The pleasures she knew she was supposed to enjoy—food, sex, art, leisure—were pale and insubstantial. Only when she ran, when she pushed her body to its limits, did she feel anything at all.

Until she'd come back here. Which was absurd, wasn't it? If she couldn't find satisfaction in one of the most beautiful, culturally rich cities in the world, how could she possibly find it here, in a dying steel town? If she didn't look forward to seeing even the colleagues she admired and liked the most, how could it be that she found comfort in her parents' company?

If she couldn't be satisfied with a man like Clay—intelligent, accomplished, handsome, wealthy—how could it be that thoughts of a rough-edged construction worker made her blood run hot?

Arriving at the back entrance to the surgery center, Gin took a moment to compose herself. She dabbed the perspiration from her forehead with a tissue—heavy clouds portended rain in the not too distant future, but for now, the humidity and heat rolled off the streets. She applied lipstick in her hand mirror and wished she'd spent more time covering the dark circles under her eyes.

Then she went into the building. She walked directly to Spencer's office, finding him with his sleeves rolled up, staring at a complex-looking spreadsheet on his large monitor.

"Spencer?"

He didn't jump so much as abruptly shut down, closing his eyes briefly before turning in his chair and greeting her with a warm smile.

"Virginia! I'm so glad you dropped by. And your timing's perfect—I was just struggling with these numbers, and I could use a break. Don't suppose you'd let me buy you a cup of coffee, would you? The cafeteria's finally started carrying Peet's."

"Actually I was hoping that I could speak to you privately. Would that be all right?"

Something flickered in his eyes—a darkness, hesitation, fear, or maybe just annoyance—but he gestured for her to come in. "Of course."

She closed the door behind her and sat in the upholstered chair, noticing that it was new and quite nice. The surgery center must be doing well, to be able to afford remodeling and the expense of carrying nonproductive staff like Tom.

"I'm afraid I have something difficult to discuss," Gin said, glad she'd practiced what she wanted to say in advance. She couldn't afford to be tentative now, not with everything that was riding on this conversation. She couldn't give the impression of weakness.

"Oh?" The smile slipped a little, and Spencer picked up a mechanical pencil and tapped it against his open palm.

"I know the truth, you see. About you and Lawrence."

The tapping abruptly stopped. Spencer stared at her, his bland smile reshaping itself into a frown. He took a deep breath and let it out slowly, then set the pencil back down on his desk, lining it up precisely with the edge of the blotter.

"Virginia, I don't have the faintest idea what you're talking about."

"I think you do."

For a moment neither of them spoke. "Well, whatever's on your mind, I'm happy to hear you out. But this isn't the time or place."

"All right." Gin kept her tone neutral, but she wasn't going to be put off. "You've already said you have time for a cup of coffee. Where would you like to go?"

"Perhaps we could find some time tomorrow—"

"Now, I'm afraid."

"I see." A tic in the corner of Spencer's mouth twitched; his eyes grew even more opaque.

A man who kills one of his oldest friends is desperate, indeed; would he hesitate to harm his children's friend? Gin never would have believed it, until this moment. The man she had grown up knowing—soft-spoken, deliberate, kind but also a workaholic, perpetually exhausted, inflexible—that man seemed to have vanished, replaced by this one with the carefully disguised exterior, the elastic features.

But that was the mark of the best liars, wasn't it? You never knew what they were capable of.

"Well, Virginia," Spencer said, recovering himself, his bland smile back in place. "Shall we go for a walk?"

Gin considered the options. The surgery center opened onto a view of the river far below, across the landscaped drive. But the neighborhood behind it had steadily eroded until it was littered with boarded-up businesses and falling-down houses and burnt-out empty lots. Not the ideal place for a conversation—unless one wanted to make sure no one would ever admit to seeing them talking.

"A drive, I think. We can take my car." Gin had already considered the options, doubting Spencer would speak freely in his office. She needed to control the conversation, however. And while she couldn't imagine Spencer trying to hurt her, she no longer believed that she really knew him.

Spencer didn't look happy about it, but he held the door for her and followed her back through the hospital. Gin made sure to greet everyone, to make sure they were seen together. Paranoid, perhaps, but she was out of her element now.

"Nice ride," was Spencer's only comment when they reached her Touareg. "I suppose the compensation is pretty good in Cook County."

"It pays my bills."

The destination Gin had chosen was only a quarter mile away. She parked right in front, gambling that she wouldn't be ticketed for the yellow curb—and willing to risk it: a parking fine would be more than fair trade for her safety.

The sign above the decrepit building read "M TTYS." At one time, it had read "SMITTY'S"—and the neon had worked, too. Gin squared her shoulders and entered the dank, dim space, grimacing at the sticky floor and the scent of stale popcorn and spilled beer.

The only other people in the place, at a little after eleven in the morning, were an elderly man playing solitaire, a sixty-something woman in a booth mumbling to herself and wildly swinging her foot, and the bartender, a tired-looking man with a crew cut and a Steelers T-shirt stretched tight over his paunch. He slapped two cardboard coasters on the bar and spoke in a monotone: "Git you something?"

"Club soda for me." She turned to Spencer. "My treat."

"Coffee?" he asked.

The bartender didn't even bother to respond, but just glared at him balefully.

"All right. A Coke."

"Ten dollar minimum on credit cards," the bartender said, not moving. Gin took a twenty from her purse, laid it on the bar, and picked up a shot glass filled with toothpicks and set it down on top like a paperweight.

The bartender moved off to get their drinks.

"This isn't exactly what I would have pictured for your kind of place," Spencer said.

"It's not. But when I had a drink with Tom the other day, I remembered that I can't stand the country club."

"Ah, right, you were having that deep conversation with Tom." Something like contempt flashed on his face.

"If you can call it that. He wasn't at his best."

Spencer sighed. "Tom is battling addiction, which as you know is a difficult disease."

Gin shrugged. She couldn't argue that point, and she'd seen firsthand how parents could defend indefensible behavior from their children. It wasn't what she was here to discuss.

She dug in her purse for the copy of the RFLP that she had made in her mother's office an hour ago, and laid it flat on the bar. "I don't know if you're familiar with old methods of DNA testing," she said.

For a moment, Spencer merely stared at the paper. Though Gin did her best to read his expression, there was little change beyond a thinning of his mouth, a hardening of his jaw.

"Now listen, Gin. This is coming completely out of left field. You'll understand that I'm . . . I'm feeling a bit blindsided."

"You are Lily's biological father."

"So it appears." Spencer pushed the paper back across the bar to Gin, who folded it and returned it to her purse. "I am obviously going to need some time to adjust to this . . . this new . . ."

He swallowed, and for a moment Gin almost felt sorry for him. It was hard to believe that his reaction was an act—except for the subtle change in his demeanor back in his office. The brief parting of the curtain that revealed the darkness inside him. The bartender slid their drinks in front of them and Spencer picked his up and drank deeply.

"You wrote my mother a note last week," Gin said. "I found it in the laundry. Telling her not to blame herself."

"Despite what you may believe, I'm not a monster, Virginia. I have . . . thought of your mother often, through the years. We were close, once."

"You killed Lawrence."

"Whatever would make you jump to that conclusion?"

"You probably won't remember this," Gin said. "But when Christine and I were in second grade, you came to talk to our brownie troop before cookie sales. You were there to tell us how to be good businesswomen. The thing I remember most of all? You held up a cookie and said, 'There are a lot of chocolate-covered cookies in this world, but only one Thin Mint.'"

"I'm afraid I don't follow."

"Your point was that our ideal customer would never be satisfied with an imitation. She would have taken note of every element of the cookie—crunchy wafer, good-quality chocolate, and yes, sold by adorable gap-toothed little girls in brown uniforms, and that would make the sale. Well, when I think about who might have wanted Lawrence dead, I guess I could think of a few other candidates. People he arrested in the past, maybe. My parents, since you could argue he botched the search all those years ago. Me, for the same reason. Even Jake, for allowing him to be the prime suspect."

"How does this relate to cookies?" Spencer's hand clenched his glass tightly.

"No crunchy middle, no chocolaty outside, no cute little girl. None of those other possible suspects have anything to recommend them." She picked a toothpick out of the shot glass and snapped it in half. "You, on the other hand . . . what do you suppose the town would think if they knew that you were the father of the murdered girl? The secret lover of our future mayor—at a time when the center's expansion plans are about to go before the city council? All kinds of well-laid plans would fall apart, I'm guessing. And that doesn't even take into account the twins. What would Tom think? I mean, some people might consider him fragile. And Christine . . . she worships you. Always has. Losing her respect would be awfully hard to bear."

Spencer shook his head at her. "You've put together a complicated narrative here, but I have to admit, it makes a certain kind of contorted sense. Except for two things. Until this afternoon, I had no idea that Lily . . . excuse me." He grabbed a napkin from the bar and dabbed at his eye. When he spoke again, his voice was thick and rough. "I had no idea that I was her biological parent. And second, Lawrence and I were *friends*. Had been for years."

"That doesn't mean anything."

Spencer downed the rest of his drink, then looked around the bar, as if he were noticing the surroundings for the first time. "So you came here to accuse me. Listen, Virginia, I know you've probably worked with a lot of cops at your job. Maybe that's given you a sense of . . . obligation, to get involved in things that aren't really your responsibility."

"My sister's *murder* is what made me get involved," Gin snapped. Spencer was trying to feel her out, find the approach that would work best with her, but she wasn't going to let him get the upper hand.

"So are you recording me right now? Hoping you'll get me to confess to this crazy version of events?"

"Nope," Gin said, though the idea had crossed her mind. The digital recorder she used at work was compact enough to fit into her purse—but her phone would have worked reasonably well in a pinch. In the end, she'd accepted what she already knew: Spencer would be too smart for that. "Let's just say I'm here to satisfy my own curiosity."

"I wish I could help you. But all I have to offer is the truth."

"You've kept yourself in admirable shape, Spencer, but even so you must have had your doubts about going up against Lawrence. I imagine you've never fired a gun, and even if he did have a couple decades on you, knowing he used to be a marine . . . well, *I* would have been intimidated. But oh, right, you and my dad have always been as thick as thieves. I remember being on vacation and Dad giving you his passwords over the phone so you could fix something in the office since we were thousands of miles away on a beach in Mexico. And knowing Dad, he never got around to changing them."

Spencer said nothing.

"Which would also explain how you were able to fake his signature. All those expense receipts that must have come across your desk, from every trip Dad ever took on hospital business. You can probably write it just as well as he can by now. I mean, I doubt that will hold up in court—no one's that good—but it did the trick." Gin considered mentioning Red and the video of the overflow lot, but decided to keep it for later. There was no doubt in her mind that Spencer had killed Lawrence, but the whole reason she was here was to learn what had happened to Lily.

"Once you had the prescription, it would have been easy enough to fill. After that, I'm a little hazy on how things went. You went to his house, maybe you chatted, a couple of old friends having a drink. Or maybe you acted all concerned about the investigation, was there anything you could do, how could you help—Lawrence would have been perfectly relaxed in his own house. He might not even have registered what you were doing when you leaned over and slid that syringe in. I'm guessing you went for the neck, knowing that the bullet wound would probably obliterate the needle mark. He might have lost consciousness without ever knowing what you planned to do."

"I don't know what to say," Spencer said haltingly. Once again his features had morphed, this time into avuncular concern. "You're a very intelligent woman, Gin, and I almost feel that might be working against you here. Fueling your desire to force this fiction to be true."

"I have to say, I'm not as impressed with the rest of it," Gin pressed on. "It's all very *Murder She Wrote*, wouldn't you agree? I mean, faking his suicide, the gun in his hand . . . and don't you ever watch *Dexter*? Those things are a lot harder to pull off than most people realize. You know, we have our own blood spatter expert in Cook County—that stuff really happens."

Spencer set down his glass. "I think this has gone far enough."

Gin stayed quiet. It wasn't as if she'd expected him to confess, to offer to go right over to the police station and turn himself in. Right now they were in a stalemate: she had proof of paternity, and he knew she lacked proof that he was the one who'd broken into the hospital. The security tape and hand-writing analysis might be enough to make the case against him, but a smart man would engage a lawyer and deny, deny, deny—and Spencer was nothing if not smart.

For Jake's sake, and out of genuine affection for Lawrence, Gin wanted justice for the man's death. But there was some-thing she wanted even more.

"So . . . was Lawrence right about Tom? Was he the one who killed my sister?"

"Absolutely *not!*"

"Really? Because, the way I see this, even if you're able to dodge arrest for Lawrence's murder, the fact that he had Tom in his sights when he died is going to make an awfully com-pelling case for the county police to go after Tom now. And Tom's going to have a hard time defending himself. His hos-pitalization could easily be viewed as an attempt to take his own life."

"He was in withdrawal!" Spencer protested, loud enough to get the attention of both the bartender and the woman at the table. Only the man at the end of the bar didn't look up from his cards. "It's a chemical response to abruptly quitting the benzodiazepines," Spencer said in a quieter voice. "Any expert would testify to that."

"Or," Gin said calmly, "as I myself have testified in court in a wrongful-death suit, it might just be the last event in a calculated act of self-destruction. Even if it can't be proved, it will plant the seed of doubt in the detective's minds. You know that there is tremendous pressure on them to come up with a suspect, now that two people are dead and the media is connecting the cases. Tom is going to make an easy target for them. How do you think he'll hold up in jail, by the way? Under interrogation? Seems like these days, at least in Cook County, they're really pushing the envelope when it comes to leaning on suspects in some of these cases. The most ambitious investigators skirt that gray area of what might be considered ethical."

She had his attention; Spencer was gripping the bar hard enough to break it, and perspiration had broken out on his forehead. How far could she push him? What would it take for him to crack?

She pressed on, deviating only a little from events she'd witnessed herself. "Personally, I think it's terrible when they extract a forced confession. Once in a while, a decent attorney can get one overturned, but that doesn't happen nearly as often as you might think from the news. Most of the time? Those poor guys rot away in jail while the world has no idea that they were left in an interrogation room for thirty hours at a time. Or denied bathroom breaks. Or humiliated, or manipulated . . . the training some of these guys get? It's on a level with what the ISIS operatives receive. Not really appropriate for domestic police work but . . ." She shrugged and turned up her hands. "Nothing you or I can do about it, unfortunately."

"Tom didn't kill Lily," Spencer said, almost pleadingly. Gin could see how close to cracking he was. "He had no reason to."

"Other than all the time my sister was spending with Jake," Gin said quietly. "I understand why he was frustrated. Honestly, when I saw her with my boyfriend, sometimes I wanted to kill her myself."

"You're not—you can't—"

"Which is what I'll have to say," Gin concluded. "When they come to talk to me. And when I start talking, I have a feeling I'm going to have a hard time stopping. Seeing as my father had to endure the humiliation of being hauled off to jail in front of the entire town. And as we both know . . . my father is an innocent man."

Gin saw the way Spencer's skin had gone gray—the tic had developed into a full-blown tremor—and decided she'd pushed him as far as she could for one day.

"Oops, look at the time," she said. "Tell you what, I've got to go. But there's probably enough left on the tab for you to get yourself another Coke. It's on me. Go ahead and enjoy it and . . . think about what we talked about."

"No, wait." Spencer looked desperate, perspiration dotting his brow, his hand trembling slightly around his glass. "I swear to you my son didn't kill Lily. I know because . . . I did it. It was me, Virginia. It was an accident."

Gin stared at him blankly, her mind refusing to accept what he'd just said. "What are you talking about?" she whispered faintly.

"I went there that night. I told the cops I was teaching Tom to drive a stick, but that was only because he was getting high with some kids from school and he begged me not to get them in trouble. I had been out walking the dog, when I saw Lily over near the water tower, where you kids used to go. I was angry, you see, because I thought Tom and she were secretly planning to meet up, and I felt they'd been spending way too much time together already. Their grades were atrocious, you'll probably remember."

Gin said nothing, barely able to force herself to continue breathing. Was Spencer really confessing to the murder of her sister?

"I confronted her. Not a good idea, with someone as temperamental as Lily. She got so upset with me—when I put my hand on her arm, just trying to get her to calm down, she started screaming at me and trying to run away. I was just trying to get her to *listen* to me. I—I don't know exactly how it happened, but I was holding onto her arm and she was flailing around and hitting me when she got her arm free and stumbled backward. She fell, and her head hit a rock. There was nothing—" He swallowed and dropped his gaze to the sticky bar. "There was nothing I could do. I tried to resuscitate her, but I could tell the damage to her skull—she was gone. Just gone."

Gin felt numb, her mind racing to catch up with what he was saying. Lily's death had been an accident. Spencer had been with her when she died.

"But . . . why didn't you call for help?"

"I panicked. I'm not proud of that. I would like to believe that if I'd taken the time to really think about it, I would have done the right thing. But—all I could think about was how it would look, and, worse, what it would do to my family. If I were to go to jail, who would have looked out for my kids? How would they have gone on with their lives? The cooler was right there, down by the creek, and it seemed, I don't know, almost like a sign. A way to make the whole thing disappear. So—that's what I did."

"But that cooler was huge. It took two of us to move it when we filled it with drinks."

Spencer was shaking his head. "I moved it empty. I went home and got a shovel and a pick, and I came back—the kids were already asleep, they didn't see me. It took me forever to dig out the hole, and then I—I tried to move the cooler with her in it, I'm so sorry, Gin."

His voice had gone hoarse, and he brushed at his eyes with his knuckles. "I had to take her out to get the cooler into the hole. Then I, I put her in it and closed it and covered it up. I pulled branches and weeds over it, tried to make it blend in, but I still thought it would get discovered within a matter of weeks, if not days. I'm not proud of this, but I thought—I thought that if she was found in Jake's cooler, that, well . . ."

"That Jake would take the fall." Gin's stupor gave way to outrage. "You would have let him go to jail for something that you did?"

"No, no, it never would have gotten that far. They couldn't have convicted him, not without more evidence. I just wanted to deflect suspicion, that's all. And then, when time went by and everyone was saying she'd run away, I just—I just prayed that no one would ever know."

"Not everyone thought she ran away," Gin said coldly. "A lot of people accused Jake. They tried to ruin his life."

"Yes, well." Spencer starred miserably at his drink. "I could tell you I'm sorry. I could tell *him* I'm sorry. It still wouldn't change anything that happened."

"It would have, if you'd told the truth," Gin countered. "You might not have been able to bring Lily back, but you would have saved everyone—Jake, my parents, me—all these years of agony."

Spencer only shrugged, refusing to look at her.

Gin gathered her purse and stood. "You know I'm going to tell the police everything you just told me."

"Do what you have to do."

Gin didn't look back as she exited the bar, the noonday sun hitting her like a fist.

*   *   *

She was running across the bridge late that afternoon, breathing in the sultry, brackish breeze, when the phone call came. She'd waited at home for as long as she could stand it, but when no new news had come in by four thirty, she'd laced up her shoes and hit the street.

She stopped next to a support beam and dug for her phone. "Mom?"

"Your father didn't go to work. He's sitting in the kitchen drinking whiskey from a juice glass," Madeleine said, as incredulously as if she was announcing that Richard was dancing an arabesque. "Oh, honey, please come home. I just— this is all too much."

"Are you . . . *crying*?"

"I just can't believe I ever thought—your poor father—but I didn't even tell you the worst part: Spencer has confessed."

"To murdering Lawrence?"

"To both of them. Spencer killed Lawrence and Lily, too."

Her mother's voice did something Gin had never heard before. She kept the phone pressed to her ear, listening to her mother's gasping sobs, while she ran as fast as she could back the way she'd come.

34

The county police held a press conference. Gin watched it on television with her parents, sitting in her mother's favorite easy chair while they held hands on the couch.

The chief spoke for only a few moments while Detectives Witt and Stillman stood on either side of her, hands clasped behind their backs, looking grim. In July of 1998, Spencer Parker had confronted Lily Sullivan in a clearing in the woods above Trumbull where local teens were known to gather. He was angry that Lily, only sixteen, was dating his son who was to start college that fall. The discussion turned into an altercation in which Lily fell and struck her head on a rock, and died. He buried her in a cooler that was left at the location, believing that if she was found, suspicion would be cast on its owner, unaware that the owner was another local teen, Jake Crosby.

As soon as the chief concluded her remarks and stepped back from the podium, the questions swarmed.

"We will share further details when we have them," the chief said, and then she and her detectives left the room.

Madeleine turned off the television.

"I'm just so glad all of this is finally going to be over," she said. "Do you think they'll release Lily's body now?"

Gin had been only half-listening, going over the chief's comments in her mind. Something wasn't lining up for her, and it wasn't just Spencer's abrupt change of heart about confessing. That, she could chalk up to pure parental protectiveness, to his giving in to panic once he realized he'd been backed into a corner.

She was quite certain he'd killed Lawrence. But his claim that he'd "run into" Lily at the creek couldn't be true, could it? Unlike Gin, Lily wasn't the sort of girl who needed time to herself. She rarely went anywhere by herself if she could talk anyone into going with her. And most compelling of all, she didn't even like the creek that much. She complained that it smelled of dead fish and rotting weeds, and she hated getting dirt on her clothes. She constantly tried to convince the others to drive to the mall or even to hang out at their house instead.

And there was something else. In the days following Lily's disappearance, Gin and her mother had discovered that some of her things were missing—her backpack and some clothing. The county police had emphasized that finding when deeming the case a runaway situation.

Spencer hadn't mentioned the backpack, and it hadn't been found at the scene or in the cooler.

Obviously, Lily had gone to the creek that day. But Gin couldn't believe she'd gone alone. Someone had talked her into it—and that someone wasn't Spencer.

"Virginia? Did you hear your mother? Will they release Lily's remains now that Spencer's confessed?"

"Oh—sorry, Dad, I was distracted. Yes, I imagine it will happen in the next day or two. But I'd hold off on finalizing plans."

As her parents discussed the interment, she returned to the puzzle of Spencer's claim. If he was telling the truth, that meant that Lily really had gone there alone. It was true that she had been behaving oddly for most of the summer. It wasn't just the increasing amount of time that she was spending with Tom—and with Jake, too, for that matter—but also with Christine, long girly chats about things that held little interest for Gin. They did each other's nails and braided each other's hair and swooned over Usher and NSYNC.

Gin had forgotten how isolated she had felt from the whole group. By the time she left for college, she was blaming Jake for everything: for driving Lily away, for keeping her secrets, for betraying Gin's trust. But that had been a convenient excuse, so that she didn't have to blame the two friends she had left. Once Lily disappeared, Tom and Christine had pulled back from her, too, and that had hurt: Gin had gone from having two best friends, a boyfriend, and a beloved sister to having no one at all.

Lily could have gone to meet any of them that day. But Tom and Christine both had given statements to the detectives that they'd been elsewhere. Spencer and Tom were each other's alibis, and Christine said she'd been scrapbooking at the house, something Spencer had confirmed.

Now, with Spencer's confession, all those alibis were worthless.

Gin got up and grabbed her purse from the kitchen counter, digging for her keys and phone.

"I'll be back soon," she called, already halfway to the door.

"Where are you going?" Madeleine called. "I thought we should all have dinner together tonight—"

"Save me some," Gin called guiltily, letting the door slam on her words. By the time she got in her car, she was already dialing Jake's number.

* * *

Jake met her at the door wearing a much-laundered apron, an expensive-looking Microplane in his hand. Issuing from the house was an incredible smell, savory and rich and definitely better than anything Gin had consumed since coming to Trumbull.

He'd shaved, and there was a smudge of something along his jawline that Gin very much wanted to wipe away, possibly with her thumb, while her other hand . . . but no. What happened yesterday had been a one-time thing, the confluence of nostalgia and shock and the remnants of chemistry between them.

She pushed the whole subject from her mind in frustration and ducked awkwardly past him into the house.

"So you just whipped this up . . . ?" she asked, and was rewarded by a long, thoughtful stare. Evidently Jake decided to follow her lead, because he merely turned on his heel and walked over to the kitchen, where he got busy at the cutting board, on which he'd grated a small mound of Parmesan cheese.

"I would have cooked anyway," he said, lifting slices of what looked like homemade pizza onto plates. "But I'm glad for the company. Help yourself to wine, it's open."

"Most guys would just stick a frozen Tombstone in the oven."

"This was just what happens when you give a man a grill and twenty years to get tired of fried chicken from the grocery store."

"You're too modest. Did you actually make that on the grill?"

"Yeah, it's really not all that hard, I've found that if you just form the dough for the grill basket—"

"Wait, and you make the dough, too?"

A smile played around the corner of his lips. "Yeast, flour, a bit of honey—it's really just a chemical reaction, Gin. I would have expected you of all people to get that. Although I suppose your job doesn't leave you a whole lot of time for domestic pursuits."

She didn't answer; there wasn't a lot she could say that wouldn't reveal that the most time-consuming thing in her life was the treadmill of her own perpetual restlessness. She sat at the table and accepted the plate laden with pizza and salad, and a rough-weave ivory napkin. The pizza was topped with olives and shaved ham and the salad was studded with pistachios.

Her mind finally stopped spinning when he handed her a knife and fork: they were the monogrammed, beaded silver pattern that had belonged to the mother he'd never known, the service that Lawrence had only used on Sundays.

He noticed her looking, and his voice went gruff. "Ah, that. You know, somewhere along the way I decided life's too short not to use the good stuff."

There was a lot more to explore in that vein. For a moment, Gin was very sorry that she'd never be the woman who got to do so.

"So," Gin said, setting her fork down after her first bite. The food was incredible, but she could barely taste it. "I assume you watched the news."

"Yeah. Pretty damn shocking. I wasn't sure if you wanted a break from it or . . ."

A break from it was exactly what she wanted, but that wasn't going to happen.

"Look, Jake," she said carefully. "The way things stand now, you're completely in the clear. I don't want to throw a wrench in that. And you know that my family is behind you now the, um, way we should have been all along."

"But . . . ?"

She sighed. "But, I don't know. I mean, we're supposed to believe that Lily just happened to go to the clearing, alone? Do you remember her ever doing that?"

He watched her steadily. "No."

"And then Spencer just *happens* to come along? On a walk, when he lived all the way over on the south end of town? His habits were so rigid—he was at the gym every morning before work, and then home every night. Remember we used to make fun of him about that? And there's also the problem of her things. The backpack and clothes. Spencer never mentioned them, and there's no reason Lily wouldn't have had them with her."

"Yeah. The out-for-a-walk thing doesn't really ring true, especially since she'd already been out once that day, with me, and I dropped her back in town. So what are you saying— he kidnapped her and took her there? Asked her to meet? Either way it's premeditated. Although, at this point, how much does it matter? He confessed to killing both of them and they've got premeditation on Lawrence—how much worse could his sentence be?"

"It's not that. It's just . . . I don't know, his whole story doesn't ring right for me. I mean . . . I've been thinking about how little attention I paid to Lily that summer. I was so focused on the future"—*our* future, she didn't say—"and she was such a pain to be around. She'd been sick so much that year, which by the way is another reason she wouldn't have gone there alone, she said it made her skin worse—"

"Wait," Jake said. "Whatever happened with that, anyway? Wasn't your mom taking her to a shrink or something?"

"She took her a couple of times, but it didn't amount to anything. Mom thought the rashes were psychosomatic, but the psychologist suggested we just go along and treat them with over-the-counter medication rather than confronting her about it. They thought that way she could work through what was really bothering her on her own."

"Which was what?"

"I don't know, growing pains? Hormones? Typical teen angst? Dad thought the whole thing was ridiculous. He always accused Mom of indulging Lily, and they both seemed to think that she'd grow out of it. I remember that's what they said to me one time when she was out with Tom—'Go easy on her, Virginia, she'll grow out of it.'" *Go easy on her*, the perpetual refrain where Lily was concerned. "I remember it pissed me off, that she got a pass for all her outrageous behavior while they still had a fit if I so much as talked back."

"She *was* kind of a bitch that summer."

"Jake . . . was there anything else you talked about that day? Anything you might have forgotten?"

He took a sip from his wine. His own food was going cold, too. "You know, I was so angry at you and everyone else, I swore I'd never tell. Typical reckless adolescent behavior— I remember telling Dad I'd rather rot in jail than cave to small minds. You know what he told me?"

"No . . ."

"He said my principles wouldn't be much comfort when I was desperate for a smoke, a steak, or a woman. Except he didn't say 'woman,' he used, ah, another word."

"Oh . . ." Gin felt a blush creeping across her face.

"Yeah. Made quite an impression on me." He laughed without humor. "Looking back, I guess that's one of those times a mom might have come in handy. Look, I'm only telling you this to explain why I retreated so far for so long."

He reached for her hand. His touch was electric, irresistible. She looked into his eyes, into the sadness that seemed permanently lodged there. "I was wrong. About just about everything. I mean, my dad could probably have expressed himself better, but my lone-wolf tendencies squashed my, uh, emotional development for a long time. Listen, I'm not much for looking back . . . but I'm sorry, Gin."

"But . . ." she whispered. It had all been her fault. It sickened her to think of how she'd blamed him.

He let go of her hand gently, and carried their untouched plates into the kitchen. With his back turned to her, he said, "Maybe sometime we can finish forgiving each other and blaming ourselves, but I guess I should answer your question."

He came back with the bottle and topped off both their glasses. "You want to know what Lily and I talked about? Well, first of all, it didn't happen nearly as often as you think. Most of the time she just wanted a ride to the Parkers', or to meet Christine at the mall."

"You were the only one with a car," Gin remembered.

"Yeah." Jake looked bemused. "Part of Spencer's whole effort to build Tom's character. Too little, too late. Anyway, I gave in about half the time, mostly because she was your kid sister and I was—well, you know. Whipped." A flash of that deadly grin, the one that could loosen her moorings. "She talked about, let's see, in order: how much of a bitch your mom was, how stupid your dad was, what a bitch *you* were, how she couldn't wait to get out of this town, how if she'd grown up anywhere else she'd already be an actress-slash-poet-slash-performance-artist-slash-whatever she'd fixated on that week."

Gin couldn't help it—a little laugh bubbled out. "Oh my God! She really was such a drama queen, wasn't she?"

"Yeah, but you just couldn't stay mad at her for long. And she usually ended up redeeming herself right before I dropped her off. Saying stuff like, '*Be nice to my sister or I'll cut your balls off.*' Sweet nothings like that."

Tears pricked Gin's eyes through her smile. "God, I miss her. Still."

"I know."

"I wish I'd tried harder to spend time with her that summer, instead of Christine. The two of them were like best friends, and I . . ."

Christine. Best friends.

"Oh no."

Jake looked at her quizzically. "What?"

"It's just—" Her mind tumbled, seemingly insignificant details lining up in new patterns, a devastating shape beginning to emerge. "It's probably nothing, but—I need to go."

"Gin, wait. Tell me what's going on."

"No, it's probably crazy. I just need . . . I'll call you as soon as I figure this out."

"I'm coming with you," he said, scooping his keys off the table by the door.

35

Olive answered the door, her hair in a ponytail, bright pink new rubber bands on her braces flashing in her smile when she saw it was Gin and Jake. "I made cookies," she said, opening the door wide. "Chocolate chip. I mean they're just the refrigerator kind, but they're pretty good. Want some? Austen's at his friend's house or he would have eaten them all already. You're here to see Mom? She should be back soon, she just went to pick Uncle Tom up from the hospital. He's going to stay with us for a while. But that was, like, hours ago, want me to call her?"

The girl's run-on exuberant speech reminded Gin so much of Lily that for a moment she had to catch her breath before she could speak.

"No, it's fine, I'm happy to wait," she said, feeling guilty for misleading Olive. "That'll give us a little time to catch up."

"By the way, look!" she said, tugging at the necklace Gin had given her. "I get so many compliments, I love it so much. Did I tell you I'm trying out for advanced drama?"

She led the way to the kitchen, but Gin had noticed something. Her forearms were pocked and speckled with an angry pink rash.

"Olive," she said, keeping her tone light, as she accepted one of the warm, gooey cookies. "Has your rash been getting any better?"

"Oh, yeah, it doesn't itch near as much. I got this stuff from the doctor. I have to put it on twice a day."

The front door opened and Christine came striding into the kitchen, Tom tottering along after her, carrying a duffle bag and looking pale and weak and as though he'd lost twenty pounds in the past week.

"Gin?" Christine said. "I saw your car out front. What on earth are you doing here?"

Olive looked from Gin to her mother and back, confusion registering on her face.

Gin couldn't look at her. "Oh, I just thought I'd stop by and—"

"Olive, don't you have homework?" Christine didn't take her eyes off Gin. She clutched her purse strap hard.

"Hey, Gin, Jake," Tom said, smiling weakly. "I'll just take my stuff to the guest room and—"

"Stay here." Christine's voice had gone shrill. "Olive, to your room please, now."

"But Mom—"

Christine reached for Olive's jacket—at least, that's what Gin told herself was happening. Calm, tightly controlled Christine, unflappable even as a teenager, would never do what happened next: Olive went staggering backward, crashing into the table, glancing off the edge and sitting down in the chair with an audible "oof," a look of shock and disbelief on her face.

But Christine turned away from her and advanced on Gin. "You have no right, you can't be here," she snapped.

Jake tried to step between them but Christine shoved savagely at him, deflecting his arm. "Calm *down*," he said. "Come on, Christine, you have to—"

"Do you have any idea what I'm going through here?" Christine demanded. "Not just dealing with Tom but trying to keep the kids from having to hear it on the news? About their own *grandfather*?"

"What the fuck is going on, Chrissy?" Tom said weakly, leaning against the counter.

"No. *No.* Just *go.* Tom just got out of the hospital and I have to, I have to—"

"You knew," Gin said. There had to be a right way to do this, but the truth was lodged in her chest like a stone. "You knew all along."

"What are you talking about?" Tom repeated. He really didn't look good at all.

"Fabry disease. It happens when there's a faulty gene in the X-chromosome. It's what caused your rash," she said gently to Olive.

"I know, the doctor told me. My stomach aches, too. My body can't make an enzyme, so I have to have shots." She grimaced. "They *suck.*"

"Don't worry, you'll be fine with treatment. My sister Lily had it, too."

Olive looked confused. "Are you sure? It's super rare. I mean the odds of it being both in my family and yours are really low, like one in a million or something."

"You had it," Gin said to Christine. "When we were middle school. Remember? You wouldn't wear shorts when it was bad. But you told me it was allergies."

"It was a really mild case," Christine said defensively. "Daddy thought it was mono, even though your father told him it wasn't. My dad took me to a specialist and she monitored it the whole time I was in school. I hated the way she called it a disease, it made me feel like a freak, and I begged Daddy not to tell anyone."

"But when Lily got that rash . . ."

"Olive. I mean it," Christine said, her voice suddenly deadly calm. "Go to your room right this second. You can watch Netflix on your iPad."

Olive's eyes widened—whether because the rules were being unexpectedly relaxed or because of her mother's behavior, Gin wasn't sure. She backed out of the room with her trembling lower lip making a final mute plea. Seconds later they heard her door close.

"I knew what it probably was," Christine said quietly, tears spilling from her eyes and forming rivulets down her face that she didn't bother to brush away. Tom looked from her to Gin in confusion. "I mean, I knew what it meant. That Lily and I were related. That we had the same father."

"Oh, fuck," Tom murmured.

"You figured out that your father had an affair with my mother." Gin forced the words out, barely able to stomach the thought. "She was taking care of all three of us when your family moved here. Our dads were at the surgery center night and day, to hear her talk about it, but I remember sometimes your dad came to get you guys when mine was still at work."

"Of all the women in this town." Spittle flew from Christine's mouth; her hair had come unclasped from her barrette and hung wildly around her face. "Dad could have dated any of them and he chose *her*."

"Yeah, well, if it makes you feel any better, he never knew he was Lily's father," Gin said, turning to Tom. "That was why Mom was so against you dating her, Tom. She was actually your half sister."

"Shit. No." Tom staggered heavily against the counter. "Jesus, that means that her baby . . ."

Christine whirled around to face him. "That's why I did what I did! God, it was so . . . disgusting. I didn't want you to have to know."

"So you murdered her?" Jake asked.

"I didn't—it wasn't like that!" Christine pleaded. "I never meant to hurt her!"

"Then tell us what *did* happen," Gin said. "You know, it's really been bothering me that Lily didn't tell anyone she was pregnant. But she obviously told you."

"She refused to get an abortion," Christine said. "I told her I'd find the money. I said that you'd drive her, Jake, if she asked. I told her no one else would have to know, and she said she didn't care, that she knew Tom would stand by her. She swore she'd never been with anyone else. I just couldn't—couldn't bring myself to tell her who he was. Her . . . her *brother.* It made me just—just so sick. I told her to meet me at the clearing so we could plan how to tell everyone, but really I was going to try to talk her into the abortion one more time. I even went to your house and got her a change of clothes. I had the bus schedule figured out and everything, there was a clinic up in Pittsburgh where we could have gotten it done and I had enough money to pay for a motel so she could recover. By the time we came back it would have been all over and we would have made up some story . . . we would have gotten in trouble, but at least it would have been taken care of."

"But she refused to go along with it," Gin guessed.

"Before I could even tell her my plan, she started telling me she'd already picked out names, that she wanted to tell Tom that Saturday, she was going to take him out to dinner, she was going to use her babysitting money to pay for it. She was—she was just *delusional.* She wouldn't listen to me. And I could see that nothing was going to change her mind. So I— I stopped her."

She turned to Tom, reached pleadingly for his hands. "I did it for you," she said. "You and Dad. If people had found out— can you imagine what they would have said? Not to mention the risks to the baby. It could have been some sort of genetic freak, I felt like I was doing everyone a favor."

"How did you kill her, Christine?" Jake's voice was calm, but Gin noticed that he was edging toward the table, putting his body between Christine and her.

Christine looked almost disappointed in him. "It was just a rock," she muttered. "Not even a very big one. Just the first one I could find. I held it with both hands and I—it caught her mostly in the back of the skull. It didn't even mess up her face. And she just fell down, you know? She didn't say anything, I don't think it even hurt. I don't think she ever knew."

Lily. Grief emanated from deep within Gin, spreading through her body. But she couldn't let go entirely, not yet.

"And the cooler," Jake pressed. "Had you planned on that?"

"No. No. After, you know, it happened, I was so upset. I went home and I was crying, I could barely talk, and Tom wasn't there, you were with your stupid friends, Tom, *God*— and I ended up telling Dad everything, I thought he would make me tell the police, but he didn't. He said he would fix it. He said he would take care of it."

The shovel. The hole he'd dug. Dragging the cooler by himself. Everything Spencer had told Gin in the bar was true— except for how Lily had died.

"He was covering for you," Gin said, putting it all together.

"He told me that we had to keep it secret forever," Christine said. "He said it was best for everyone. He said it was the only way."

Christine reached in her purse for tissues, and Gin dug out her phone. It was time to end this. Time to call for help.

"Put that away, Gin." Christine's voice was suddenly clear— and her hands were wrapped around a little gun she'd taken from her purse. "You know what, I knew you were going to be trouble. I've been carrying this ever since you came back to town."

"What are you going to do, Christine?" Gin demanded. "You can't possibly kill all of us. There aren't enough coolers in this whole town."

"Not all of you. Just you and Jake. I mean, it's kind of a nice ending, don't you think? The two of you, back together at last. And when you go missing, it'll make a nice epilogue to the whole Lily story. Kind of poetic. And everyone will just think you ran off to start a new life." She stared Gin straight in the eye. "Just like last time. Only this time, you get to keep the guy. Much better, don't you agree?"

She swiveled and pulled the trigger. To Gin, it almost seemed like Jake staggered backward before the shot echoed through the room. A trick of perception, the speed of sound. She was on the floor with him before she realized that the screaming she heard was her own.

"Call nine-one-one, Tom," she pleaded. She could see that the bullet had entered Jake's shoulder; his face was already going pale.

"Oh, you're not going to have time for that," Christine said in a voice that was almost bored, as she crouched down next to Gin and pressed the gun up against her head. Gin could feel the metal, hot from the first shot, pressing against her temple. "Let's see if we can make a little less mess with this one, shall we?"

And then she fell sideways, the gun clattering to the floor.

Gin looked up to see Tom standing above her, holding the heavy wooden knife block that he'd struck her with. Some of the knives were still lodged in their slots. "Oh," he said, sinking to his knees. They both looked at Christine: her hair was matted with blood, and a thin, bright white shard of bone was visible. A voice in Gin's mind, the voice of a thousand autopsies, was automatically running, documenting the damage, the negligible chances of her survival.

Tom crawled over his sister, and Gin thought he was going to cradle the dying woman in his arms. Instead, he picked up the gun. "I'm sorry," he gulped. "I'm so sorry, Chrissy."

Then he shot her in the forehead and she went still.

Gin tried to get to her feet, but the floor was slick with blood and she slipped and fell back down. Jake was motionless, and she couldn't reach his wrist to see if he had a pulse. She had to get her phone, had to call for help—

Tom, directly in front of her, had the gun pressed to the underside of his chin. "This family is cursed," he mumbled. "All of us. Cursed."

"Don't you do it," Gin ordered him. She managed to get her hand around his splayed leg, saw the streak of red her palm left on his khaki pants. She squeezed as hard as she could, trying to get his attention. "Don't you dare. This has to end now."

Only his eyes moved, rolling in their sockets. For a moment they focused on Gin, and then his hand slipped. The gun slid down his chest, his hand coming to rest in his lap. Gin took it from him and he didn't resist.

She pushed it into her purse as she finally got her phone out. The 9-1-1 call was quick—Gin knew precisely what to say to convey the gravity of the situation. The paramedics would be here soon to care for Jake; there was nothing she could do for him until they arrived. She left the phone lying on the table and walked out of the room, knowing there was one person who needed her the most right now.

Olive had opened the door a crack and was staring out with wild eyes. "What happened?" she demanded. "Were those gunshots?"

"Oh, sweetheart," Gin said, picking the girl up despite her size. Olive didn't resist, wrapping her arms tightly around Gin's neck and beginning to sob. Gin carried her back into the room, closing the door behind them with her shoulder. There was no way she was going to let the girl see the carnage in the kitchen.

They sat on the bed and Gin rocked Olive and crooned softly into the girl's hair, promising her that it would be all right, her heart breaking at the lie.

36

On a gray morning the following week, Gin stood between her parents at the back of the small group gathered near the fresh grave. Olive held her father's hand, and Gin prayed that Brandon Hart would be strong enough to be the man his children needed him to be. Each of them carried a white rose that they would lay on the casket when the priest was finished with the service.

Gin would be back here in a few days' time, when Lily would finally be laid to rest on a sunny slope in the old section of the cemetery, near where her grandparents were buried. By then, she hoped that Jake would be able to attend. The doctors had assured him he'd be well enough to be at Lawrence's funeral, which had been delayed a week to ensure Jake's presence, but they were making no guarantees that he'd be allowed to leave the hospital before then. Still, in the hospital, Jake had promised Gin that nothing would hold him back.

But he'd also promised that he'd never again allow her to leave Trumbull. Either the man was reckless with his promises, or . . .

She couldn't think about that today, not even with the ghost of his kiss on her lips. It hadn't been much of a kiss in some ways—kisses delivered in busy hospital rooms over the tangle of IV tubes rarely are—but it had certainly been memorable.

The priest invited the mourners to prayer, and Tom sobbed audibly.

Of everyone gathered here, he was the one that Gin doubted would ever recover. But in some ways, his fate had been set long before his spiral into addiction and depression. It had started when a lonely man attempted to compensate with work, borrowing a family that could never really be his. It had escalated when that man poured all his hopes and ambitions into one child, while cruelly ignoring the other. Christine had devoted her life to trying to build a happy ending, to assure her brother's success.

It was possible to feel compassion for her. Gin thought back to a day in early summer, seventeen years ago, when Lily had come clattering down the stairs with her Walkman earphones jammed in her ears, singing out of key. The rest of them had been playing cards, and as they all looked up, Gin watched their faces, rather than her sister.

Tom had been entranced, the glow of Lily's irrepressible beauty seeming to light him up. Jake had laughed and shaken his head, the response of a big brother, a buddy, a tolerant friend.

Only Christine had faltered. The pain that had passed over her expression had been easy to dismiss as annoyance, a match to Gin's own irritation at having to include her annoying kid sister in everything they did.

But it hadn't been annoyance, Gin understood now. It had been a bewildered sort of envy, the excruciating knowledge that she—who had tried so hard, who had given her all— could never compete with Lily, who simply *was*.

It was impossible to say whether Lily would have grown up to master her own untamed energy or if, in the end, it would have been her downfall. But then, on the cusp of adulthood, the seed of new life already growing inside her, she had been magnificent. And Gin might have been the only other person in the world besides Christine who understood how much that hurt.

Something that her mentor used to say, during Gin's fellowship, came unexpectedly to mind. *Amor est vitae essentia*— Latin for *Love is essential to life*. Perhaps, in the end, that was where life had failed Christine: she had not known enough love. Her mother had died before she could hold her infant twins; her father had found comfort in his work and in the son he hoped would grow up to carry on his legacy. Christine had been left alone and bereft, doomed ever to try to win the attention of men who paid her too little mind.

Lily, on the other hand, had never doubted her place in the world. She had seized and savored, loved and delighted, run as free and far as her feet could take her. She had easily eclipsed them all, burnt more brightly than the rest of them even dared to dream.

But now, it was as though Gin was only beginning to wake up to the world. Lily was gone, but her memory finally had a place of honor in Gin's heart. Letting her rest had freed Gin to begin living. In the last week, she had extended her leave of absence; moved some things over to Jake's house, where she was staying so she could care for Jett while Jake was in the hospital; and covered more ground strolling with her mother than she had running. She had no idea what would happen next—and she didn't really care at the moment.

The pastor finished his remarks, and Olive and Austen stepped forward, holding their father's hands. They dropped their flowers into the grave, the white petals fluttering in the breeze. As Olive turned back, her gaze caught Gin's, and she gave a tiny wave.

Gin nodded back. In the months to come, she would offer to bring the girl here, if she wanted to come. Gin had helped usher hundreds of people out of their life on earth, and while she didn't know if that qualified her to soothe someone else's grief, it surely couldn't hurt.

Gin's job had taught her that there was no recipe for saying good-bye, no best practices for letting go. But she could try. And in trying, she might finally learn to be free.